THE DIVA WRAPS IT UP

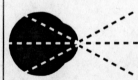

A DOMESTIC DIVA MYSTERY

THE DIVA WRAPS IT UP

KRISTA DAVIS

WHEELER PUBLISHING
A part of Gale, Cengage Learning

GALE
CENGAGE Learning·

Farmington Hills, Mich • San Francisco • New York • Waterville, Maine
Meriden, Conn • Mason, Ohio • Chicago

GALE
CENGAGE Learning

LIBRARY OF CONGRESS CATALOGING-IN-PUBLICATION DATA

Davis, Krista.
  The diva wraps it up / by Krista Davis. — Large print edition.
    pages ; cm. — (A domestic diva mystery) (Wheeler Publishing large print
  cozy mystery)
    ISBN 978-1-4104-7355-4 (softcover) — ISBN 1-4104-7355-4 (softcover)
    1. Winston, Sophie (Fictitious character)—Fiction. 2. Murder—
Investigation—Fiction. 3. Large type books. I. Title.
PS3604.A9717D65 2014
813'.6—dc23   2014031540

Published in 2014 by arrangement with The Berkley Publishing Group,
a member of Penguin Group (USA) LLC, a Penguin Random House
Company

Printed in the United States of America
1 2 3 4 5 6 7 18 17 16 15 14

To my readers, with love and appreciation.

ACKNOWLEDGMENTS

Over a year ago, I put out a call for recipes from readers. I asked for their favorite family Christmas cookie recipes. So many people responded! They shared a little bit about themselves and their cookies. They offered an amazing variety of cookies, many handed down for generations. I am delighted to share their recipes at the end of this book. Very special thanks to all my cookie recipe contributors: Ellen Marie Knehans, Nancy Foust, Kathy Kaminski, Michelle Melvin, Jeanne Schutts, Margaret F. Johnson, Jessica Faust, James Ashcroft, Elaine Faber, Roberta Daniels, and Kitty Free.

I am always so grateful when experts take the time to enthusiastically share their specialized knowledge with me. Seth Guggenheim, assistant ethics counsel for the Virginia State Bar, was kind enough to set me straight about Alex German's ethical responsibilities. I hope I got it right and that Alex makes Seth proud. Thanks also to Lucy Zahrey, aka the Poison Lady, who is helpful, gracious, and fun. Any mistakes are, of course, my own.

The title for this book posed some challenges. Thanks to readers Lori Meadows-Clark and Wendy Robbins, who suggested the title *The Diva Wraps It Up* without having read the book. How very appropriate it is! And for those who may wonder, the title does not mean the end of the series. Rest assured that another Domestic Diva Mystery is in the works.

Thanks also to my many friends who patiently answer questions and offer suggestions, Leslie Budewitz, Perry Garson, Betsy Strickland, Janet Bolin, Janet Cantrell, Laurie Cass, Daryl Wood Gerber, and Marilyn Levinson. Very special thanks to my friend, Peg Cochran who gave me some clever ideas for Gwen's Christmas letter and to Teresa Fasolino for painting another beautiful cover. As always, I owe deep gratitude to those who provide so much support and friendship, my mom Marianne, Susan Smith Erba, and Amy Wheeler.

I would be lost without my wonderful editor, Sandra Harding, and my incredible agent, Jessica Faust. They're always there with the unvarnished truth, delightful humor, and, when warranted, cupcakes and champagne!

Thank you all!

MARS'S LIST

Mars Winston and Natasha
Bernie Frei
Nina Reid Norwood
Gwen and Baxter Babineaux
  Bethany, Bradley, and Katrina
    Babineaux
Patty Babineaux (Baxter's ex-wife)
Elvin Babineaux (Baxter's brother)
Sugar (Elvin's girlfriend)
Liza and Luis Simon
Twiggy and Jonah Lawrence
Claudine Lawrence (Jonah's mom)
Horace and Edith Scroggins
Phyllis Tate (Horace's secretary)
Jill Kinghorn (owner of Fleur de Lis)
Mabel Akins (Horace and Edith's house-
  keeper)

Dearest Friends and Family,

We moved into our dream home in Old Town Alexandria, this year. Built in 1847, it just drips with historic splendor, majestic moldings, and the kind of craftsmanship you simply can't buy anymore. We had to rip out the kitchen, of course (can you even imagine the mess?), but now it's so beautiful that it's being featured in Charming Homes Magazine*!*

We Babineauxs know how boring these Christmas letters can be, so this year we're including one fib about each of the five of us. We'll let you guess what's true and what's not!

Bethany adores her new room. We built a special study nook for her, which turns out to have been a brilliant idea. She's so far ahead of all the other tenth graders in her prestigious nationally ranked private school that we've been advised to homeschool her so she can move at a faster pace. She'll miss being a cheerleader, of course, but she's so involved with her nonprofit company that makes shoes for underprivileged children in third-world countries that she barely had time to be on the homecoming court or edit the newspaper anyway.

Little sister, Katrina, is already being called an art prodigy and sold a painting for a thousand dollars! We're told she has incred-

ible abilities. Can you believe that she's start-ing school next year? She works part-time, too, testing toys at a local store.

Bradley has been the most valuable player on the football team this year. He's the school's track star, as well. They're begging him to play basketball, but he's taking so many college-level courses that we can't see how he can make the time for it, especially now that he reads to children at the library. This year he painted low-income housing units, collected winter coats for those in need, and spearheaded the planting of cherry trees along the river.

Baxter barely has time to use the movie room we outfitted with a popcorn machine and candy dispensers. He is living proof that what goes around comes around. All those years of hard work are really paying off now, if you know what I mean! Baxter has broken all the sales records at Scroggins Realty, and has been made vice president! But he found time to take me to Paris for nonstop partying. We even had dinner with Kenny G and Liza with a Z, who couldn't keep her hands off Baxter! Ooh-la-la!

Baxter's brother, Elvin, is on a cross-country trip with his new girlfriend, Sugar (a profes-sional ballet dancer!), to promote healthy eat-ing and fight childhood hunger. If he comes through your town, I hope you'll turn out and support these important causes.

In between herding the kids, I wrote a cookbook, lost twenty-five pounds, had an affair with a yummy neighbor, was president of the PTA, and won the Mother of the Year award. (They must have known about Katrina's impetigo. The poor child looked like a leper with all those blistery sores. No one else would touch her.) But the highlight of my year had to be the invitation to decorate the White House. Yes! That one! The First Lady selected humility, harmony, and hope as the theme and for a few glorious days, I had the honor of preparing our nation's finest residence for the holidays. I was even invited to eat lunch at the White House! What a fabulous experience. I am truly humbled by the opportunity to serve my nation in this way.

The enclosed photo was taken at the mountain cabin Baxter bought me for our anniversary. Now that we're in our fabulous and huge historical house with so many extra bedrooms, we hope you'll stop by for a visit.

May you all have as wonderful and magical a Christmas as the Babineaux family!

Baxter, Gwen, Bethany, Bradley,
and Katrina Babineaux

CHAPTER ONE

Dear Natasha,
My son-in-law is quite a cook. I would love to give him a set of professional-quality knives for Christmas. Can you recommend some good brands?

Hungry Mom in Turkey, Arkansas

Dear Hungry Mom,
Never give knives as presents. The gift of a knife is believed to sever the friendship. In this case, it might even sever the relationship between your daughter and her husband! Unless, of course, that's what you had in mind, in which case any old knives would do.

Natasha

Horace Scroggins poured hot chocolate into a mug. "It's my own special blend." He glanced out the door of his office as if he thought employees might be eavesdropping to hear his secret ingredients. "I add vanilla! Learned it from my true love."

He was too cute. I accepted the mug and made a fuss like I thought vanilla in hot chocolate was very special indeed.

Horace had always reminded me of Santa Claus. A petite man with rosy round cheeks and a belly that jiggled, 364 days of the year he wore a bow tie and suspenders, and at Christmastime they were inevitably red. On the day of the Scottish Christmas Walk, he donned a kilt and proudly paraded through the streets of Old Town.

I had never heard Horace utter a bad word about anyone. In his early sixties, he had a head of fluffy hair as white as snow. He always smiled, amazing in itself since he was married to Edith Scroggins, the most odious and unfriendly woman imaginable.

As an event planner, I didn't typically handle small company gatherings, but for the past few years, Horace had talked me into arranging his real estate company's Christmas party. It kicked off the Christmas season in Old Town. Horace had bought a magnificent historical town house for his real estate business many long years ago. His staff delighted in decorating it with a towering balsam fir in the two-story foyer. Scottish tartan ribbons curled through wreaths in the most tasteful and elegant manner, and groups of ruby red poinsettias graced antique tables and mantels. The muted colonial green walls provided a perfect backdrop for the tartan ribbons and bold reds.

It was Horace's habit to invite people to whom his company had sold homes in Old Town Alexandria, which included half my neighbors.

He sat down in his desk chair. The weathered leather gave, soft and cushy under his weight. He drank from his mug like he was thirsty and smiled at me. "Always settles my stomach. There's nothing like hot chocolate to cure whatever ails you." He held a pink box out to me. "Peanut brittle?"

"No, thanks. Do you have a queasy tummy?" I asked. "The party is going very well. You needn't worry."

"You did a lovely job, Sophie. I'm just getting older, I guess. Can't eat everything I used to."

Luis Simon, a distinguished psychiatrist who had bought a home on my street through Scroggins Realty in August, popped his head in the doorway. With prominent cheekbones and sultry bedroom eyes, Luis was worthy of posing for the cover of a romance novel. He carried a cup of English

Bishop, a flaming holiday punch loaded with rum and oranges studded with cloves. "Horace! Where's the Scottish dirk you were telling me about?"

"Dirk?" I asked.

Horace jumped up. He steadied himself briefly, his fingertips on his desk. "A traditional Scottish dagger, my dear." He turned to the bookcase behind him, took a tiny key from a book, and unlocked a desk drawer. He removed the knife gingerly and proudly presented it in his open palms as though it were a prized possession.

"An antique. The sheath bears sterling silver thistles."

Probably hand carved, the sheath appeared to be ebony. I didn't have to be an antiques expert to see that it bore the hallmarks of age.

He grasped the handle. A silver crown on the top held a large amber stone. Horace withdrew the handle to reveal a gleaming knife. "I like to imagine that it was really used, and not just worn for ceremonies."

Luis whistled his admiration and took the knife from Horace. "It's sharp! And heavier than I expected. You could do some damage with this thing." He danced backward and extended his arm as though it were a sword.

"They made things to last in the old days,

didn't they?" Horace beamed. "Let's find Babineaux. He wanted to see it, too." He locked the drawer again and tucked the key back into the book.

They scuttled out of Horace's office with the enthusiasm of little boys who had found a shiny object. I moseyed toward the buffet to check on the food. Guests couldn't seem to get enough of the oysters on the half shell and rolls of salmon on pumpernickel with pink peppercorns and crème fraîche. The baked Brie with toasted pecans and fig glaze was always a hit. I couldn't resist a taste of the melting cheese with a hint of salt and a smidge of sweet fig. Heavenly! And I had to try the seared foie gras with caramelized pears. The caterer had outdone himself.

I spotted my ex-husband, Mars Winston, gabbing with my best friend, Nina Reid Norwood. Everyone appeared to be having fun. I checked my watch, grabbed my pashmina, and slipped out the front door in search of the carolers I'd hired, shivering at the chill. Mother Nature had cooperated beautifully, sending us sparkling snowflakes. Not enough to have to shovel, but the right amount for perfect ambiance. In the spirit of the season I'd worn a red velvet dress, but it lacked sleeves. No matter. The pashmina would cover my bare arms. Besides, I

21

didn't plan to be outdoors long.

The carolers hurried along the street toward me. Dressed in traditional Victorian garb, with white faux fur trim on their clothes, they fit in perfectly on Old Town's colonial streets.

They gathered in front of the door, and at the signal, I opened it and stepped aside on the sidewalk to watch them.

They began with "Deck the Halls." The doors to the upstairs balcony opened, and Horace led a small group out to watch. I didn't care for the blanched color of his normally rosy face. He still smiled, though, and listened to the voices blend.

But then he grasped the railing with both hands and appeared to sway. None of the people behind him seemed to realize that he wasn't well.

Only when he leaned forward did they finally cluster around him in concern. With an enormous snap, the railing split, and Horace plunged headlong onto the sidewalk, landing directly in front of the carolers.

CHAPTER TWO

Dear Sophie,
My sister was stationed in Germany and brought me a nut-cracker as a gift. I'm not quite sure what to do with it. It looks sort of awkward and lonely standing there by itself.

        Clara in Nut Plains, Connecticut

Dear Clara,
The height of most nutcrackers makes them wonderful anchors for vignettes. Use him to give your mantel arrangement height. Or cluster him with some candles for a charming centerpiece on your dining table. I love them set next to poinsettias, too.

        Sophie

For a few eternally long seconds, everyone watched in shocked silence. A horrific red stain seeped onto the brick sidewalk.

Screams sounded all around me.

"Nooooo! Horace!" his secretary, Phyllis Tate, shrieked from the balcony.

I rushed to Horace, not knowing what to do. If he had broken his spine, then moving him would be the worst possible thing.

"Horace?" I whispered into his ear. "Can you hear me?"

He lay facedown. A couple of people wanted to turn him over, but I didn't let them.

Phyllis arrived at the scene and moaned his name over and over again, tears etching trails through her makeup.

Placing my face close to the sidewalk, I tried to see his eyes. He didn't appear to be bleeding from his nose or mouth. Where was the blood coming from?

Sirens sounded in the distance, and I thanked my lucky stars that Old Town wasn't very big. They would arrive momentarily. "I think we should leave him this way," I said to no one in particular.

There wasn't much I could do except cover his hand with mine and murmur encouragement. "You'll be fine, Horace. The ambulance is on the way."

Horace's hand twitched. He whispered something in a voice too faint to hear.

"They're coming, Horace. Hang in there!"

He pressed my hand feebly and tried to speak. I lowered my head as close to his as possible.

He murmured, "In the desk drawer. Edith must never know. Tell her I always loved her."

"Fool!"

I looked up to see Horace's wife, Edith, looming over us. Tall and slender, a permanent scowl creased her face. She regarded her husband with frigid eyes.

Officer Wong arrived at the same time as the ambulance. She shooed everyone back to make way for the emergency medical technicians to work.

They immobilized him with some difficulty. When they finally turned him over, I saw the problem. Horace's prized dirk jutted from his chest. He had fallen on his own sword, so to speak.

Screams and gasps echoed again as onlookers saw the knife handle. In minutes, Horace was loaded into the ambulance and it rolled away, picking up speed.

Edith returned to the building. I hurried inside, dodged her, and made a beeline for Horace's office. I took the time to close the door, quickly wiped my hands on tissues, and located the key in a book of poems, on the page with Elizabeth Barrett Browning's

"How do I love thee? Let me count the ways."

Moving in haste, I fumbled with the key, finally opened the drawer, and found only one item inside — an aging envelope.

I wrapped the pashmina around it and slid the drawer closed just as the door swung open.

Edith stared at me, cold as ice. "What are you doing in here?"

I sniffled, pulled another tissue from the box on Horace's desk, and turned my back to her. "I needed a moment alone." Wiping my eyes, I turned to face her. "He said to tell you he always loved you."

"Get out." She couldn't have said it in a more demeaning and hostile manner if she had tried.

I hurried past her into the hallway, clutching the pashmina carefully so I wouldn't accidentally drop Horace's precious letter.

Wong pulled me aside. "Sophie," she said calmly, "you do know that you have blood on your dress?"

I glanced down and shuddered. *Gross.* "From kneeling on the sidewalk, I guess. How is Horace? Did the EMTs tell you anything? Can a person survive that kind of wound?"

"Wish I knew. What happened exactly?"

"He was carrying the dagger around to show everyone. When the carolers came, a group of people crowded onto the balcony to listen. Horace looked ill, then the railing broke and he fell."

"How come no one else fell?"

"Come to think of it, that was a little bit odd. Maybe they held on to the side railings?"

"Did you see anyone plunge the knife into him?"

"No. It wasn't like that. He was in the front of the crowd on the balcony. He must have fallen on the dagger."

She pulled out a notebook and scribbled in it, her plump face contorting at the thought. Wong had kept her former husband's last name, which often surprised people when they met the short African-American policewoman. She wore her hair in curls, longer toward the front and trimmed in the back, with one sassy curl tickling her forehead. It suited her. She was a no-nonsense police officer who often saw through flimsy explanations.

Edith Scroggins approached us. "I thought I told you to get out." She eyed Wong. "You, too." Not even a hint of emotion showed on her stony face. She held herself painfully erect. She spat the word, "Now!" and watched us, waiting.

"Ma'am, I need to examine the balcony," said Wong.

"Not without my permission. Get out of my building."

"Ma'am, I can get a warrant to look at it." Wong sounded stern yet factual.

"Out!" Edith screamed like a wild woman.

Wong's mouth dropped open. Our eyes met. Without another word, we turned and walked through the empty hallway to the foyer. Edith had cleared the building. As far as I could tell, we were the last to leave.

When we reached the front door, I glanced over my shoulder. Edith held a glass of punch in her hand and watched us imperiously.

We'd barely made it outside when we heard the door lock behind us.

"Whoa!" Wong shook her head. "What a witch. She better hope her husband doesn't die. She'll be the prime suspect if there's any indication that someone tampered with that railing."

A few people still lingered on the sidewalk. "Can you believe how fast she got rid of us?" I asked. "It's been less than five minutes. Wonder what happened to the caterer?"

Wong huffed. "She's not through with me yet. If she wants a warrant for me to look at that balcony, then I'll get one."

"That was the oddest thing I've ever seen. Wouldn't you have gone to the hospital with your husband?" I shivered in the cold but didn't dare unfold my pashmina.

Baxter Babineaux, who had bought a home on my block, joined us. "That was quite the act, wasn't it? I have to agree with you, Sophie. Who doesn't go to the hospital with an injured husband? Horace might die from that stab wound! I'm not related to him, but you bet I'll be keeping tabs on his condition."

Tall and portly, Baxter exuded authority in a grandiose way. He was certainly friendly enough, but he had a pretentious manner about him, which always made me feel like I might not live up to his high standards.

He frowned. "With all those HIPAA regulations, I wonder if they'll tell us anything. Old Mrs. Scrooge certainly isn't going to keep us posted on his condition."

Baxter gazed at the wreath that had hung on the balcony but now lay on the sidewalk. "Horace loved Christmas like a little kid. I never met another human being who was as generous or good as that man."

"I hope he recovers." I couldn't take the cold on my bare arms anymore. I unfolded the pashmina to wrap it around my shoulders, taking care not to drop the letter. "My coat is in there."

Baxter nodded and took a deep breath. "Mine, too. And my wife's. She hurried home because she was freezing."

The caterer, surprisingly slim for such an outstanding chef, strode up to us. "Why aren't you answering your phone?"

I smacked my forehead. "It's inside."

He snarled, "Along with all my gear."

I turned to Wong. "Isn't there anything you can do?"

She marched up to the front door and knocked firmly. "Mrs. Scroggins! This is the police. Answer the door, ma'am."

The front door opened just wide enough to see Mrs. Scroggins's bitter face. We couldn't hear the conversation, but after a minute, Wong motioned to us.

The chef, Baxter, and I hurried to the front door.

Wong spoke with authority. "You have five minutes. Babineaux and Sophie, collect all the coats. Caterer, get your stuff and high-tail it out."

Baxter and I rushed to retrieve the coats.

Baxter had parked his metallic midnight-plum Cadillac SUV in back of the building. I carefully wrapped the pashmina around Horace's letter and stashed it under my purse on the front seat.

Unfortunately, my dress was still wet with Horace's blood. I carried coats in my outstretched arms so I wouldn't get it on any of them. We piled coats into the back as fast as we could, dodging the caterer and his staff as they ran in and out.

Edith Scroggins observed us with a steely glare. Wong helped us carry the last load. We had barely stepped out the door when we heard Edith turn the lock.

Baxter offered to give me a ride home. I hesitated, looking down at the blood on my dress.

He retrieved a throw from the back of the car and covered the leather passenger seat with it. "Try not to get blood on anything?"

I did my best.

As Baxter drove, he asked, "Would you mind taking care of the coats? My wife gets a little hyper about clutter."

Truth be told, I would rather be in charge of the coats. Most of them belonged to neighbors and people I knew anyway. Plus, that way, I knew the coats would wind up with their owners. Not that I didn't trust Baxter, I just knew I would get it done.

My classic Ocicat, Mochie, greeted us at the door. He had the distinctive *M* on his forehead but instead of spots, the necklaces and bracelets of his American shorthair ancestors decorated his chest and legs. He rubbed against my calves. I dropped the pashmina on the console in the foyer before helping Baxter carry coats into my dining room.

"Whoa! This place is huge. Ever think about selling?"

"Never." I wouldn't give up my beloved house with its creaks and quirks for anything, even if the one and a half ancient bathrooms *were* in desperate need of renovation.

I thanked him for his help, and insisted on washing the throw. "I'll bring it over when I come to the cookie swap," I promised.

As soon as he left, I rushed upstairs to take off my dress. "I'm not ignoring you," I told Mochie. "But I want to get cleaned up first."

After a hot shower, I soaked the dress in cold water and searched my closet for something warm and comfortable while Mochie sniffed the corners. I pulled on fuzzy dark green pants and a cream-colored sweater and swung Mochie into my arms for a snuggle.

"Brrrr," I said into his fur. "It's cold out there. Be glad you were in a nice warm house. What do you think, bake Christmas cookies by the fire or decorate?"

His head raised, his eyes bright.

"Aha. You'd like to do more investigating. Decorating it is."

He raced up to the third floor ahead of me. As if he knew what we were going to do, he waited by the door to the little attic room that I used for storage.

I had barely opened it when he sprang inside and disappeared. I pulled out boxes of Christmas items, leaving them in a mess on the floor. Opening each box was a treat. They held old friends that brought the joy of cherished memories. I carted a box of nutcrackers, garlands, and snowmen downstairs to the kitchen.

Definitely time for a mug of hot tea to take off that chill. If only I could call someone to find out how Horace was doing. I shook my head. How could he have stayed with a woman like Edith for all those years? What had made her such a bitter shrew? Yet even when Horace was so horribly injured, his thoughts were of her.

Nina Reid Norwood, my across-the-street neighbor and best friend, rapped on the kitchen door.

A gust of cold air blew in when I opened it.

"I thought you must be back by now. That was quite a scene Edith made, throwing everyone out like we were teenagers who'd raided someone's house while they were away." Raised in North Carolina, Nina would never lose her Southern accent.

"I have everyone's coats. Spread the word, okay? And don't forget to take yours home. They're in the dining room." I lifted a snow woman in a red felt hat and a green muffler out of the box and set her on the table. "What's Edith Scroggins's problem? Do you know why she's so cross all the time?"

Nina peered in the box of Christmas items. "Glass-half-empty person is my best guess. The woman is never happy about anything." She lifted out two nutcrackers. "These are so cute. But I'm still glad *I* don't have to decorate."

"I thought you were staying home for Christmas. Did you change your mind?"

"I wish. We're having a full house this year. I hired Jill from Fleur de Lis to do it for me."

"I need to stop by there for pine roping and wreaths. Do you know anyone we can call to find out how Horace is doing?"

"Maybe his secretary, Phyllis? I think they're good friends." She looked around my kitchen. "Did you bring home any goodies from the party?"

"Not a thing. I have water boiling for tea. Why don't you snoop through the freezer while I bring down a couple more boxes?"

"I have to do *everything,*" she teased.

I was carrying a third box downstairs when Nina met me at the foot of the stairs, holding Horace's letter in her hand.

"Is there something you'd like to tell me?" she asked.

"Don't read that!" I set the box down and reached for the letter.

"Too late."

CHAPTER THREE

Dear Sophie,
I dearly love baking Christmas cookies with my mom and sisters. It's an annual tradition. But Mom insists on using her old, blackened-from-use cookie sheets, which always make the cookies too dark on the bottom. We've bought her new baking sheets but she won't use them. Help!

Tired of Burned Cookies
in Mistletoe, Kentucky

Dear Tired of Burned Cookies,
Bring Mom parchment paper. No more greasing the baking sheet and the cookies slide off perfectly every time.

Sophie

"That's not mine. It's none of our business," I insisted.

Nina stepped away, still holding Horace's

letter in her hand. "Really? Then what are *you* doing with it?"

"Did you really read it?" Even though Nina was my dearest friend in the world, I felt an obligation to protect Horace. After all, he'd said Edith should never know about it.

She eyed me. "Okay, it probably isn't yours. You couldn't have kept this a secret from me."

"Nina, you have to promise me you won't tell anyone what it says, or, for that matter, that I even have it."

"You haven't read it, have you?" She held it in the air, as if taunting me.

"No. And I don't plan to."

"Allow me."

My sweetest Moondoggie,
Despite my pleas, we are moving away. They won't tell me where for fear you will follow. My life is over. I don't know how I will manage without you. No one can ever replace you. I shall hold you in my heart and think of you each day. When you gaze at the moon every night, know that I am also looking at it, and for that brief moment, our hearts will

meld across the miles.

Yours forever,
Your Brown-Eyed Girl

I shrank against the newel post. No wonder Nina was making such a fuss about it. What was Horace doing with it? "Is there a date on it?"

"Nope." She checked the envelope. "No address, either. It must have been hand-delivered or left somewhere for Moondoggie." She giggled. "I should have known it wasn't yours. You have green eyes. Brown-Eyed Girl drew a broken heart on it."

"Broken?" I held my hand out for it, and Nina handed it to me. Brown-Eyed Girl had drawn two sides of a heart, separated by a jagged edge. "This is so cute. How old do you think she was? Fifteen or so?"

Nina crossed her arms over her chest. "I assume you know the identity of one of them."

"Why would you think that?"

"Where did you get it?"

"Very nice. You're some friend. Trying to trick me into telling you what I know."

"Why won't you tell me?"

"Look, someone gave this to me for safe-keeping. *I* never would have read it. I'm serious. It's really none of our business."

She wrinkled her nose and flicked the end of her tongue out at me. "But it's so charmingly schoolgirlish and romantic."

"I'll make a deal with you. *If* and when I can share what very little I know, then I'll tell you. Okay? You'll just have to trust me."

Thankfully, the kettle screamed and the phone rang with the distinctive jingle I had assigned to my parents. I moved the kettle off the burner and answered the phone, folding the letter neatly and storing it in a cookbook for safekeeping.

"Sophie, sweetie," said Mom, thereby alerting me that she wanted a favor. She never called anyone *sweetie* unless she was buttering them up. "Do you remember Aunt Louise?"

Of course I did. She knew that, but she had to work up to the favor that was coming. She'd elevated it a notch by mentioning Louise, her best friend in the world from her college days. I poured water over Twinings Christmas Tea into a teapot with a red spout and handle. The middle was supposed to look like an ornament with the words *Merry Christmas* written in jaunty letters. Cinnamon and cloves instantly perfumed the kitchen. Nina had her head in the freezer, in search of something to nosh on.

"Her daughter, Patty, is on her way to Old

Town," continued Mom.

She paused, and I knew what was coming. Since it was located just outside of Washington, DC, a stay in Old Town Alexandria could run into serious money.

"I told her you would be thrilled to have Patty bunk with you while she straightens out her problems there."

It was a done deal. I didn't even have an opportunity to make a bogus excuse and wriggle out of it. "Problems? What kind of problems?"

My kitchen door flew open. My ex-husband, Mars, short for Marshall, burst in with our hound mix, Daisy. His significant other, Natasha, charged in after him, shouting, "Just say no, Sophie!"

Mars glared at her. "No fair, Nat. Let Sophie decide."

Daisy romped to me, her tail spinning with joy. Still holding the phone, I bent to hug her.

"Is that Mars?" asked Mom. "Let me say hi to my favorite son-in-law."

And there it was. The motherly twist of the knife in my back. I didn't bother correcting her by pointing out that he was no longer her son-in-law.

"Just a second. When is Patty coming? I have a date in a couple of days."

"A date! With that cute lawyer?"

I could imagine Mom salivating. "Yes."

"Don't worry about Patty. I don't know when she'll be there. Let me talk to Mars."

I handed the phone to him. "It's Mom."

Natasha immediately said, "I want to say hello, too!"

Nina asked, "She doesn't want to talk with me?"

I preheated the oven and told Nina where she could find mushroom-and-leek turnovers in the freezer. I had made them in advance so I would have something on hand in a pinch. This wasn't the sort of event I'd had in mind, but I could always make more.

Natasha demanded the phone from Mars.

Natasha and I had grown up together and competed at everything except the beauty pageants she loved. My mother once had the nerve to say Natasha had made me a better person by always pushing me to try harder.

After my divorce from Mars, he and Natasha set up housekeeping together and bought a home on my block. It made sharing custody of Daisy easier, but it also meant they were still part of my life.

It had been pointed out to me by friends and family alike that there must have been some hanky-panky between Mars and Natasha prior to the divorce. Some blamed Natasha for breaking up my marriage. I didn't know if she had or not. Some days I thought she might have.

But mostly I had moved on. Although there were moments when I wondered if everything was truly over between Mars and me. For some reason, I pushed those thoughts away and didn't want to face them head-on. Because I was afraid to open that door and find out what was behind it?

For several years I had dated Wolf Fleishman, a local homicide investigator. When that broke off, I met Alex German, the drop-dead-handsome attorney I hoped to get to know better.

Mars and Natasha promised Mom they would entertain Patty so I wouldn't have to cancel my date.

I poured tea for the two of them, smiling at the Spode mugs with candy-cane handles. They heralded the official arrival of the season for me.

Mars, a political advisor, wore jeans and a funky multi-colored sweater that Natasha must have foisted upon him. It wasn't his taste. "I see we came to the right place. I'm starved. Any word about Horace yet?"

"What a tragedy. I can't imagine he'll survive." Natasha was one of those people who never had a hair out of place or a jagged nail. I couldn't remember seeing her without makeup. Her robin's-egg blue sweater must have been an angora blend. I would have looked like a chubby blue bird, but she was tall and slender and carried it off beautifully with matching wool trousers. The silver beading on the sweater set off her almost black hair.

"I'm just sick about it. Horace is such a nice man." I placed the turnovers on a tray covered with a sheet of parchment paper and slid them into the oven. "I don't know who to call. I'm guessing neither of you is close to Edith?" I didn't think she was close to anyone.

"I've never had any problems with her," said Natasha. "Oh! You mean you want someone to call her and inquire about Horace. No thanks, I don't need my head snapped off."

Mars opened the doggy cookie jar on the counter and slipped a treat to Daisy. "Sophie, I need a favor."

"Don't do it, Sophie!" Natasha hissed like an angry cat.

Aha. Now we were getting to the reason for their visit.

"Don't do what?"

"Have you heard about the Christmas

Decorating Contest?" asked Mars.

The First Ever Annual Christmas Decorating Contest had spurred great debate. Old Town was known for its colonial elegance. Many residents argued that the tradition of a candle in every window should be promoted instead of modern decorations. If they weren't arguing about that, they were discussing whether *first ever annual* was an oxymoron. Someone in charge had wisely decreed that the three judges should remain anonymous to eliminate any possibility of bribery or inducement.

A very clear image of an embarrassing number of holiday lights neatly stored in boxes in my basement flashed into my head. Of course. He wanted the lights! "I presume you want to borrow my Christmas lights?"

Mars shook his head from side to side. He wiped his fingers on a napkin. "I want to borrow your house. But now that you mention the lights, I could use them, too."

I choked on my tea. I hadn't expected *that*. By all rights, it should have been Mars's house. We had inherited it from his Aunt Faye, whose portrait hung over my kitchen fireplace. I had bought out his share fair and square in the divorce. It set me back financially but I loved the almost two-hundred-year-old house — uneven floors and all.

"Natasha won't let me decorate our house," Mars explained, cocking his head sideways and giving me the same look Daisy used when she wanted a treat.

"Mars, please. I don't understand why you can't be reasonable about this." Natasha turned on her pouty face, but she must have overused it because it didn't appear to affect Mars. Her lips drew into a thin line. "Honestly, Mars, I'm not letting you go whole hog with our house. Do you know how fast that would make the newspaper?" She lifted her hands in the air as though picturing a headline. "Domestic Diva's Cheesy Christmas."

Mars snorted. "My holiday decor might improve your reputation."

She clutched her throat like she was gagging. "Oh, pul— ease! You're like Clark Griswold. No restraint whatsoever!"

"Funny you should mention that," Mars cackled. "There's a Clark Griswold award!"

Offering a prize in a Clark Griswold category begged for outrageous lighting effects, like the Clark Griswold character had put up on his house in the movie *Christmas Vacation*. I debated silently. Was Mars just yanking Natasha's chain a little bit? There were prizes for the best traditional house, the best colonial decorations, and a kids' favorite category, in addition to prizes for the best decked out businesses. Mars didn't have to go bananas in Clark Griswold style. The prizes were fun and sensible — a plaque, a yard sign designating the house as a winner, and dinner for four at one of the participating restaurants.

"So how about it, Sophie? Loan me the house to decorate? I used to do it when we were married."

I nodded for Natasha's edification. "He did."

I try to be a nice person. Really, I do. But the way I saw it, my house would be decorated to the hilt by Mars, and it would aggravate Natasha no end. Win-win all the way around. A surge of wicked Scroogishness overcame me. It was typical of Natasha to think she was the only one who could pull it off. "You're on. As long as you pay my electric bill."

"Oh, Sophie!" Natasha shuddered. "The neighborhood will be so tacky!"

"It's all in good fun, Natasha. Lighten up," said Mars. He slapped a hand in the air and waited for me to high-five him.

I smacked his hand before taking the turnovers out of the oven.

Natasha glared at me, but I was long past being swayed by her. It was my year to host my family for Christmas, and I had planned to go all out anyway. It would be fun to have a house covered in lights!

Natasha choked on her tea and coughed. "It's appalling."

Nina laughed. "Everybody wants to win. Bernie, Luis, Baxter, all the neighbors."

When it came to Christmas, I was a traditionalist. But sometimes it was fun to go overboard. Besides, I'd seen Natasha's version of Christmas décor, and it was usually a little offbeat. She wasn't in any position to complain.

"Can I use the lights in the basement?" asked Mars. "I could wrap them around the trees on the street."

"Sure. Help yourself. A lot of them are little fairy lights, though."

"C'mon, Daisy. Let's have a look."

As soon as they disappeared into the basement, Natasha said, "I wish you wouldn't encourage him. That contest is a nightmare. I think the women on this block should protest and put an end to the whole thing."

Nina grinned. "Not a chance. I wish my husband weren't off to San Diego tonight. I'd love to join in. Maybe I can hire someone to string lights for me. That would still count, wouldn't it?"

Natasha's eyebrows rose. "I have you on the list of houses the neighborhood will decorate during the block party. It would free up a lot of our time if you hired someone. I'm furious with Gwen, though. I've had the block party planned since last summer, and now she has the nerve to schedule her cookie swap before the block party."

Like it mattered? I threw a red retro-style tablecloth over the kitchen table. Tiny Christmas trees dotted the fabric. Around the edge, the scalloped white border was printed with Christmas trees bearing old-fashioned red candles. I placed the turnovers on a white platter and set it on the table. I added small white hors d'oeuvre dishes, forks, and white napkins.

We heard Daisy's paws and Mars's feet coming up the stairs.

"Flying reindeer!" Mars was giddy with excitement. "Everyone loves reindeer. Maybe I can find some with moving lights so they look like they're taking off!"

"Mars! Talk about uncultured. You're as bad as Gwen Babineaux." She turned her attention to Nina and me. "Did you see that ridiculous pack of lies Gwen sent as a Christmas letter?"

Nina snorted. "That was the point. There

are five lies in it."

Natasha sighed. "Well, I can tell you which one is the lie about Gwen. Decorated the White House, my foot! Like they would let just anyone do that."

"Actually, they do." I sat down at the table, and they took seats, too.

"What?" The tea in Natasha's mug swayed precariously. "You're kidding."

"Nope. They invite people from all over America to come to decorate each year."

"Why haven't I been invited?" Natasha held up her hand when I offered to serve her. "None for me, thanks."

"Probably because you never applied."

She frowned at Mars. "Did you know about this?"

"Yes, Natasha," he said sarcastically, "I spend a lot of time worrying about how they're going to decorate the White House for Christmas."

"I still think it's a lie. Just the way Gwen lies about her age. That business about little Katrina being an art prodigy and selling paintings? She's six! And there's no way Bethany has surpassed the capabilities of her school. That girl couldn't figure out how to light a candle."

"I wouldn't be so sure about that," said Mars. "She leaves plenty of cigarette butts in our alley. She's lighting them with something."

"Obviously Gwen's lie is about having an affair with a neighbor." Nina cut into her turnover and took a bite.

Natasha nearly choked on her tea. "I wouldn't put that past her. Who do you suppose it is? I'm thinking Horace."

"Natasha!" I protested. "That's the lie. What married woman would say that in a Christmas letter if it were true?"

"I wouldn't be so sure. Gwen's quite the flirt," said Mars.

Natasha set down her mug with a *thump.* "Well, I suppose I'd better take a stroll by the Scroggins house. Looks like we might have two widows to decorate for this year." She set down her empty mug and left in haste.

Mars flipped his hand impatiently behind her back. "Bah humbug to you, too. The real reason she won't let me decorate our house is because everything has to reflect *her* and *her* taste. It was more fun when you and I did it together. I miss that."

Nina raised an eyebrow and glued her eyes on me, but said nothing.

Truth be told, I missed it, too. "You don't mind if I buy pine roping and wreaths, do you?"

"Not at all." Mars fetched paper. In between bites, he made a rough sketch of the house, showing us what he had in mind. "I'll help you with the pine and hang the wreaths for you."

Nina glanced at her watch. "Better go. I have to take my husband to the airport. Call me if you hear anything about Horace."

Mars left with her, eager to work out his sketch in greater detail on his computer. It was his week to have Daisy. She bounded out with him.

"Looks like it's just us, Mochie." I spent the evening decorating the interior of my house.

In each guest bedroom, I placed a teeny Christmas tree with lights. In the small bedroom where my niece would sleep, I had begun a tradition of arranging a street of five North Pole houses on the dresser. They were on a timer so she would see them when she went up to bed at night. Even though she was a teenager now, I knew she still got a kick out of them. The little buildings were lovingly detailed, from the reindeer stables with some open stall doors, to the elves' favorite after-work gathering hole.

As I set up the Christmas Village in the living room, I couldn't help thinking about Horace and his Brown-Eyed Girl. Clearly,

51

he must have been Moondoggie. When was that character popular? In the sixties? The early seventies? Horace must have been very young. And very much in love to keep that letter all these years. I had no idea he was such a romantic.

I gasped, startling Mochie during his careful prowl through boxes on the floor. I'd told hateful Edith that Horace said he always loved her. *Always!* What if he hadn't meant Edith? That would certainly be understandable. She probably didn't treat him much better than she did anyone else. What if he had meant Brown-Eyed Girl?

On the other hand, maybe he did mean that he had always loved Edith. Just because I found her to be caustic didn't mean she acted that way toward everyone. He had stayed with her all these years. Maybe he really did love her. Seemed doubtful, though.

Had he meant for me to find Brown-Eyed Girl? Was I supposed to relay his message to her? He'd said Edith must never know. That made sense. Whether it was Edith whom he had always loved or not, he probably didn't want her to realize he'd been in love with someone else.

I set figures of an older couple in the village. Maybe Brown-Eyed Girl felt the same way and longed to see him. What if he died from the stab wound? They would have missed their chance to see each other one last time. I cupped my forehead in my hand. Why hadn't I realized this sooner? I had to find Brown-Eyed Girl. But Edith must never know. Aargh. This wouldn't be easy.

I phoned the hospital before I went to bed, but they wouldn't give me any information about Horace. During the night, I tossed and turned, imagining Moondoggie and his Brown-Eyed Girl. How would I ever find her? There were millions of brown-eyed women around Horace's age.

The sun shone in the morning, giving me fresh hope. Still dressed in my flannel nightshirt, I stumbled down the stairs, put on the kettle, and immediately placed a phone call to Wong, who confirmed that Horace had survived the night but remained in critical condition. I cracked the window to let in a little fresh air, then stirred sugar and milk into my morning tea.

Nina tapped on the window of my kitchen door. She had dashed across the street wrapped in a fluffy lavender robe. I had barely opened the door when she demanded, "It's Horace, isn't it?"

I played coy for just a moment longer in

case she meant something else. "What is?"

"Moondoggie. Horace is Moondoggie. It came to me in the middle of the night. You worked on his party yesterday. No one at the party would just hand you that note to carry around. No, no, no. It was Horace!"

She beamed at me and poured herself a mug of tea. "We have to go see him. I wonder if he can speak."

I gazed down at her feet and giggled. "What are those?"

"Christmas slippers. They're reindeer heads. Aren't they fun?"

Outside someone screamed in terror.

CHAPTER FOUR

Dear Sophie,
My son will be on leave from the military for Christmas, so my husband wants to decorate the house from top to bottom. I'm scared of the electric bill. Which lights use the least electricity?
Proud Mom in Lightsville, Ohio

Dear Proud Mom,
Solar lights don't use any electricity but will cost more to buy. There are also battery-operated lights, some of which operate on built-in timers! If Hubby really wants to go overboard with electric lights, LED lights are your best bet.
Sophie

If I hadn't cracked a window earlier to let in some cool winter air, we might not have heard the scream at all. Mochie jumped onto the banquette and peered out the picture window.

Nina and I rushed to the front door to look outside. A few houses down, I thought I saw something in the bushes. I grabbed a coat, and the two of us dodged traffic to cross the street. We ran like clowns in our slippers, the bells on Nina's jingling all the way.

Baxter Babineaux appeared to be stuck on his back in the grip of boxwood bushes. He called his wife's name feebly. "Gwen? Help! Gwen?"

A ladder pinned him down and strands of Christmas lights draped over him like a colorful web. "Are you okay?" I asked as Nina and I wrestled the ungainly wooden ladder to the ground.

"Sophie! Nina! I was afraid my family wouldn't hear me."

I wasn't surprised. Trendy teen music blared right through the walls of their elegant historic town house.

He tried to disengage himself from the strings of lights but only succeeded in creating bigger knots as they caught on one another.

I did my best to lift them straight up, but they had twisted around his legs and torso. "Can you hold on to me? Let's get you out of the bushes first, then we'll tackle the lights."

I wedged my hands under his arms and pulled. Baxter had to be almost twice my weight and a good foot or more taller than my five feet. Nina tried pulling away the lights that entangled him. I tugged, and he rolled up to a sitting position. Branches cracked under him and broke as he kicked at them to free his legs. When he tried to stand up, he collapsed into a heap on the ground.

Nina rushed to his front door and rang the bell. "Should I call an ambulance?"

"No! I'll be quite fine. I just" — he pulled a strand of lights that tugged at another strand of lights — "need to catch my breath."

The sight of the staid and slightly pompous businessman sitting on the ground wrapped in Christmas lights *was* a little bit amusing. The next time he prattled on about the best meal he ever had in a tiny village in Tuscany, I would remember this moment. "Would you mind if I cut these lights off you? They're caught on each other. How many strands are there?"

"Twenty."

"Decorating for the Christmas contest?"

"Gwen's been pestering me about it. She

has to have the best house on the block. Better than Natasha's. And" — he grunted when he tried to stand and failed — "my brother is coming for the holidays. I guess I have a little Clark Griswold in me after all."

The homes in Old Town Alexandria were gorgeous. Many of them, like those on our street, had been built in the 1800s in typical colonial styles. But they were tall and hard to climb. Baxter's house was three full stories with dormer windows on the third floor. Very difficult to cover in lights.

"Have you heard anything about Horace? You work for him, don't you?" Nina asked.

Baxter scowled. "I haven't heard beans about poor old Horace. There won't be a business if he dies. His insufferable wife had the locks changed on the building. No one could go to work today." He shook his head. "We have deals pending," he whined. "Everyone has to work from home. It's unbelievable."

The front door swung open. Gwen Babineaux seemed surprised to see Nina. A bottle blonde, Gwen had gone too long without a boost of color. Dark roots gave away her true brunette color in spite of the dark blond curls that cascaded around her shoulders. Tall and curvy, she prided herself on her cooking and baking skills, and the resulting extra pounds enhanced her voluptuousness. She tended to squint, hiding eyes the color of milk chocolate. With her long straight nose and thin lips, the squint sometimes gave the impression that she was being critical. She wore an oversized green flannel pajama top with the sleeves rolled up. Pictures of the Grinch and wrapped presents alternated all over it. "Baxter? What have you done now?"

"Do you have scissors I could use to cut the lights off him?" I asked.

She huffed, shook her head and went inside, returning in a minute with shears. She handed them to me and pulled twigs of boxwood from his thinning hair.

"Honestly, Baxter is about the least handy man I've ever known."

"You're the one who wants to win the contest," he protested.

She took a step back. "I don't see a single light! What's that on the roof?"

"The staple gun."

"You were on the *roof?*" she shrieked. She shook her head. "And I'm the one who goes to a shrink! Well, he'll be hearing about this."

"How else am I supposed to put lights up there? I took the ladder upstairs and pushed it out the window. Then I set it up so I could string lights on the dormers, but when I stepped on it, a rung broke. I fell down, but managed to grab hold of the ladder. It slipped at first, but then it caught on something. If Bethany didn't crank up her music so loud, you would have heard me yelling for help. Then the whole thing gave way."

I snipped faster. "If you fell all the way from the roof, you really should go to the emergency room. You're incredibly lucky the bushes broke your fall. Did any branches stab you in the back?"

Gwen appeared more irritated than concerned. "Looks like he was protected by this horrible old leather jacket that I keep trying to throw out. Good thing he wrapped up."

I cut a few more light strands. They finally dropped off Baxter and fell to the ground. Nina gathered them in a pile.

"What kind of idiot takes a ladder up on the roof anyway?" muttered Gwen.

Baxter sounded tired. "Didn't you tell me you wanted lights on the dormer windows? Did you think I could just toss them up there?"

Time to get out of their squabble. "I'm glad you're okay."

Nina frowned at him. "Sophie is right. You ought to get checked out. That was a long fall."

"Nonsense. If he can argue with me, he's fine." Gwen sounded like a mom talking about a kid who'd taken a little tumble.

"I guess we'll head home, then." Turning as I spoke, I stepped over the ladder. My father had owned one very much like it. Long and battered from use, various colors of paint had dripped on it over many years. My breath caught in my chest at the sight of the broken rung.

It hadn't worn out in the middle from years of use. It broke on the side where it connected to the ladder. I was no expert, but only part of the rung had splintered as wood should. The top portion of the break appeared almost smooth, as if it had been sawed.

CHAPTER FIVE

Dear Sophie,

I'm married to a Christmas nut. For years my husband has wanted a lighted Christmas wreath attached to the front of his car. I'd like to surprise him, but I don't know where to start. Do they sell wreaths for cars?

       Santa's Helper in Bow, Kentucky

Dear Santa's Helper,

You can buy prewired artificial wreaths for cars at many automotive stores. If you would rather use a fresh wreath, then use a string of battery-powered lights, or twelve-volt LED lights that plug into the car's cigarette lighter.

       Sophie

My gaze drifted to Gwen, who fussed at Baxter. "I'm behind schedule now," she complained. "There's so much to do. My cookie swap is tomorrow. I don't have time to coddle you. Can you walk? And Nina, don't you dare bring store-bought cookies."

Their front door opened again. Katrina, the Babineauxs' youngest daughter, viewed the scene. Six years old with an adorable mischievous face and pudgy cheeks, she ventured toward her parents, her auburn tresses unkempt as though no one had bothered to comb her hair. "Mom? Mom! What if I promise —"

"Really, Kat. Can't you see that I'm busy? The subject is closed. There will be no animals of any sort in my house. You're allergic to them. End of story. Now get out of your father's way."

Baxter stood up unsteadily.

Kat watched with a crestfallen expression and whispered to no one, "But I'm *not* allergic."

A tinny rendition of "Jingle Bells" played on our street, distracting us. A faded red and white VW camper pulled up in front of the Babineauxs' home. A lighted wreath covered most of the front under the window and between the headlights. Colorful lights twinkled around the windows. A sign on the side read *No More Hungry Children.*

Gwen's mouth hung open. "Noooo," she breathed.

A man leaped out of the driver's seat and yelled, "Baxter, baby!" He held his fists over his head and did a little dance of joy, rotating his ample middle.

Gwen hissed, "Please tell me that's not your brother, Elvin."

Baxter probably didn't hear her. With a joyous cry, he charged toward the dancing man and held him in a bear hug. The guy looked suspiciously like a younger, chubbier version of Baxter. I'd have bet on them being related.

The passenger door opened and a long shapely leg emerged, followed by another. The owner wore her skirt too short, her makeup too heavy, and her sweater far too tight on the most ample bosom I could recall seeing.

Gwen gasped.

The woman's curves made Gwen's shapely figure seem positively scrawny.

The woman smiled and issued a happy little scream. "Gwen!" She sauntered toward Gwen on high heels and held out her arms for a hug. "I feel like I've known you forever!"

"Are you my Aunt Sugar?" asked Kat.

The woman released Gwen and placed her palms on the sides of Kat's face. "Aren't you the prettiest little angel? You must be

Kat! Can I have a hug?"

Gwen pulled Kat to her, interrupting any attempt at a hug for Aunt Sugar. "Honey," Gwen said to Kat, "why don't you help your daddy and uncle park that, that bus?"

Kat eagerly ran toward her father.

Gwen hustled along behind her to Baxter and said, loud enough for everyone to hear, "They cannot stay here. And move that embarrassingly unsightly vehicle to the alley this instant!"

Undoubtedly having forgotten all about us, Gwen propelled Aunt Sugar into her home as though she meant to hide her, much like the bus.

I rubbed my arms against the cold. A glance at Nina reminded me that we wore fuzzy slippers. But I paused anyway for one more moment. Now that they were inside, I dared to look at the ladder more closely. I nudged Nina. "Did you notice the ladder?"

I knelt beside it and examined the break. The second rung had given way. I didn't want to touch anything in case the police could get prints off it. The closer I looked, the more convinced I was that someone had weakened the rung by sawing it.

Nina shrugged. "Old ladders break. I'm freezing. Let's go."

Back home in the warmth of my kitchen,

I closed the window, fed Mochie minced turkey in gravy, and pulled out bread for cinnamon- and nutmeg-laced French toast.

"Seriously, Nina? You didn't think it looked like someone cut that rung on the ladder?"

"You're turning into a buttinsky, Sophie, one of those people who report neighbors to the police. Before long, everyone will run from you, shrieking."

I whisked the eggs, added generous doses of cinnamon and nutmeg as well as a drop of vanilla, and dredged the bread through the mixture.

Had I become overly suspicious of everyone and everything, seeing maliciousness everywhere? Maybe I was wrong and no one had tampered with the ladder. Then I'd have egg on my face and permanently alienate the entire Babineaux clan. What if I *was* right, though? I would never forgive myself if someone meant to harm Baxter, and I could have prevented it. I heated the griddle and added oil. "Baxter could have been killed!"

"Okay, I'll grant you that." Nina poured water for hot tea. "But I hardly think Gwen is trying to knock him off. Not that I know them very well. Besides, we have something more important to do — find Brown-Eyed

66

Girl for Horace!"

I grinned at her eagerness and handed her a plate with French toast that I had topped with dots of butter and maple syrup. We took mugs of tea and settled at the table. "How are we ever going to find a girl Horace loved thirty or forty years ago? She could be anywhere."

Nina cut a piece of French toast and devoured it. "Mmm. So good. We could start by paying Horace a visit."

"Think they'll let us in?"

"Why not? We're friends of his. Isn't that what people do? Visit their friends in the hospital?"

If Horace was conscious, maybe he could point us in the direction of Brown-Eyed Girl. I supposed Edith had the power to chase us away, but it was worth a try. I couldn't think of another way to follow up for him, and Horace certainly couldn't do it himself.

After breakfast, Nina rushed home to change. I promised to meet her in fifteen minutes. I pulled on a white turtleneck sweater and my favorite stretchy jeans with an elastic waist. My boots were more functional than high fashion, but my jeans fit into them nicely, making me feel quite trendy. I added a warm black suede jacket, and an ultrasoft long white scarf that wrapped around my neck loosely twice and folded over itself in front. After a quick good-bye to Mochie, who lounged happily in the sunroom, I dashed out to my garage. Nina waited for me, wearing a beige corduroy skirt, boots, and a dark green jacket with a red and beige plaid muffler.

I drove to the hospital, planning to stop to buy pine roping and wreaths on the way back.

The woman at the front desk told us Horace's room number without hesitation. The silence in the intensive care ward emphasized the dire condition of the patients housed there.

A nurse was exiting the room when we arrived. "Are you here to see Horace?" There was no mistaking the hope in her expression. "I'm so glad." She lowered her voice to a whisper. "Doesn't he have any family?"

"He has a wife," blurted Nina.

The nurse stared at her. "Does she know he's here?"

Nina and I exchanged a glance.

"She hasn't been to see him?" I asked.

"No," whispered the nurse. "Not a soul has come to visit."

She ushered us to the door of his room, chattering the whole way. "He's not responding at the moment. We don't know if he can hear us or not, but it's important that you talk to him. Okay?"

She watched as we turned our attention to Horace. He lay still and pale with his eyes closed, a mere ghost of himself.

Nina set her purse in a chair, and in such a cheerful voice that it almost sounded like she had burst into song, she said, "Hello, Horace! How are you feeling? You look wonderful. I hear you did splendidly in surgery yesterday and that you're healing well."

I threw Nina a questioning glance. Why hadn't she told me? "Where did you hear that?" I whispered.

Clearly annoyed, she grabbed a pad of paper from her purse and scribbled, *You're supposed to say encouraging things to a patient!*

"Hi, Horace. It's Sophie."

Nina rotated her hand in front of her face. Evidently I was supposed to say more.

Instead I reached for his hand and clasped it in mine. "We're so worried about you." His cold hand lay in mine, motionless as a dead fish.

Nina babbled brightly, telling him what a glorious day it was and that his Christmas party had been fabulous. Throughout her cheerful rambling, Horace showed no recognition that we were in the room. I feared for him.

When Nina ran out of steam, I sat in the chair and spoke with him softly, holding his hand and telling him to be strong and that we were all pulling for him.

I couldn't help noticing that the nurse hovered protectively just outside the door.

And then Nina leaned over him and, right in his face, said, "Moondoggie, we're looking for Brown-Eyed Girl. I'm sure she'd want to know that you need her now."

To my total amazement Horace's fingers curled just enough to give my hand the slightest squeeze.

"I saw that!" gasped Nina. "Horace, I know you're in there. I know you can hear us. Does Brown-Eyed Girl live in Old Town?"

The soft pressure pressed my fingers again. It was nothing more than an attempt to curl his fingers really. I gazed at Nina and said in a low voice, "You have to tell him what a squeeze means. One squeeze for yes, and two for no."

The nurse interrupted. "Did he really squeeze your hand?"

We nodded.

"Have you been having a good visit, Horace?" she asked. "I'm afraid it's time for me to change your bandages."

She shooed us out in the nicest way, saying she hoped we would return because Horace needed interaction with his loved ones.

As we walked down the hallway, Nina said, "He needs Brown-Eyed Girl."

"Isn't it interesting that horrible Edith hasn't been to the hospital?" I didn't think I was particularly critical of people, but I couldn't imagine anything harsher or more cold. "She must despise him," I said. "Maybe Edith knows about Brown-Eyed Girl and that's why she's so unhappy."

"He squeezed your hand. I saw him."

"That doesn't mean anything. Let's be realistic. If Brown-Eyed Girl lived in Old Town, wouldn't he have contacted her?"

"Maybe not." Nina scowled at me. "You know things are different when you're married. Most people don't go calling up old flames. That's extremely poor form." Nina grabbed my wrist. "Look! That's her! How could we have been so blind?"

Horace's secretary, Phyllis, walked toward us. "Have you seen Horace? How's he doing?"

We filled her in, omitting the fact that his wife hadn't paid him a visit yet.

Nina widened her eyes and tilted her head toward Phyllis in little jolts. Phyllis definitely had brown eyes. She wore her hair yellow blond, but her dark eyebrows gave away her natural color.

When I didn't take Nina's oh-so-obvious hint, she burbled, "Phyllis, do you know the song 'Brown Eyed Girl'?"

Phyllis smiled. "I do! It's one of my favorites."

Nina turned a smug, satisfied face toward me.

Nina was such a romantic. We couldn't walk around questioning every woman in Horace's general age range. I asked Phyllis to keep in touch and let us know if she heard about any changes in Horace's condition.

Nina didn't say anything until we were out of earshot. "We found her! Right under our noses. Why didn't you say something?"

"First of all, everyone likes the song 'Brown Eyed Girl.' That doesn't prove anything. Second, unless I'm mistaken, over half the population has brown eyes. Are you planning to ask every brown-eyed woman in Old Town if she likes that song?"

"We'll know soon enough anyway. I bet if she's Brown-Eyed Girl, he'll respond to her and get better right away."

We drove out of the parking lot, Nina still insisting that Phyllis had to be Horace's long-lost love. "Horace is such a nice guy. I can't imagine how he tolerated Edith all these years."

I couldn't help thinking about Horace's upset stomach the day before. "I don't want to be swayed by the fact that Edith is such an unfriendly person, but the spouse is always the first suspect when something happens. It would be so easy for her to slip something into his food."

Nina dreamily said, "He and Phyllis worked next to each other all along, never able to share their true feelings." She choked. "Is Phyllis married? Do you know?"

"I have no idea." I parked the car close enough to my house to have walked easily, but I needed my hybrid SUV to transport the pine roping and wreaths home. I thought I'd better get them up before Mars covered the house with lights.

Old Town was beginning to put on its Christmas finery. Lush pine boughs surrounded store windows and cheerful wreaths seemed to have appeared overnight. Even though it was early afternoon, lights sparkled everywhere I looked. Nina and I peered into a paned store window. A silver and white winter wonderland glistened inside. Giant three-dimensional snowflakes hung from the ceiling, lights glinted off their fuzzy spokes and gleamed on little beads. Stunning silver pieces graced a table set as though for a holiday dinner. The centerpiece took my breath away. Two elegant silver reindeer pulled a foot-high silver sleigh filled with white blown-glass ornaments. On the buffet behind it, silver candleholders in the shapes of stag heads with antlers held white candles laced with tiny silver stars.

"Ohh," sighed Nina. "Do you think Jill could do my house in silver and white? There's something so clean and wintery about it."

I understood completely. It sparkled in a crisp, elegant way, making me long to change my traditional red and green Christmas décor to silver and white. "Can't hurt to ask."

We moved on to Rocking Horse Toys.

Jonah and Twiggy Lawrence had outdone themselves decorating the window of their new toy store. Jonah had been a sales representative for a major toy company in Arizona. He'd bucked the corporate life to pursue his dream — a toy store of his own. He and his wife, Twiggy, opened it with great fanfare in June, but this was their big season. They had re-created Santa's workshop. Two-foot-tall elves wearing red and green outfits wrapped packages. Dolls in lacy dresses looked on. The giant unicorn and huge pony behind them were so cute I wanted to buy them. Colorful books lay in artistically arranged piles, waiting their turn to be wrapped. Gleaming red fire trucks competed for attention with a four-foot-tall sailboat. If none of that was enough to lure children inside, bright gift tags bearing names like Emma, Sophia, Kat, Jacob, and Michael were scattered around, as if they were waiting for the elves to assign them to gifts. A tower of colorfully wrapped gifts with mysterious contents waited to find homes.

It was that wonderful time of year again. I took a deep breath of the frigid air and couldn't help smiling. There was simply something magical about the Christmas season.

Nina tugged me inside, and I didn't resist, even though my niece had outgrown the toy stage. A collection of huggable white snowmen, polar bears, and dolls had been arranged in a pyramid. A train circled in the store, tooting its horn, and in the background, soft music played "Santa Claus is Coming to Town," which I remembered from my childhood.

Twiggy was decked out in red and white striped tights, green elf shoes that curled at the toes, a green jumper, and a green elf hat. Her name suited her perfectly. Almost as slender as a young boy, Twiggy sparkled with enthusiasm and seemed far younger than her forty years. Her cropped hair, the color of chestnuts, followed the shape of her head. Today wisps stuck out from under her hat. There wasn't a child in the world who wouldn't confide in this adorable elf.

"You look so cute," I said.

"Thanks, Sophie! We have children coming by any minute. Santa will be here soon, so I thought I'd dress in the spirit of things. This is my official helper. You know Kat, don't you?"

Kat Babineaux wore an outfit exactly like Twiggy's, but she held a live long-haired white cat who appeared to be very much at home in her little arms.

"Who is this pretty kitty?" I asked.

"Snowball."

Maybe she was right about not being allergic to animals. She didn't seem to be in any distress at the moment, and she couldn't get her nose any closer to Snowball if she tried.

A loud cantankerous demand stilled the

other voices in the store. "Just how long do you expect me to stand here?"

CHAPTER SIX

Dear Natasha,
My daughter has been begging for a bicycle. We think wrapping it is the best way to hide it, but how do we wrap something so awkward?

> One of the Elves in Santa Claus,
> Indiana

Dear One of the Elves,
Disguising gifts takes cardboard boxes, masking tape, and a little creativity. It's easiest to slice one side off a large box and tape two sides or three from another box to the first one, thus creating a new shape that fits around the item. You can even bend one into an arc, or use another household object like a ball or a lampshade to give it a different shape. Then wrap with gift wrap.

> Natasha

Twiggy's eyes flew open wide. "Heaven preserve us," she muttered, adjusting her hat. She hurried to the cash register, where her mother-in-law, Claudine, was ringing up someone else's purchases. "I'm sorry, Mrs. Scroggins. We're a small store and only have the one cash register."

Petite Claudine had turned the color of beets. Silver hair in a bob style that she'd tucked behind her ears emphasized the blaze on her face. The gentleman customer before Mrs. Scroggins grabbed his purchase and practically ran for the door, brushing by me in his haste.

Claudine rang up the stuffed mouse Mrs. Scroggins wanted to buy. It wore glasses and a Santa hat.

"The price is wrong. I *have* a coupon!" Mrs. Scroggins couldn't have spoken louder without yelling. Although she could certainly make a big fuss, she was actually fairly scrawny. Even her bulky wool coat didn't add much to her girth. But her scowl and contemptuous manner were enough to intimidate anyone.

The other customers stared. Kat retreated to safety behind the counter with Snowball.

The deep red color drained from Claudine's face. "I'm so sorry, Mrs. Scroggins. This coupon is for another store."

"That makes no difference to me." She reminded me of an unpleasant school-teacher who could make a student squirm with a mere glance.

Mrs. Scroggins wasn't physically imposing, but Twiggy looked to Claudine in desperation and hissed, "Give her a discount." She smiled sweetly at Edith. "Mrs. Scroggins is an excellent customer."

Claudine stared at Mrs. Scroggins for a moment, her eyes narrowed. "I'm sorry. We cannot honor this coupon, Mrs. Scroggins. If you want to use the coupon, you'll have to go to that store. I believe the closest branch is in Falls Church."

"Why, no one has ever been so rude to me. You'll rue this day. I shall inform my husband and from here on out, we'll do our shopping elsewhere. How ungrateful! I'll go on the Internet and tell everyone what a despicable store this is. I'll run you right out of business. How dare you treat me like this? You'll wish you had given me a discount when you're sitting in the poorhouse all alone. All you Lawrences deserve to be cold and hungry!" Mrs. Scroggins smacked money on the counter, turned on her heel, and marched out of the store gripping the mouse.

Twiggy called out a weak, "Merry Christmas!"

"Wow. That was quite a scene."

In the commotion, I hadn't noticed my new neighbor Liza Simon, who always introduced herself as *Liza with a Z, like Minnelli.* Reddish blond hair curled into her face in an unruly manner that gave her the appearance of being carefree and fun. She made little effort to tame it, other than pushing parts of it back with her hand, which emphasized the roundness of her face and a slight double chin. She was married to Luis, the psychiatrist who had wanted to look at the dirk at Horace's party.

"People say New Yorkers are rude, but I never saw anything like *that* in the city. I thought Southerners were supposed to be super-polite. What's Scrooge's excuse?"

"Scrooge?" asked Nina.

"That's what people call her. Luis gets mad at me, but the woman is always a grump. What is her problem?"

"Maybe she's stressed because Horace is in the hospital." My path had crossed with Mrs. Scroggins's several times, but only on a surface level. I had no idea what her story was.

Nina leaned in and whispered, "But she hasn't been to see him."

81

"Could she have bought the mouse for him?" I suggested halfheartedly.

"Do you think she ever gets away with that coupon scam? I'm not much of a coupon clipper, but if I could use them anywhere, it might be worth it." Liza laughed aloud, which assured me she meant it in jest.

The hostile air left in Mrs. Scroggins's wake dissipated, and it wasn't long before shoppers were merrily enjoying hot cider that Twiggy brought around on a tray.

"Are you three invited to the cookie swap of all cookie swaps?" asked Twiggy.

"You mean at Gwen Babineaux's house?" Liza sipped a little cup of cider. She held her free hand up in the air and waved it. "Please explain this to me. Why on earth am I supposed to bake thirteen dozen cookies?" She looked up toward the ceiling and moved her fingers as though she was counting on them. "One hundred forty-four . . . that's like a million cookies! What is she going to do with all those cookies?"

"She's having twelve guests," I explained. "One dozen of each type of cookie will be shared at the cookie swap, so we can all try them. Then everyone gets to take home one dozen of each type of cookie."

"Instead of you baking a dozen kinds of cookies for yourself, everyone bakes enough to share, and we all end up with a variety of cookies." Twiggy grinned at her. "With the store so busy, I don't have time to do a lot of baking this year, so I'm thrilled. I'm bringing no-bake cookies," said Twiggy. "They're our favorites."

"No-bake? Why didn't I think of that?" Liza pouted. "I'm not much of a baker. Gwen is out of her mind crazy! It would take me *months* to bake that many cookies. And I'd have to go to a spa for another month just to recover. Do you think anyone would notice if I brought store-bought cookies?"

Twiggy nodded. "Natasha and Gwen will know the difference. And believe me, they'll say something. We've been renting the apartment over Natasha and Mars's garage since June, and she has the nerve to sneak in there when we're not home. Can you believe she told me I don't fold my towels correctly? Like anyone cares? It's not as though *she's* the one using them!"

Liza moaned, turned her eyes up to the ceiling and cringed. "They're such domestic divas! It makes me crazy. I think they've rubbed off on Luis. The man was always content with a fake Christmas tree and an artificial wreath slapped on the door. This year he's completely consumed by the

Christmas decorating contest, and he expects *me* to be a holiday domestic goddess. I told him I'm a goddess all right, and he'd better remember that, but not a domestic one."

Twiggy gasped and focused on me.

Looking slightly sick, Liza said, "Oh no! You're one of them, too, aren't you? I feel like I've moved onto the *Stepford Wives* street!"

"Not to worry," I said. "There are plenty of people on our block who don't cook and bake, and frankly, I'm not much into cleaning."

"Cleaning?" Liza's eyes swept heavenward again, and the corners of her mouth plunged. If nothing else, she was amusingly dramatic.

"I'm not joking when I say I'm not a domestic type. What am I going to do?" Liza asked.

Nina giggled. "Shh. Don't tell, but you won't be the only one. I won't be baking cookies for the swap or for any other reason. Buy cookies from a bakery and put them in cute little containers. Gwen and Natasha will be so absorbed with their own cookies that they probably won't notice."

"Nina, you're a doll! Finally, a woman after my own heart."

The door banged open and adorable children trundled in bundled up in colorful coats, boots, and hats.

"They're so sweet it *almost* makes me wish I had one of my own," said Liza.

Wistfully, Twiggy said, "We've been trying to have one but no luck yet. We've put in an application to adopt."

"You'd make great parents. Besides, what kid wouldn't want to have his or her very own toy store in the family?" I asked.

"That's what I think!" Twiggy smiled broadly. "I swear we'd keep Kat if we thought Baxter and Gwen wouldn't notice!" Twiggy excused herself and flitted over to the kids.

"I'm off to buy pine for my crazed husband." Liza frowned like a clown.

"At Fleur de Lis? That's where we're headed," said Nina.

A hearty *ho ho ho* boomed from the rear of the store. Santa had arrived, complete with red suit, fuzzy white beard, and Jonah's kind brown eyes. A few children squealed at the sight of him. Some drew away to the safety of their parents.

Nina, Liza, and I slipped out and headed next door. A cascade of ready-to-use arrangements for front doors and walkways flanked the entrance of Fleur de Lis, Old

Town's floral and garden supply store. Evergreens spilled out of the tops of Santa's boots. Bells, hearts, and stars made of birdseed hung from jaunty red bows on miniature Christmas trees, and stunningly elegant topiaries of greens that alternated with rings of rosy apples were topped off by the traditional colonial sign of welcome — a pineapple. I loved them all. A thick garland decorated the doorway. Huge magnolia leaves twined with holly, various kinds of fir, red berries, giant pinecones, green and red apples, and mistletoe. It was nothing short of amazing. I studied it for a moment, wondering if I could re-create it.

Stepping inside was like walking through a portal to a winter wonderland. Glitter sparkled on poinsettias, and bare white branches dripped gleaming icicles and ornaments. I selected plain white pine roping and balsam wreaths that I could decorate myself.

Thinking I should add some holly and magnolia leaves, I strayed to the back of the store in search of florist wire.

Liza Simon studied boxes of rat poison with a steady eye. Silver tinsel roping draped over the top shelf, and Burl Ives sang "A Holly Jolly Christmas" over the speaker system in the store.

I watched the incongruous scene longer than I should have. She selected a box, tucked it under her arm, and ambled away. I wanted to ask if she was experiencing a rat problem — after all, I lived across the street and two houses down. If she had rats, I would too. I hesitated only out of sheer politeness. Gasping, *Good Lord! You have rats?* seemed the height of rudeness. Especially in front of so many shoppers. No need to embarrass the poor woman when she was still new to the area. Maybe I could ask her in private at the cookie swap.

I found the wire and hummed along with Burl as I picked out a few Christmas decorations in the front of the shop. I didn't need them, but half the fun of the holiday was decking out the house, and really, shouldn't everyone have a tiny puffed-up bird with a red and green knit stocking cap on his head?

Nina spotted the bird in my hand. "Where did you find that? I have to have one!"

I pointed her in the right direction. "On the left, just past Jill Kinghorn."

Nina elbowed me. "Jill has brown eyes, and she's about the right age."

"What if 'Brown Eyed Girl' was their song but she really had blue eyes?"

Nina scowled at me. "Spoilsport. Jill says she can decorate my house in silver and white. My monster-in-law should be duly impressed. And FYI, you and I just invited Liza to lunch on Saturday. She seems like a lot of fun."

I should have stopped shopping, but Christmas was just too tempting. I added a few sprigs of mistletoe to my selections and then pretended to be like a horse wearing blinders so I wouldn't be seduced into buying anything else.

Nina helped me load everything into my car. Minutes later, we pulled into a parking spot in front of my house to unload. Across the way in his tiny snippet of a front yard, my new neighbor Luis wrestled with a blow-up reindeer so large that it looked like a balloon from the Macy's Thanksgiving Day Parade had broken loose and landed on our street.

Mars and Bernie, who was the best man at our wedding, glared with outrage at the mammoth creature.

Nina and I stepped out of the car, focusing on the leg that blocked traffic. The reindeer dwarfed Luis, who had to be at least six feet tall. The eyes could have peeked into Luis and Liza's second-story windows.

"How big *is* that thing?" asked Nina.

Mars growled, "Eighteen feet."

"He can't leave it there," I said, watching cars slow to veer around it.

Bernie, whose British accent made him sound brilliant no matter what he said, raised his eyebrows. "He's talking about putting it on the roof, which is simply ludicrous. The first strong wind would blow it off."

Luis dodged traffic and jogged across the street to us. "Looks like my eyes were bigger than my front yard," he joked. "I'm envious of you two and Baxter. I think outdoor decorating is best done in teams."

"Horace was supposed to help you, right?" asked Mars.

"That was the plan," Luis sighed. "Did you hear the latest about Horace?"

My breath caught. "What?"

"That fall probably saved his life."

Nina and I exchanged a confused look.

"Turns out," said Luis, "that he had taken too much of his blood-thinning medicine. He could have died from internal bleeding if he hadn't gotten immediate medical attention. Ironically, the dagger wound might have helped save his life. They caught the blood-thinning medicine overdose just in time."

"Everyone's saying it was a close call for Horace. Poor bloke." Bernie cocked his head toward the sidewalk, prompting us to turn around.

Edith Scroggins walked along the sidewalk toward the monstrous reindeer. With a dirty look at Luis, she walked underneath it, her head high and her back ramrod straight.

"Is she spying on us?" asked Mars. "She's been by a couple of times."

"She probably thinks Horace is the one having an affair with Gwen." Nina turned her head to watch Edith. "The Christmas letter Gwen sent has half the women in Old Town spying on their husbands."

Bernie chuckled. "Maybe she's planning to replace Horace with you, Mars."

"Very funny."

"Oh, that's right. You're already busy having a fling with Gwen."

"So you're the one!" Luis laughed.

Nina shook her head. "What a stupid thing to say in a Christmas letter. Didn't Gwen know that she would worry wives all over the neighborhood?"

"Oh, come on, Nina. No one has to worry," said Luis. "That was obviously the lie about Gwen. But what was the lie about Baxter?"

"There were so many details in that letter that I can't remember them all." I thought back. Hadn't she heaped praise on Baxter?

"I'll give you a hint," said Luis. "It involves a mountain cabin."

A car screeched to avoid the large reindeer leg that still jutted out into the street.

"Hey, guys, would you mind giving me a hand? I could use some help deflating that thing. I'm afraid it will come down on cars."

The three men headed across the street, and Nina went home with her purchases.

It seemed like old times when I draped the pine around my doorway and added bulk with glossy magnolia leaves. Neighbors drifted by to pick up their coats and ask about Horace. Mars puttered around the house with lights and occasionally stopped to give me a hand. Daisy sniffed the pine and decorating items I had bought.

We were chuckling about Mrs. Scroggins striding by yet again, when we noticed Natasha hanging a giant purple wreath on the door of Francie's house. My elderly neighbor had been away visiting friends over Thanksgiving and was due home any day.

"Purple?" I whispered to Mars. "Really? Natasha knows Francie hates it when Natasha decorates for her."

"Give Nat a break. She's trying to do something nice. She knows Francie doesn't have the energy to do a lot of decorating anymore. This is Nat's gift to Francie."

"If she brings topiaries, there will be big trouble when Francie comes home. I can't wait to hear what Francie thinks about the purple color."

Natasha left and returned shortly. With great care, she set two large topiary raccoons on either side of Francie's front door. They wore Santa hats.

Natasha stepped back to admire her work. She ambled over to Mars and me. "Mars, when we have the block party, could you add some string lights to Francie's door and maybe the front windows? I have some in purple that will go perfectly with her décor."

"Why don't I wait until Francie comes home and find out what she would like?" asked Mars.

Natasha pretended to pout. I hoped he didn't fall for that ridiculous gag.

"Can you imagine, Gwen told me I shouldn't let Mars work over here by himself. She thinks you're going to steal him from me, Sophie!" Natasha chortled. "Isn't that a hoot?"

CHAPTER SEVEN

Dear Sophie,
I live in an apartment and can't do much exterior decorating. I have a very wide living room window but I never know what to do with it. Do you have any suggestions?

Noel in Joy, Illinois

Dear Noel,
One of my favorite decorating tricks is to use multiple wreaths. Either hang three straight in a row or stagger them with the middle one higher or lower than the others.

Sophie

Suddenly, I felt terribly guilty for enjoying Mars's company.

"At least I don't have to worry about him having an affair with Gwen. I have my money on Bernie." Natasha brushed a fiber off her jacket.

"Bernie? Why would you think that?"

"He's a bachelor. He's not bad looking, though *I* certainly wouldn't call him yummy. Hey, where's Humphrey? He usually likes to join in when you decorate."

"Still at his mom's house in the country. He's probably helping her decorate. Should be back any day."

Across the street, Kat Babineaux skipped along the sidewalk, still wearing her assistant elf costume and chattering gaily at Sugar, who held her hand.

"What do you know about the Babineauxs?" I asked, still concerned about the ladder that broke under Baxter.

"Not much," said Mars. "They moved here from California."

"Their kids play their music too loud," complained Natasha. "Drives me up a wall. Who were those people making all the noise in front of their house this morning? That old VW bus looks like it's ready for the junkyard. I'm hoping the trash collectors will take it by mistake."

"Baxter's brother and his girlfriend, Sugar."

"Are you going to the cookie swap?" asked Mars, shooting a peeved look at Natasha.

"Do you mean me?" I asked. "Of course!"

Natasha heaved a huge sigh. "I'm only invited because Gwen wants a celebrity guest, and she knows I'll bring gourmet cookies. What will I get out of it? Nothing."

"She invited friends from the neighborhood." If Natasha was going to have that kind of attitude, I hoped she wouldn't attend. She did have a local cable TV show about all things domestic, but that hardly qualified her as a celebrity. The two of us wrote competing advice columns about domestic issues, which irritated her. Natasha thought of everything as a contest.

Mars wound lights into the pine around my door. "It's the neighborly thing to do, but Natasha doesn't care for Gwen."

Natasha pumped her fists on her hips. "She's such a braggart! She thinks she does everything better than anyone else."

I had to bite my top lip and turn my back to hide my amusement. Natasha had just described herself. I pretended to search for another string of lights so she wouldn't see my expression.

"Seems like you would want to prove you can bake the best cookies, then."

Whoa. Mars knew how to pull her chain!

The edge of Natasha's mouth twitched. "I don't know why you're so intent on me going to that thing."

"Maybe he wants you to bring home twelve dozen cookies," I teased, although I wondered if that wasn't part of his motivation.

"I shudder to think what they'll be like." Natasha regarded my house. "I could do so much with this place. We should have lunch and talk, Sophie. You could make a lot of improvements." She strode away, passing Mrs. Scroggins, who was making yet another pass along our street.

"Any yelling at the Babineauxs'?" I asked Mars.

"Not more than you'd expect with a couple of rowdy teenagers in the house." Mars stepped on the ladder and attached pinecones to the greenery. "Why all the questions?"

"Baxter fell off their roof this morning when a rung on his ladder broke. I'm not sure, of course, but it looked like someone might have tampered with one of the rungs."

Mars gazed toward their house. "That's a heck of a drop."

"Luckily, the bushes broke his fall. I thought he should go to the emergency room, but neither he nor Gwen felt it necessary."

Mars raised one eyebrow. "This isn't their ladder, is it?"

I laughed at him. "No. But be careful anyway. If you take a spill, you won't get all these Christmas lights up."

"*That's* what you care about?"

"I thought you wanted to trump Natasha."

"I do." Mars snickered. He lowered his hand to me, ready for more pinecones. "Are you suggesting Gwen *wanted* Baxter to fall?"

"I'm simply making a discreet inquiry."

Mars tucked a bit of ribbon into the corner. "I think you miss Wolf."

"What? Why would you say that? You hate Wolf."

"Do not. He turned out to be a decent sort. Why else would you be imagining murder and mayhem?"

"You think it's so I can call Wolf? Don't be silly. I cannot imagine any circumstances that would prompt me to call him. Besides, I'm not imagining anything. Maybe I should show you the ladder."

"This date you're going on — is it with Alex German?"

"It is."

Mars stepped off the ladder and eyed the remaining items I held. "If you need mistletoe to get him to kiss you, then I would recommend knocking off the murder and mayhem talk. Honestly, Sophie! *'Tis the*

97

season to be jolly and all that."

"Come look at the ladder with me."

"Excuse me, Baxter," Mars quipped, "Sophie wants to know if I think Gwen is trying to kill you. You don't mind us inspecting your ladder, do you?"

"You're going to feel pretty rotten if she does kill him."

"He's fine. I can see him on his roof — with someone else."

"Probably his brother."

"See? You're imagining things. He'll be fine."

Now that he pointed out Baxter's brother, I felt relieved. Surely Gwen wouldn't try anything when his brother was visiting. There really was safety in numbers. Wasn't there?

"We only have an hour or so of daylight left anyway. Let's finish this and the bay window. Maybe get the wreaths hung? Bernie agreed to come over tomorrow afternoon to help with the roof. Much easier with two people."

I was glad he wasn't enlisting my help on the roof.

When we finished, I stood on the sidewalk admiring my house. A wreath hung from a wide red ribbon in each window. We had filled the flower boxes under my bay window with evergreens that spilled over them. Red and green apples adorned them, and the ubiquitous colonial pineapple sat prominently in the center. Small Christmas trees loaded with white lights sat in two large pots that flanked the front door. Red apples filled the tops of the pots hiding the electrical connections. The wreath on the front door and the thick roping Mars and I had adorned with magnolia leaves, pinecones, ribbons, and apples had never been more lush.

Mars slid an arm around me. "We still make a pretty good team, Soph. The house looks great."

I nodded. "I think your Aunt Faye would be proud." There were those who thought her spirit still inhabited the kitchen. Sometimes I thought so myself.

"Wait until she sees it tomorrow night with all the lights on it!" Mars pecked my cheek. "I'm beat. See you tomorrow. C'mon, Daisy!"

Before I cooked dinner, Mochie accompanied me through the house as I added a single battery-operated candle to each window. They would turn on automatically at dusk and stay on well after Mochie and I were tucked in bed. I couldn't imagine that Mars would want to run his lighting extravaganza for hours on end. The candles would provide ambiance when his lights weren't on. Besides, I loved walking into a room that was lighted by the glow of a candle. It was one of the joys of the season.

For dinner, I whipped up one of Mochie's and my favorites. He turned up his kitty nose at the salad of crisp mixed greens, but he loved Julia Child's Chicken Suprême. I had modified it to suit my casual lifestyle. While I readily admitted that it tasted more delicious sautéed in butter, the olive oil I used instead was supposed to be healthier and the chicken breast still turned out soft and delicious. It cooked in minutes, but not fast enough for Mochie, who sat on a chair next to the fireplace, his tail twitching impatiently.

I tossed some kindling into the fireplace and lit a rolled newspaper underneath it. The blaze warmed my kitchen. The crackle and occasional hiss was so comforting that I wanted to stay put.

I cut a piece of the juicy chicken into cat-bite-sized pieces and placed them in a small red bowl. Mochie wasted no time eating. He finished before I ate my first bite. I watched him wash his face in the glow of the fire while I ate my dinner.

After cleaning up the few dishes, I draped

leftover pine roping along the top of the window over my kitchen sink and around the bay window in my kitchen. I was hanging gingerbread stars and hearts from delicate red ribbons when I heard a soft tap at the door. A woman peered through the glass.

I opened the door to Edith Scroggins, who said, "My husband is trying to get rid of me."

CHAPTER EIGHT

Dear Sophie,
My in-laws are coming to Christmas dinner this year. At our wedding, my mother-in-law complained that the centerpieces were too high and discouraged conversation. How do I impress her with a low centerpiece?

Nervous in Holiday, Florida

Dear Nervous,
Double the depth of your centerpiece with a mirror. Use a framed or unframed mirror as the base and add low items. They can be as simple as red berries, gold ornaments, or a cluster of votive candles surrounded by twigs of evergreen.

Sophie

Edith stared at me, wrapped in a black wool coat with a mink collar that had probably been the height of fashion once. A mink band ran around the black hat she wore. Also vintage, it was adorable, with the brim curling up on the right side and down over her face on the left. I didn't much care for the black veil, but I suspected she'd worn it over her face instead of sunglasses since it was pitch dark outside. It was a classic outfit. Except for the mink and the veil, I could imagine women buying it today.

Her chest heaved, and I heard her breath shudder. She was scared.

In spite of my feelings about her, I invited her in.

"Would you mind drawing the curtains?" asked Edith.

"Has Horace been released from the hospital?" If she thought he was trying to harm her, she didn't need to worry while he was incapacitated. Unless she thought he had hired someone. What was I thinking? Horace wouldn't hurt anyone. He didn't even want her to know about Brown-Eyed Girl!

"No. But he has friends."

I was one of them. Surely she realized that. "May I take your coat?"

"Yes, thank you. You certainly have a lot of friends. I thought they would never leave."

I drew the curtains closed. "Could I offer you some hot chocolate?"

"No. Have you a bottle of water with an intact seal?" She didn't bother removing her black gloves.

"Probably. Would you like ice?"

"No."

I fetched a bottle of Perrier and a glass. I placed a few sugar cookies on a small porcelain cookie plate shaped like a star, and added a napkin.

When I set them on a small table next to her chair by the fire, she said, "Thank you. I haven't eaten since yesterday."

I didn't know quite what to make of that. Had Horace's hospitalization caused her lack of appetite? If she thought he was trying to get rid of her, more likely her lack of appetite stemmed from worry about him coming home.

"I thought it safe to eat what the caterers had prepared for everyone else. Otherwise I would not have attended Horace's party."

She wasn't going to eat the cookies. Poor woman. I felt sorry for her even though I seriously doubted that Horace planned to harm her.

"Can you help me or are you one of Horace's adoring minions?"

"If you suspected me of being one of his

104

minions, I don't believe you would be here."

She nodded. "Astute. Apparently you *do* have a brain."

I let it slide. "Mrs. Scroggins, I have to be honest with you. If you fear for your life, you should go to the police."

Her mouth twitched downward. "I am seventy years old, but I'm not stupid. If I go to the police and tell them that items in my home aren't where they're supposed to be, the police will think I have simply misplaced them."

"What kind of items?"

"First my medicine. It is kept on the third shelf in the medicine cabinet, yet it moved to the second shelf with Horace's medicines. Second, the cash that I placed in an envelope for my cleaning woman's Christmas bonus vanished from my desk. I found the empty envelope later in my nightstand. Third, a mirror that has hung on the left wall of the back hall since I was a child, suddenly hung on the right. Fourth, the ringer on the telephone was turned off so one could not hear it ringing. Fifth, and possibly the most disturbing to me, which leads me to believe that it's Horace or someone he's paying, a small statuette of a boy that Horace gave me as a gift has disappeared from our garden."

"Was it valuable? Perhaps it was stolen."

She scoffed. "Only sentimental value."

It was difficult for me to imagine Edith Scroggins being sentimental over anything. I could understand her problem, though. With the exception of the mirror that moved, all of those things could happen due to sheer forgetfulness. My own mother had turned the ringer off her phone by accident. And who had never misplaced something? Putting medicine on the wrong shelf wasn't a big deal. Losing the money was odd, but Edith could very well have thought she placed money in the envelope but have forgotten to do it. I was quite a bit younger than Edith, but it wasn't unusual for me to misplace things.

"Did you ask Horace about any of those items?"

"I'm not daft! Of course I did. Horace denied knowledge of any of them."

"He didn't notice that the mirror moved? Wasn't there a spot on the wall where the paint was a different color?"

"We had the painters in last summer. Horace said he couldn't recall where the mirror had hung. I am correct. I found a photograph from 1985 that showed the mirror hanging on the left." She poured water into the glass with a trembling hand.

The veil did a good job of hiding her face, but I knew she was aging well, without the ravages of the sun wrinkling her skin. I wouldn't have put her at seventy. She was right, of course. The police would likely believe exactly what I was thinking — that we all misplace things.

"Why do you think Horace did these things?"

"No one else has access to the house, except for the cleaning woman. She has no reason to wish me ill."

Unless she acted a great deal nicer toward the cleaning woman than she did to everyone else, I wasn't convinced that her housekeeper didn't harbor resentment. Moving things would be a simple enough way to take revenge. "That wasn't quite what I meant. It sounds like someone is gaslighting you," I said, in reference to the Hitchcock movie *Gaslight,* in which a husband tricks his wife to make her think she is going mad. "Why do you think the goal is murder?"

"I'm glad you're familiar with that film. What other reason would there be? He plans to get me out of the way."

Oh no. I wished I didn't know about Brown-Eyed Girl.

Edith paused. I waited quietly to see if she would divulge anything more helpful.

"I own our house and the majority of Scroggins Realty. They belonged to my parents."

Okay, that was a motive, but I thought Horace had done pretty well for himself financially. "I'm under the impression that Horace could buy another house if that's what he's after."

She folded her hands in her lap. "I suppose that's true. It wouldn't be quite as simple to get me out of the business, unless . . . unless he's trying to make a case that I am incompetent. I don't know what to do. I hoped you could help me."

"Do you know Officer Wong?"

Edith frowned. "No."

I probably shouldn't mention that she had thrown Wong out with the rest of us after the party, and that Wong was the one who had threatened to get a search warrant for Horace's office. "She's very sharp. Maybe you could tell her. I would feel better if the police were on notice."

"In other words, *you* won't help me."

"Mrs. Scroggins, I don't know what I can do." I shrugged. "Unless you stayed here with me, I couldn't keep an eye on you." The words had slipped out of my mouth. I hurried to add, "I'm certain you don't want a babysitter. And I'm not big or strong enough to stop anyone who might mean you harm."

Her eyes focused on something past my shoulder. "I don't think I would be comfortable here. Your cat has been staring at me."

I turned. Mochie sat on the banquette in classic Egyptian cat position, his tail wrapped around his front paws. Alert, yet with superior feline aloofness, he studied Edith. *Good kitty!* I didn't think I would be comfortable with Edith staying with me. I hadn't meant to invite her, merely to make the point that I didn't know what anyone could do short of a bodyguard.

"Isn't there someone who might come to stay with you? A family member or old friend?"

"No." She said it simply, directly, and to the point.

"Maybe you could hire a bodyguard."

Edith rubbed her temple. "I prefer my own company. I loathe the notion of someone hanging around. And how would I know that person wasn't on Horace's payroll?"

"How about a hotel?"

She raised her eyes to meet mine. Her fingers coiled into fists. "May I call on you again if there are further developments? Much to my surprise, I have found it useful to discuss this with someone."

"Yes, of course" — I turned the tables on her — "but only if you promise to share this information with Officer Wong."

She rose. "Very well. Thank you for the water."

I helped her with her coat and showed her to the front door.

"I always liked this house," she said. "I'm glad you didn't rip everything out. If one wants a modern house, one ought not buy in Old Town."

"Would you like me to walk you home?"

"You would do that for me?"

"Of course." I tamped down the fire to barely burning embers, grabbed a coat from the closet, and slid it on. I seized my keys, locked the door behind us, and strolled along the sidewalk toward Mars and Natasha's house.

Luis had given up on the giant reindeer. Next door, the lights Gwen had wanted on the dormer windows glowed in the night. It appeared every light inside their house had been turned on. Strains of music reached the street. "The Babineauxs have a lively household," I observed, making small talk.

"Their household is in a state of permanent chaos." She sounded angry.

Natasha had gone minimalistic with

Christmas lights. They outlined her front door and wound along the railing of her stairs. In pink and orange. They were bright, they were pretty, they were most certainly merry, but they made me want to ask when the circus was coming to town.

Edith stopped to stare at it. "Good lord, it looks like Natasha is advertising a bordello."

I bit my lip. I could see exactly what she meant. But I didn't think she intended to be funny.

We didn't speak much as we turned onto her street. The Christmas decorations on Edith's home reflected Horace's love of Scotland. Next to her front door, a giant tartan bow graced a balsam wreath that held pinecones, little black Scottish terriers, and red berries.

She let herself in, said good-night, and closed the door. Locks clanked into place promptly.

I took my time walking home to enjoy the Christmas decorations. Much to my surprise, I found myself feeling sorry for the grouchy old woman. She had alienated everyone, and now that she needed a friend, she had none. It made me appreciate my friends all the more, even Natasha, who, obnoxious as she was, would be the first in line if I needed help.

When I passed the entrance to the alley behind Mars and Natasha's house, I heard murmuring voices. I slowed and looked, expecting to see them.

Instead, I caught Sugar with a man in what appeared to be a rather personal moment.

CHAPTER NINE

Dear Natasha,
My siblings make a lot more money than I do. Every Christmas they give my parents pricey electronics and antiques. I can't begin to compete. What's a fabulous gift that doesn't cost much?
                    Broke in Humbug, Arizona

Dear Broke,
Bake a gingerbread house that looks like your parents' home. Draw a sketch to guide you, bake the walls, and decorate with candy and white icing. You'll steal the show.
                                        Natasha

His back to me, the man leaned against the wall of Mars and Natasha's garage. It had been decorated to look like a gingerbread house. Jonah and Twiggy must have done it, because it was far too cute and traditional for Natasha. The two-story building housed the garage, an incredibly opulent crafting workshop for Natasha, and, on top, the apartment that Jonah and Twiggy had rented.

Lights ran across the top of the roof. Icicle lights dripped along the gutters. More white lights lined the corners of the structure and the windows. Red and white candy canes stood on each side of the back door. Lighted mock hard candies dotted the sides of the house. It was darling.

Unfortunately, the bright lights illuminated Sugar with her hand on the chest of someone who looked all too much like Jonah. My heart plummeted for Twiggy. I didn't know Sugar. Maybe she was the sweetest woman on earth, but anyone with a figure like that who was so willing to show it off was a man magnet.

Jonah's head bent forward. Sugar looked up at him coyly. They were deep in conversation about something. The shadows probably hid me somewhat. I didn't think they noticed me at all.

I strolled on quickly. It was none of my business. But it pained me to know what might be in store for Twiggy.

It was still early enough to bake cookies for Gwen's cookie swap extravaganza as I had planned. I had been experimenting with a chocolate gingersnap cookie that I thought would fit the bill. Normally I would drizzle the tops with chocolate, but that could take some drying time. I decided to bake them anyway and see how it went. If I had enough time, I would add the drizzle.

I turned on an old Christmas CD, tossed a log in the fireplace to get it going again, and preheated the ovens. Eggs, butter, flour, baking powder, salt, chocolate chips, a bottle of homemade vanilla, and ginger went on the island, ready to be used.

But before I began, I phoned Wong. She answered her phone right away. It must have been a slow night for the police in Old Town. I told her about Edith's visit.

"She agreed to talk to me? Are you sure?" asked Wong.

"Absolutely."

Wong snorted. "She's going to expect a Chinese cop. This should be interesting."

I had done everything I could for Edith. I measured butter and sugar and my Christmas red KitchenAid mixer went into overtime. The recipe was simple enough. Creaming butter and sugar was a cookie basic. I rolled the dough into balls and placed them on a tray covered with parchment paper. In minutes the first baking sheets slid into my ovens. Only one hundred twenty-six more to go.

I mixed ingredients for the next batch, thinking about Edith and Horace. I found it unfathomable that someone as kind as Horace would play pranks on his wife to scare her. As far as I knew, Edith lived a fairly solitary life. Why would anyone want to make her think she was losing her mind?

I shook my head, removed the baked cookies, and placed more trays in the ovens. That was preposterous. Most likely, Edith was just getting forgetful. Maybe the painters moved the mirror last summer when they painted. Maybe the little statuette broke, and Horace threw it out. There were a million perfectly reasonable explanations.

Then why did it worry me? I used a specially thin cookie spatula to lift baked cookies off the parchment paper and place them on racks to cool. The cookies only baked for twelve minutes. With fifteen cookies on each baking sheet, the whole process was going much faster than I had expected.

I stopped cold. Surely Edith hadn't planned all this. Could she have weakened the balcony in the hope that her husband would fall? Could she have made up the story about her medicine being on the wrong shelf as a cover for sneaking extra blood thinner into his food?

Scratching my forehead, I sat down in the chair next to the fire. It was almost too clever. Edith could easily move anything around and pretend to be afraid. Why would she have chosen to speak to me today? Was I part of her plan to create an alibi? The timer went off again. I removed the baked cookies and slid another batch into the oven.

Suddenly, I was extremely glad that I had called Wong. Something strange was happening with the Scrogginses. I just didn't know which one might be trying to get rid of the other one.

The scents of vanilla and ginger wafted through the air from the cooling cookies. I prepared two more trays for the oven and considered making myself a drink.

Mochie lifted his head and focused on the kitchen door as though he expected someone to arrive.

Wong and Nina showed up less than a minute later. Frigid night air blew through the kitchen when they bolted inside.

"When did it get so cold?" asked Nina.

"I was just getting ready to make some hot cider."

Wong sniffed and surveyed my production line. "Ginger? Wow, but that's a lot of cookies."

"I'm almost done. They're for a cookie swap. I just need to drizzle chocolate over them to make them pretty. I don't suppose you two would like to taste them to be sure they're edible?"

Nina and Wong each grabbed a cookie before removing their coats.

Nina groaned with satisfaction. "Umm. Perfect for a cold night. And it's so Christmasy in here already." She slung their coats on the banquette, picked up Mochie, and nestled into a fireside chair with him on her lap.

Wong drummed her fingertips on the island. "That Mrs. Scroggins is a piece of work."

I poured melted chocolate into an icing bag with a small round frosting tip and let the chocolate fall onto the cookies in a zigzag pattern. "Did you ever get a search warrant for Horace's office and have a look at the balcony?"

Wong smiled, her round cheeks puffing up. "Wasn't necessary. I sent the building inspector around to have a look. I just happened to be there on the sidewalk when he arrived." She flipped her hand casually.

Nina and I giggled at her planned coincidence.

"The railing had rotted through. Even I

118

could see that it hadn't been tampered with."

"And I was so sure that wicked Mrs. Scroggins was trying to do her sweet husband in. Did you tell Wong about Brown-Eyed Girl?" asked Nina.

I glared at Nina for a moment, frustrated that she'd so readily revealed Horace's private letter. On the other hand, given what Edith had told me, Wong probably should know. I suspected she could keep a secret better than blabbermouth Nina.

While Nina told Wong all about Brown-Eyed Girl, I poured apple cider into a pot to heat and tossed in two sticks of cinnamon, juicy orange slices, a pinch of cloves, and a teeny bit of nutmeg.

Wong appeared incredulous. "That's so sweet. And so sad. I can't believe he kept the letter all those years."

I added chocolate to the last tray of cookies. When I was finished, I turned in a circle, looking for any I might have missed. There wasn't a square inch of countertop that wasn't covered with cookies. No wonder Wong had been impressed.

I poured the cider into footed glass mugs and garnished them with orange slices. After handing them to my friends, I sat down and relaxed. "So what did Edith say?"

Wong tilted her head. "You know I can't talk about that." She grinned at Nina. "But I wouldn't stop *you* from telling Nina about it."

Good grief. I filled Nina in as fast as I could.

"She came here?" asked Nina. "Was she nice?"

"Stiff. But for once, she wasn't horribly hostile."

Wong's lip twitched upward.

"Can you tell us anything about what she said?" I asked.

"Did you notice her eye color?"

I thought a moment. "She was wearing a veil — but you wouldn't mention it unless they were brown!"

Nina's forehead wrinkled. "I need a real drink. She rose, displacing Mochie, who yawned before the fire. Nina doctored her cider with bourbon and butterscotch schnapps. "Anyone else?" she asked.

Wong declined. "I'm on duty."

"Maybe a little bit of the schnapps," I said.

Nina complied. "This is boggling my mind. What you're saying, Wong, without actually telling us, is that you think Edith Scroggins is Brown-Eyed Girl. But then why would he say Edith should never know?"

Wong cocked her head again. "Can you

imagine what it must be like to be married to her? It's a mystery to me that they're married at all, but I can imagine that she responds to any display of affection with criticism or hatefulness."

Nina curled her fingers around her mug of cider. She shook her head in disagreement. "Nope. I'm not buying it. She couldn't have been a wonderful, warm — scratch that, *normal* — person in her youth and a colossal crab now. People don't change that drastically. Horace has a long-lost honey somewhere."

I wasn't sure what Wong could or would say about Edith, and I wanted to respect her position as a cop, but I asked anyway, "What do you think about the things that are moving around in Edith's house?"

Wong sipped her cider while she considered. "It's troubling. I'll keep an eye on her place and pass the word along."

"I think she's doing it to get attention." Nina eyed another cookie. "Why would she come to your house? Because she's alone. There's no one at home to yell at. You saw the commotion she made at Rocking Horse Toys today. She craves attention, and apparently she'll do anything to get it."

"I love that place. It's the best toy store anywhere. Makes me wish I were a kid again." Wong sucked in a deep breath. "You're being mighty deep tonight, Nina. Maybe you're onto something."

"Do they socialize with anyone?" I asked. "Someone who might know more about Edith? Horace always came to parties and events by himself. I rarely saw her with him."

Wong asked, "When does Francie get home from visiting the Greenes? I bet she knows the scoop."

My neighbor Francie had lived on our block longer than anyone else. "She's due home soon."

Wong snagged a couple more cookies and got back to patrolling the neighborhood. Nina headed home, and I finally hit the sack, leaving the cookies out so the chocolate would harden enough for me to package them.

Mochie jumped on top of my bed and curled up. The battery-operated candle in my bedroom window glowed as I snuggled under the down comforter.

I drifted off to sleep, thinking about brown-eyed girls, Edith, and poor Twiggy. This wasn't turning out to be a happy holiday at all.

The cold air left a frosty glaze of snow on

the ground during the night. Snow flurries blew outside when I rose in the morning. I made a mug of steaming tea and indulged in a three-cheese omelet. Mochie turned down canned turkey and chicken. He communicated his displeasure by lifting his dish and letting it drop with a *bang* until I finally got it right with canned salmon.

I packaged my chocolate gingersnaps in red boxes with snowflakes around the sides. I tied each one with a white satin ribbon, adding a recipe card and a glittering white snowflake that could be hung on a tree. When all thirteen boxes stood on my dining room table, ready to go, I took a second mug of tea into my office. Mochie settled on my desk and groomed himself while I got some work done in my pajamas.

Even though I applied myself, Edith Scroggins weighed on my mind. At noon, the sun returned and the icy glaze on the sidewalks had disappeared. Dressed in soft, stretchy jeans, boots, and a dark green turtleneck that was too warm to wear indoors, I walked to the Scrogginses' house.

Their home was decked out with a surprising amount of Christmas décor for a house belonging to someone as unhappy and disagreeable as Edith. I wondered if Edith appreciated Horace's happy touches. I knocked a lion's head door knocker nine inches wide that gleamed in the sunshine. Someone kept it very well polished. The detail on the lion's face was astounding.

I heard footsteps on the other side of the door, but no one opened it. "Mrs. Scroggins?" I called.

CHAPTER TEN

Dear Sophie,
I have been invited to a cookie swap. I would love to attend, just to get together with friends and relax from the holiday craziness for a couple of hours. But when will I find the time to bake all those cookies?

Busy Mom in Candlestick, Georgia

Dear Busy Mom,
The dough in many cookie recipes needs to be refrigerated before it can be rolled out or sliced and baked. Choose cookies that do not need to be frosted. Make all the dough one night. Package it in waxed paper and store in the fridge. Bake the cookies when you have a free evening, or over a couple of days when you have a little time. If you have children, they might be willing to help you put the

cookies into containers in exchange for a cookie snack.

Sophie

The door swung open to reveal a woman with a pleasant face, and — good heavens — brown eyes! She smiled at me. "I'm sorry, dear. Mrs. Scroggins is out. I'm Mabel Akins, the housekeeper. May I tell her who called?"

"I'm Sophie Winston. I just wanted to check on her."

The woman's eyes widened in shock. "Check on Edith? That's a first. This is a day just full of surprises. Come in out of the cold, sweetheart. Mrs. Scroggins wasn't here when I arrived this morning. That was a first, too."

"You have a key?" I inquired casually.

"Shh. Now, don't you tell her, but Horace gave me a key years ago. I carry it with me even though I know she leaves the key to the back door over the ledge. But Mrs. Scroggins has always been here to greet me at the side door. Never let me out of her sight — until today."

"I think the cat might be out of the bag when she comes home and finds the house clean."

She laughed. "I suppose so. I reckon she's

over at the hospital checking on Horace."

I doubted that but kept my suspicion to myself. "Have you heard anything about his condition?"

"They say he's having a rough time of it. I can't imagine a more terrible thing to happen to such a good man. Falling is bad enough, but landing on his own dagger! It breaks my heart to think of it."

"Have you worked for them long?" She seemed willing to gab. I felt a little guilty taking advantage of her, but I knew so little about Edith.

"I cleaned this house for Mrs. Scroggins's parents, and when they passed, I kept right on cleaning for Horace and Mrs. Scroggins. Goodness, it's at least twenty years or more now. Fine people, her parents were. It's a shame Edith turned out so . . . oh my. You must be a friend to come around checking on her. I didn't mean to say anything unkind."

"It's all right. I know she's crabby and unfriendly."

"You said it!" She leaned toward me. "That's why I didn't open the door right away. In all the years I've been cleaning for her, no one has ever knocked on the door! Not even to bring a package. When you knocked, I was afraid it might be her, testing me in some way."

I took a stab. "Has she been acting unusual lately?"

She gasped. "How did you know? Meaner than a snake is what she's been. She's colder than ice anyway and prone to yelling, but lately, she's been intolerable! Accusing me of all kinds of things. Honestly" — she swirled her finger in the air near her ear — "I think the old biddy is losing it. I'm closer to Horace's age, so heaven knows what I'll be like at her age, but she's started accusing me of moving things. And stealing my own bonus!"

"Horace's age?"

"You didn't know? She's ten years older than Horace."

"The mirror in the hall . . . ?"

"She told you about that? I didn't think she talked to anyone." She placed a hand on my shoulder. "Oh, darlin', it does me good to know that she has one friend in the world. Now, that mirror, I'll admit, that was awful strange. One day it was on one side of the hall and the next day it was on the other. I don't clean but once a week — it's not necessary more often as it's just the two of them — but I did a double take when I went to dust it and it was on the other side. She says she didn't move it."

"Did you talk to Horace about it?"

She pulled her chin back. "He said to humor her. What does that mean? I didn't need to humor her, because I agreed with her. Somebody moved that mirror!"

"Do you think it could have been Mrs. Scroggins?"

She blinked at me. "Then why would she complain about it?"

"Because she's confused?"

"Oh, that's sad. You could be right. Maybe that's why Horace suggested I humor her. It fits in with her misplacing things." She heaved a sigh. "Poor Mrs. Scroggins, losing her mind and going bonkers. I hope you won't mind if I don't tell her that you stopped by. Maybe you could call her later? I don't want to set her off. In fact, I believe I'll leave early so she won't know I've been here. No point in upsetting the poor dear. Goodness me. I've spent all these years disliking her, but then something like this happens" — she snapped her fingers — "and all I feel is pity for her."

I thanked Mabel and assured her I would call Edith later. They kept their house warm, and I felt like I would bake in my heavy sweater. It was a relief to step out into the cold air again. I wondered, though, what had prompted Edith to leave the house unattended when she knew Mabel was coming. Maybe Edith really was confused.

I probably shouldn't have, but out of curiosity, I cut through the walkway that led past the house and into the back garden. Even though winter had ravaged the garden, it offered a private respite. Beautiful bushes and old trees stood stark against the fence, their bare branches reaching out like comforting arms around the expansive garden. Boxwoods lined redbrick walkways and a small herb garden had been put to bed for the season. Only the markers with herb names remained. Totally symmetrical, another patch of the same size and shape lay asleep on the other side. A fountain stood in the middle, surrounded by a circle of the red bricks that led like spokes on a wheel to the north, south, east, and west. I imagined that it must be even more impressive from the upstairs windows. Where had the statuette of the boy been? I walked through the garden to the back gate and let myself out into the alley.

The old VW camper that had horrified Gwen was parked outside their gate on the other side of the alley. I turned left and walked by Mars and Natasha's gingerbread garage. I paused for a minute where I'd seen Sugar and Jonah the night before. My cell phone rang, startling me.

"What are you wearing on your date?"

I recognized Nina's voice. "I don't know. Probably something black."

"I have your dress and there's a woman eyeing it. She looks like she wants to grab it out of my arms. They only have one. Get thee to Sweet Belle right now."

"Nina, that's thoughtful of you, but —"

She spoke to someone else. "I'm trying this on." Into the phone, she hissed, "Hurry!"

The store was only a few blocks away. I stopped by my house, grabbed my wallet, and walked over, knowing full well that I wouldn't buy it. It was Christmas, for heaven's sake. I needed to buy gifts for other people, not shop for myself.

The second I opened the door to the shop, I knew I was wrong. Nina had me pegged. She held out the hanger so I could see the entire 1960s-style dress. Blue velvet on top, the color of the fabric grew darker in the tapered bodice until it ended up midnight velvet in a flared skirt. Silver sparkles clustered around the scoop neck and grew more sparse as they descended toward the bottom of the dress. It reminded me of a twilight sky with stars.

Nina handed it to me and smiled a bit too

condescendingly at a woman who looked on with annoyance. I gathered she was the one with her eye on the dress.

Happily, it zipped up with no problem. The skirt flattered my figure by fooling the eye and making my waist look smaller. It was exactly right for the formal bar association dinner that I planned to attend with Alex.

When I paid for it, the owner of the store said, "It just came in this morning as a sample from a young new designer. All the employees have been gushing over it. There's something so feminine about it."

"Where were you?" asked Nina.

"I went over to check on Edith Scroggins."

The shop owner's head snapped up. "Is something wrong with her? I know Horace is in the hospital. I hope she's not sick, too."

What? Someone who actually liked Edith? "Are you a friend of Edith's?" I inquired.

"Not exactly. She's a very good customer. Won't buy anything that's on sale. *There's* a quirk every boutique owner loves! We always serve her a glass of champagne and bring out the classic clothes we know she likes. She won't paw through racks like the rest of us do, and she has exquisite taste. She'd like this dress. I hope she's okay?"

I didn't feel that I should go into details.

"She wasn't home. Probably at the hospital."

Nina's eyebrows shot up, giving my lie away. I grabbed the hanging bag that contained the dress and propelled her out the door before she could say anything. Somehow I felt it would be wrong to spread word of Mrs. Scroggins's problems all over town.

"She finally went to the hospital to see Horace?"

"I don't know that. It just seemed a reasonable thing to say." We walked toward our block. "I did speak to her housekeeper, though. The mirror really was moved. But after talking with her, I'm inclined to think that poor Edith is suffering from a failing memory. That seems sort of consistent with Edith making such a big fuss about using a coupon yesterday at Rocking Horse Toys, yet she won't buy anything on sale at the boutique. She's confused."

Nina's lips puckered. "Or she does what gets her the most attention."

"What?" Maybe Nina was right. That would explain her erratic behavior, too. "Funny. Most people try to be superfriendly to get attention."

Nina snorted. "The squeaky wheel. Everyone always makes a big fuss over the people who complain the most. Haven't you ever noticed that? If you're nice about a problem, they're grateful. If you're mean about it, they give you stuff for free and try harder to make you happy."

"How do you know that? Do you make scenes when I'm not around?"

"Just observation of human behavior. I should have been a shrink. People are so fascinating! Mars and Natasha, for instance. Wouldn't you think she would do anything to keep Mars at home? Instead, she drove him back to you, and you very generously embraced what he wanted to do to your house — almost like you're still married. I don't think Natasha thought that one through. Seems pretty foolish to me."

Mars stood on a ladder hanging lights around my front windows. Daisy sniffed the bushes underneath. I gauged my response carefully. "Maybe Natasha is comfortable with the friendship between Mars and me."

Nina laughed so loud that Mars turned to look at us. "Then she's a dolt of the highest order. See you at the cookie swap."

Nina's reaction made me feel guilty again. I crossed the street thinking I had no reason to feel that way. The fact that Mars and I had shared a kiss a couple of years ago in a moment of enormous stress meant nothing. It had never happened again.

Daisy ran to me for dog hugs. She wiggled from one end to the other. "Only a few more days before you come back here to stay with me," I whispered. She must have understood, because she licked the side of my face.

I said hi to Mars. Daisy followed me into the house. Mochie must have been watching Mars from the living room. He dashed in to see us, stopped, stretched, and then pretended he wasn't really that interested but finally wound around our legs.

I hung the dress in the hall closet so it wouldn't wrinkle. Daisy and Mochie followed me into the kitchen where Mochie head-butted me, prompting me to give him a few dried salmon kitty treats. Daisy waited patiently. She sat next to the counter where I kept the dog cookie jar and raised her paw without my asking. I shook it and handed her a large carrot and bacon cookie in the shape of a dog bone.

They raced up the stairs with me when I carried the new dress upstairs to my walk-in closet.

At four o'clock I donned a red and white Christmas sweater my mother had knitted. White on the shoulders and red in the body, she had sewn on iridescent white beads that made it perfect for the holidays. With a pair of winter white slacks, I thought I looked festive but not overdressed for a holiday cookie swap party. A pair of silver earrings were all the jewelry I needed.

The *tack, tack, tack* of Mars's staple gun hammered outside my window. I didn't mind leaving that annoying sound. Poor Daisy would have to stay inside with Mochie and listen to Mars work on the roof. Daisy and Mochie followed me downstairs.

I took the bags packed with cookies, along with the throw I had washed for Baxter, apologized to Daisy and Mochie for leaving them in the house with that racket going on overhead, and hustled out the door. Light snowflakes blew, and I debated wearing a coat. Gwen's house wasn't far, though.

The same *tack, tack, tack* resounded across the street at Liza's house. Luis appeared to be setting up a rooftop nativity scene.

I shivered in the cold wind, crossed the street, and looked back at my house.

Mars had deviated from his plan considerably. A plump Santa Claus had one leg in my chimney. Bernie clambered around, apparently fastening a sleigh on the roof. I hoped they would be okay. It was a long way down.

I hurried toward Gwen's house, relieved

to see that no one pounded on her roof. It was bad enough that the sound of staple guns reverberated through the neighborhood. Gwen's front door bore an oversized wreath of greens covered with shiny pink and orange balls. A wide orange bow bordered with gold dominated the top. I rang the bell, and Gwen opened the door as if she had been waiting on the other side.

"Sophie!" She leaned toward me and kissed the air over each of my shoulders.

It took me exactly one second to realize that she had a pink and orange Christmas theme going. She wore an orange Christmas sweater that looked to be hand-knitted. A vivid pink border ran along the V-neck and the sleeves. A row of lime green Christmas trees lined the bottom and matched the color of her leggings. She twirled around. "I made it myself."

"It's lovely." Behind her, though, I couldn't take my eyes off something I had never seen before — an orange Christmas tree in her living room.

She followed my gaze. "Isn't the tree incredible? It's flocked!"

"Amazing," I murmured, handing her the throw Baxter gave me to sit on in his car. "Baxter lent this to me. Where do I put my cookies?"

"Natasha is coming up the walk. The cookies go in the dining room, dear."

So Mars had finally guilted Natasha into attending the cookie swap after all.

I had to give Gwen credit for one thing. Orange and pink were certainly festive. She had used a long orange tablecloth with a pink topper and tied it in swags with lime green bows. Except for the incredible silver sleigh centerpiece loaded with pink and orange ornaments, it could easily have been set up for a birthday party or a bridal shower.

Liza stood next to the table, arranging her cookies. "Do you believe this sled? Gwen says it's sterling."

"It probably is. I saw it in a store just yesterday. It's gorgeous. Look at the detail. The bell on the front, the ornate scrolls on the sleigh. The reindeer are unbelievable."

"They must have some kind of money," she whispered. "There are matching deer-head candlesticks on the mantel in the living room. Luis would die of a heart attack on the spot if I brought home something like that in sterling."

"It certainly wouldn't be in my budget."

Liza leaned toward me. "Don't you think orange and pink are bizarre Christmas colors? To think that I was worried about using brown kraft boxes!"

She had tied the kraft paper boxes with plaid red and green ribbons and added a candy cane to the top of each one.

"What do you think?" she whispered. "Will I get away with it?"

"They're adorable."

"Get away with what?"

I looked up. Sugar observed us from the kitchen doorway. Her black leggings were as tight as Gwen's. A long red sweater almost covered her derriere. A thick swath of fuzzy black trim ran around the bottom and up the zippered center of the sweater, which hadn't been zipped quite as far as most women might have closed it.

Liza's eyes went wide, and she shifted uncomfortably. "Um, I'm not much of a domestic type. Everyone else is so talented in crafting. Look at these tins with pinecone reindeer. That must have taken someone hours!"

"Those are mine." Twiggy joined us, bashfully running a hand over her pixie haircut. "I'm so glad that you like them. I was up late last night gluing on the pipe cleaner antlers."

"You should have followed my example." Sugar grinned at us. "When you show up before you're expected, you get to eat the cookies without any of the work."

Nina charged into the dining room. "I'm making note of that and doing it next year!"

"I hear you're a ballerina," said Twiggy to Sugar. "I dreamed of being a ballerina when I was a little girl. It sounds so glamorous."

"Keeps me in shape so I can eat all the cookies I want." Sugar tossed her hair and eyed the table. "Are those Whoopie Pies? I haven't had one since I was a kid."

I didn't think that was very long ago. She appeared to be about thirty. Not a single wrinkle creased her face yet.

"That was quite a scene with Mrs. Scroggins in your store, Twiggy. Why did you give her a discount? I would have thrown her out." Nina reached for two Whoopie Pies, handed one to Sugar, and bit into the other one.

"Her husband is one of our biggest customers."

"Horace?" I asked. "I didn't know they had children, or grandchildren."

"He — I guess I should say *they* — bought a couple thousand dollars' worth of toys and had us deliver them to the Christmas toy drive for underprivileged children," said Twiggy. "We can't afford to lose that kind of business! We gave them a discount for that. I mean, who wouldn't when they were buying so much and for such a wonderful cause? Maybe she thought she would always get a discount?"

"No Whoopie Pies yet!" Gwen sashayed in with Natasha. "As soon as Natasha's cookies are on the table, I have to photograph them all! What a gorgeous display."

Nina stuffed the rest of her Whoopie Pie into her mouth like a little kid caught at the cookie jar.

Gwen paused and stared at Liza's contribution. "Goodness, Liza! You're putting us all to shame with those cookies. It must have taken you hours to pipe snowflakes on the icing."

Liza froze.

Since she was at a loss, I jumped in. "I love sugar cookies iced with blue frosting and decorated with white snowflakes. I try to make them every year because they're so beautiful. Thanks for bringing them, Liza."

Natasha's nostrils flared. I suspected she was irritated that she wasn't the one getting attention. She placed deep pink boxes on the table. Wrapped with lacy golden orange ribbon, they matched Gwen's odd Christmas décor perfectly.

Gwen opened one box and organized them on a platter. "These are fabulous, Natasha!" She tilted her head to read the ornate label affixed to the box. "*Balsamic Jalapeno Crisps Enrobed with Salted Dark Chocolate.* Are these sweet or savory?" Gwen arranged the light brown cookies, half-dipped in chocolate, on a platter.

Her lips drawn thin and tight, Natasha uttered, "Both."

Natasha tugged at my sleeve and drew me into the kitchen. It was worthy of a magazine spread. Ultra-fashionable with clean lines, a giant island dominated the room. The cabinets gleamed white. Two hefty pendant lamps shone over a white marble countertop. The gray in the marble picked up the silver of the aluminum bases on four stools with black leather seats. The steel theme repeated in a huge backsplash and range hood behind the stove. The only pop of color came from an orange-flocked Christmas tree in the corner of the room near what appeared to be a back stairway.

"She stole my Christmas colors," hissed Natasha.

If anyone else had said something so utterly ridiculous, I would have laughed. But Natasha wasn't joking. Her dark eyes sparked with fury. I half expected to see steam shoot out of her ears.

"How many colors are on a color wheel? If you won't use red and green, don't you think the odds are pretty high of choosing the same colors as someone else?"

"I do *not*! She waited to see my colors and stole my idea."

"Pink and orange?" I said it sarcastically, but she evidently didn't grasp that.

"It's tangerine and magenta," she said through gritted teeth.

"What's the big deal? Let it go and enjoy the party."

She squared her shoulders. "In the spirit of the season, I shall refrain from mentioning it today. But I'm not letting it go. It's an outrage. She lives next door, for heaven's sake. I work very hard at keeping my themes fresh, and I resent Gwen seizing my ideas."

I tried one more tack. "Don't they say that imitation is the most sincere form of flattery? You set the trend. She's just following it."

Natasha stepped back and touched the base of her throat with her fingers. "Don't I feel the fool? Of course that's what it is. Just this once, I believe you're right."

Laughing privately about her little slight implying that I was never correct, I headed for the living room. From the foyer, I hadn't seen the second tree. I knew people who decorated a tree in every room of the house, but two huge trees flanking the fireplace was a new twist to me. A wreath hung over the mantel, cedar branches draping from the bottom of it in both directions. A gold-flecked orange ribbon undulated the length of the mantel. Flanking the wreath were the two silver deer-head candlesticks I'd seen the day before in the store. They held pink candles with an orangey-bronze swirl cascading down them. Tiny lights shone in between pink and orange ornaments. It was lush and tasteful, if not exactly traditional.

"There you are!" said Gwen. "We're just starting my favorite Christmas game. I'll be the timekeeper, Sugar, you join Natasha, Sophie, and Liza's team. Each team needs a leader. Volunteers?"

"I think it goes without saying that I am the leader of this group," said Natasha.

"Okay!" Gwen handed Natasha a pair of pantyhose fresh from a box and gave me a bag of balloons.

Natasha held the pantyhose by the tips of her thumb and forefinger, as though thoroughly disgusted.

"When I sound the whistle, teams blow up the balloons and leaders stuff them into the stockings to make antlers. The first team to get the loaded antlers on the team leader's head wins! Ready?"

She blew on the whistle. Liza, Sugar, and

I huffed into balloons while Natasha insisted she was not wearing pantyhose on her head for any reason. Ever.

I tied a knot in a red balloon and handed it to her, muttering under my breath, "Be a sport."

It took only minutes for us to fill all our balloons. All Gwen's guests smiled and laughed, with the exception of Natasha, who dutifully, if a bit grumpily, rolled the pantyhose over the balloons. We were neck and neck with Nina's group. Good-natured banter flew around the room. Cheering grew louder for each team. Natasha balked at actually wearing the antlers, but Liza and Sugar seized the pantyhose and plopped them on her head. Gwen swirled toward Natasha with a camera and was snapping shots when the doorbell rang.

Gwen turned to me and asked, "Would you mind getting that, Sophie?"

I slipped away from the gaiety and hysterical laughter, and opened Gwen's front door.

A disheveled brunette with weary eyes appeared surprised to see me. "I'm so sorry. I thought this was the Babineauxs' house." She fumbled in a large purse and withdrew a tattered envelope.

"You're in the right place. Come on in."

"Oh no. Sounds like a party. I couldn't

barge in uninvited. I'll come back later." She peered inside. "Looks like everyone is having fun."

"Come in out of the cold and join us."

"Uh, well, if you're sure." She held her hand out to me. "I'm Patty. Bethany and Bradley Babineaux's mom."

I shook her hand. "Sophie Winston."

Patty gasped and slapped a hand against her chest. "I'm Louise's daughter! Our mothers were sorority sisters. I was going to your house next!" She clasped her hands together. "I don't know how to thank you for putting me up. I hit the road without a clue of where I would stay. And look, you're here! It's like you were waiting for me." The smile on her face faded, and her tone sounded like she was doomed. *"Oh noooo. You're friends with Gwen."*

She didn't seem at all happy about that. It *was* a little misleading. It wasn't like Gwen and I were bosom buddies. "We're neighbors."

That didn't appear to console her. "Maybe I should stay somewhere else. Is there a Y in town? Someplace, you know, cheap?"

"Nonsense. We don't dare severe the ties of Phi Mu sisters! Perish the thought of our mothers involved in such a scandal. You'll stay with me." I didn't quite understand her

146

reluctance. She came to Gwen's house on her own. Mom had mentioned that Patty had some sort of problem. I deduced that it might be with Gwen.

"You're as nice as my mom said you'd be." Patty removed a navy peacoat and tugged her Christmas sweater straight. It bore a snowman and snowflakes on a sky blue background. "I must look a mess. I just drove nonstop from Chicago." She fluffed her hair. "Are Bethany and Bradley here?"

"I haven't seen them." I took her coat and ushered her into the living room.

Gwen gasped at the sight of Patty, and a hush fell over the guests.

CHAPTER ELEVEN

Dear Natasha,
I'm throwing a cookie swap. My sister says it's silly to offer prizes for the prettiest cookie and the tastiest cookie because it pits friends against each other. I say it will improve the cookies they bring! What do you think?

Loves Competition in Antler,
North Dakota

Dear Loves Competition,
I agree with you. Spark up the cookie swap by letting everyone vote. There's no question that it will improve the cookies. No one will dare cheat with store-bought cookies!

Natasha

Gwen recovered her composure quickly but her narrowed eyes and tight lips gave away her discomfort. "Patty! What are you doing here?"

"I'm sorry. I didn't mean to interrupt your party." She laughed uncomfortably and pointed at a woman wearing balloon antlers. "The antler game. I bet you learned that from my kids."

Gwen didn't respond. She seized the coat I held. Towering over petite Patty, she ushered her into the dining room.

In hushed whispers, other guests asked who the newcomer was. "Apparently, she's the mother of Gwen and Baxter's two oldest children," I explained, setting off a new round of whispering.

Sugar sauntered toward the dining room but did a poor job of hiding her attempt to eavesdrop.

I couldn't remember seeing Natasha quite so angry. She ripped the reindeer antlers off her hair, which frizzed out loaded with static. I had to choke back a giggle at seeing Natasha so undone.

She strode to the deer-head candlesticks on the mantel. Methodically, and with savage glee, she plunged each balloon on an antler point, popping them in a rapid staccato rhythm.

Gwen glided back into the room, snapped a photo of Natasha looking like she'd stuck her finger into an electrical outlet, and announced that she thought it was time to sample cookies.

"I had no idea that you're Bethany and Bradley's stepmother," said Twiggy.

Gwen smiled with her lips pulled tight. "Surely you didn't think I looked old enough to have a teenage daughter!"

"Well, yeah, you do," Nina murmured into my ear.

I elbowed her, even though I thought Gwen looked old enough to have grown children. I had put her at about fifty.

There was no sign of Patty. Had Gwen ushered her out the back door or sent her upstairs to visit with her children?

Other guests were busy sampling Gwen's minipizzas, which were no larger than a cookie and decorated with a melted cheese Christmas tree on top. They tried an orangey dip and cut into a wreath of miniature sausages in pastry garnished with a red-pepper bow. Meanwhile, I hustled into the kitchen in search of Patty.

I was right! She had been banished. From the kitchen window, I could see Patty trudging through the backyard, turning now and then to look up at the windows. Snowflakes drifted down on her. She wiped her face. Was she crying?

I flew out the kitchen door and down the deck stairs to the backyard. "Patty!"

She turned, her expression momentarily hopeful.

"What happened?"

Tears trickled along her cheeks. "I'm sorry," she snuffled. "Are you sure you still want to put me up?"

"Absolutely." I shivered in the cold. "Where are you parked? We'll get you settled right now. Come on. I could use a hot drink."

We entered the alley, walked behind Natasha's house and circled around to the front. We shivered and hurried down my street. I was half-frozen by the time we reached Patty's car. We carried her bags to my house as fast as we could.

"I'm freezing!" I said as we entered the foyer.

Mochie greeted us, happy to have company. I didn't hear any hammering and there was no sign of Daisy, so I presumed Mars and Bernie had left.

"This way."

She followed me upstairs to the second floor and into the bedroom with the four-poster bed.

"Ohhh, this is beautiful."

"Wait until you see the bathroom," I

151

joked. I only had one and a half bathrooms. While they were quite functional, they still had ancient green and black tile. If I waited any longer to renovate them, it would be back in style again.

"Make yourself at home. I'm going to change, then I'll heat milk for hot chocolate."

"That sounds good." She blew her nose.

I headed to my bedroom and peeled off my sweater and trousers. Donning olive green fleece pants and a red turtleneck still didn't warm me.

Mochie trotted downstairs with me. I lit a fire in the kitchen to thaw us. Mochie immediately curled up on one of the chairs that flanked the fireplace.

Should I call Gwen now to apologize for leaving so suddenly or wait until the party was over? Most of the guests probably wouldn't even notice that I was gone, and I hated to interrupt Gwen when she was so busy. Hah. Modern technology held the answer. I texted Nina, who was rarely without her cell phone. If anyone asked, at least they would know why I had departed.

I mixed a little bit of cold water into powdered unsweetened chocolate in a pot and stirred to dissolve it. I added a teaspoon of vanilla, which reminded me of Horace, poured the milk over top, and heated it on the stove. Happily, I'd counted on needing whipping cream, and had some in the fridge. I beat it, adding a touch of vanilla and powdered sugar.

Gwen arrived in the kitchen as I poured hot chocolate into mugs with candy-cane handles. I plopped a dollop of whipped cream into each mug and handed her one.

All we needed were napkins and something to nosh on.

"Are you hungry?" I asked. "It's dinnertime."

"I don't want to put you to any trouble," Patty protested.

"No trouble at all," I assured her, pulling steaks, mushrooms, and carrots from the fridge.

She sipped her hot chocolate. "I feel terrible. You left your party because of me." Patty set her mug on the counter. "I could go out for a while, and you could go back."

"Don't be silly." I cleaned and sliced the mushrooms. "I'm sure Gwen will understand."

Patty warmed her hands on the mug and assessed me, her brown eyes cautious. "No. She won't. You don't know her well, do you?"

"They only moved here a few months

ago." I stopped peeling carrots and met her gaze. "Is there something I should know?"

"Other than the fact that she's a liar and phonier than a two-dollar bill?" Patty slapped a hand over her mouth. "I don't believe I just said that. I don't even know you. You must think I'm a horrible person."

I sliced the carrots and tossed them into a pot. "I don't think anything of the sort. I'm beginning to think you have a problem with Gwen, though."

She sagged into one of the chairs by my fireplace. "She ruined my life. And now she's destroying my children."

"I gather you were Baxter's first wife?" I cut up sweet potatoes, tossed them with oil, rosemary, and salt, and popped them in a hot oven.

"And I have all the bruises to show for it." She glanced up at me. "Oh, not physical bruises — he was never violent. I meant I got beat up by an ace divorce lawyer. After twenty years of marriage and two kids, all I have left are memories. His lawyer got *him* the kids. I couldn't afford to fight him. Plus he and Gwen made me sound like a nut. I mean, who doesn't act a little crazy when another woman comes along and steals your husband, then takes your kids, too? Right?"

"That must have been very hard for you."

"It was! It would have been hard to raise them as a single parent, but not to raise them at all?" Patty sniffed. "It's brutal!"

"You do get to see them . . . ?"

"For a few weeks during the summer." She pushed her dark brown hair behind her ears. "This is a perfect example. I drove all the way from Chicago, and now that I'm here, Gwen won't even tell me where they are! Not that I don't appreciate your kindness to me, but I'd like to see my children!"

I could understand that. I joined her at the table. "You came to visit them for the holiday?"

She sighed. "Gwen and Baxter take advantage of me because they know I don't have the money to contest anything. It's not fair because they push me around and do whatever they want, and I just have to take it. They were supposed to send the kids to me for Christmas this year, but Gwen said I couldn't have them. How rotten is that? They're not *her* children! I can't believe that Baxter would be so cruel to me. And to them! Don't they have a right to spend *some* holidays with their mom? And then Gwen sent that Christmas letter."

Patty leaned over the table. "Homeschooling?" she snarled. "It's sure not Baxter who's going to stay home and teach Bethany." Her hand shook when it touched her forehead. "Can you imagine the kind of education she'll get from Gwen? I'm no genius, but at least I recognize my own limitations. I am *not* letting her homeschool my child!"

She frowned and stared at the floor. I wondered what I could say to console her. I rose to start the mushrooms and press cracked pepper into the steaks.

"And think what she'll miss by not being in high school. Prom and graduation with her friends, all those junior and senior traditions that mean so much to teenagers. This is such an important time for her. I have to stop this nonsense. It would be different if she were a little kid or if Gwen were . . . smarter. But at this point, Bethany should be taking important classes. *I* never could grasp calculus, and it wouldn't surprise me if Bethany struggled with it, too, but I hardly think Gwen will be able to do better than an experienced teacher."

The kitchen door burst open. Mochie lifted his head to observe the commotion Nina and Liza made coming through the door loaded down with shopping bags.

Nina set hers on the floor. "Look at this! Gwen had shopping bags made in her pink and orange theme for everyone to take home their cookies."

Liza sniffed the mushrooms that were cooking.

"You're back awfully soon," I observed.

Nina snickered. "Things went downhill fast when you left. Gwen threatened to put a picture of Natasha on Facebook. Her hair was standing on end from static. It was hysterical!"

Liza continued the story with the drama of a natural storyteller. "Natasha issued a few choice threats to Gwen, who retaliated by calling Natasha a 'domestic deadhead.' Then she went for the jugular, saying Natasha couldn't even get Mars to marry her. Natasha stormed out. It was like an episode of *Desperate Housewives*! And I thought living on this block was boring."

"Everyone was very uncomfortable, and the atmosphere was deadly, so we packed it in. You should have seen Twiggy. I thought she would collapse. I don't think she's used to shouting and ugliness," said Nina, handing me a bag. "We brought you your share of the loot."

"Have a seat." I threw on some extra steaks. "We can sample some of the cookies for dessert. Hot chocolate doesn't really go with steak. Would anyone like wine?"

"I would!" Nina selected a bottle.

I fetched red cut-crystal wineglasses. "Is anyone onto you two?" I asked.

While they filled Patty in on their trick of buying bakery cookies instead of baking their own, I slid the steaks onto a platter and placed the mushrooms, carrots, and roasted sweet potatoes on the table with red dinner plates and green napkins.

"The only problem was appending a recipe for them," said Nina.

Liza pointed at Nina. "She's so devious! She copied a recipe off the Internet and pretended it was for her cookies."

"Nina!" I cried. "What if someone tries that recipe? What a surprise they'll get when they turn out completely different."

"No one will care except for Natasha, and you know she won't bake them. In fact, I don't think she took her share of the cookies home with her."

Patty had been surprisingly quiet but wore a Mona Lisa smile. "What a shame that Gwen ruined the party."

"Isn't it funny that none of us knew Bethany and Bradley were Gwen's stepchildren?" Nina poured the wine.

With a heavy sigh, Patty launched into her sad tale.

Liza said, "Why don't you call Baxter? Maybe they're with him."

I loaded a plate with a variety of cookies to try and brought it to the table for dessert.

Patty's mouth shifted. "He's the reason I'm in this mess. We don't communicate very well. I tried calling the kids from the road, but they don't answer, and their mailboxes are full."

Nina cut a bite of the steak on her plate. "Sounds like the evil stepmother took their cell phones away."

Liza snorted. "I'd like to know on what planet Gwen looks too young to have teenagers. If anything, she looks too old to have a six-year-old."

"She's in great shape," I said. "Maybe she's younger than we think."

"Hah! Gwen's had work done. I'm sure of it. She's not as young as everyone thinks. I've seen her up close without makeup. I bet I'm happier, though, and I never go to the gym." Liza stuck out the tip of her tongue in disgust. "Stinky, sweaty places where everyone wears spandex and makes you feel bad for not being a size two. No thanks!" Liza reached for a second helping of mushrooms.

"Did either of you see my kids there? Maybe they're home and hanging around

upstairs in their rooms." Patty seemed hopeful.

"I didn't see them," said Nina. "If I had
been them, I would have been downstairs
sneaking cookies."

Patty laughed. "That's what my kids
would normally be doing. If . . . if Gwen
hasn't turned them into little robots."

A siren pealed outside, too close for
comfort. We peered out the bay window in
my kitchen and watched an ambulance as it
came to a halt.

"That's *my* house!" screamed Liza.

CHAPTER TWELVE

Dear Natasha,
You are always on the cutting edge with clever, fresh ideas. I love Christmas lights, but I'm tired of the same old thing. All the houses look alike. Help!
                    Christmas Elf in Joy, Illinois

Dear Christmas Elf,
Use rope lights to write a holiday message on your house. Naughty or Nice come to mind!
                              Natasha

Liza ran out the door with the rest of us trailing behind her. For someone who disliked gyms, she could move pretty fast in an emergency. She yelled, "Luis! Luis!" as she sped across the street.

We piled into Liza's living room. Three emergency medical technicians surrounded Luis. One was checking his blood pressure.

Luis perched on the edge of a leather sofa, holding up his hands as if he wanted everyone to go away. "I'm okay," he insisted. But he spoke in a weak voice and rubbed his chest.

"What happened?" demanded Liza. "You better not be having a heart attack! It's the job, isn't it? The new job. I knew it was a mistake."

Baxter looked on over Liza's shoulder. "He got shocked putting up Christmas lights."

"What?" Liza placed her palms on the sides of her face, her long sparkling white nails jutting out well beyond her fingertips. "The lights? Who gets shocked by those flimsy lights? You scared me half to death." She gazed at an EMT. "How bad could it be? Those lights barely carry any electricity in them."

"You'd be surprised how often this happens, ma'am," he responded. "People think that they're not dangerous, but they can pack a punch."

Baxter gazed over at us. His eyes widened, and he looked as though *he'd* had a shock when he saw his ex-wife, Patty. He did a double take. "What are you doing here?"

"I came to see my children." Patty crossed her arms over her chest defiantly and lifted her chin.

"Where are the lights?" asked Liza. "I'm throwing them out right now."

"No, no, no." Luis hadn't moved, except for the hands that scratched his chest.

Liza narrowed her eyes suspiciously. "If you're not having a heart attack, how come you keep massaging your chest?"

"It itches." Luis unbuttoned the top of his shirt.

"Good grief!" Liza pushed aside the medical technician. "What did you have for dinner?"

"Oh, Liza. Don't start." Luis sounded tired.

"I'll get it out of you. You might as well tell me now."

"Looks like an allergy?" asked the medical technician.

"He's allergic to soy." Liza shook her finger at him. "It's in everything now. Even in salad dressings! Who would suspect that?"

Baxter asked, "Where's the fuse box? After I make sure there's no juice, I'll climb up there and take those lights down." He pointed at Patty. "And then you and I will have to talk."

"No!" Luis started to stand but fell back onto the sofa. "Still a little dizzy."

"It's all right, Luis. I'll just remove the

lights that caused the problem, okay?" said Baxter. "Where are the breakers in this house?"

Liza led the way, and I followed them but stopped in the kitchen to stuff ice cubes into a plastic bag.

In a hallway off the kitchen, Baxter said, "Hah! Look at this. It threw the switch. Don't worry, Liza, we'll get you straightened out."

I returned to the living room and handed Luis the ice. "This might make you feel better."

He held it to his forehead. "Thanks, everyone. I'm not going to the emergency room. I'll be fine. Really."

The glint in Liza's eyes suggested she didn't agree. "You're such a stubborn old goat. It's a good thing you're gorgeous or I would have left you years ago."

A glimmer of a smile crossed Luis's lips. "Really," he said to the EMTs, "you guys go on and help someone who needs it."

Liza pulled one of them aside. "Is he going to be okay? Should I drag him to the hospital?"

"It's always wise to get checked out. His vital signs are normal, though."

The EMTs were packing up when Baxter returned. "I've switched the breaker back on." Baxter held a string of Christmas lights in his hand. "Guess this was the culprit. There's a long spot where the coating over the cord is missing."

One of the EMTs asked, "Were the lights on something metallic?"

Baxter seemed surprised. "How did you know?"

The EMT nodded his head. "We see it every Christmas. Faulty lights can charge a metallic object. It's usually a metallic tree, but it could be anything."

"Who knew?" asked Baxter. "I'd better tell Elvin. He's been stringing lights on things for as long as I can remember, and I bet he never knew that. I think he even dressed up in them once as a gag. Luis had these wrapped around a real fancy metal railing up on the roof."

"Sounds like the widow's walk," the EMT clarified.

Liza clasped her hand to her bosom. "Widow? I don't want you up there again, Luis."

"Liza, calm down." Luis sounded tired.

"Maybe we should go," I said, motioning to Nina and Patty.

Nina reached for Liza's arm. "I'm right next door. Call if you need anything."

We walked outside and clustered in the

cold as we watched the ambulance drive away.

"Why didn't you tell me you were coming?" asked Baxter.

"It was a last-minute thing." Patty sounded defensive. "Could I please visit with my children now?"

"Well, sure. I don't see why not."

Patty flashed a look of surprise my way and grinned. She walked next door with her ex-husband. Nina and I scurried across the street to my house and finished our dinner.

"Is it just me, or has this been a very strange few days?" asked Nina.

"I was just thinking the same thing. Too many odd accidents seem to be happening."

"It's this crazy Christmas decorating contest that has people scrambling around on rooftops. I'm glad I've hired someone to do my decorating. I don't think I'll ever look at a strand of Christmas lights quite the same way again." Nina slid on her coat and picked up her shopping bag loaded with cookies. "Liza forgot her cookies."

"I'll bring them over to her tomorrow. I'm sure cookies are the last thing on her mind right now."

"Don't forget, lunch with Liza at The Laughing Hound tomorrow."

"Assuming she's still up for it," I said.

Nina hustled home, and I turned my attention to Mochie, who waited patiently next to his empty food dish.

"Turkey or tuna?" I asked.

He stared at me like he thought I should know the answer without having to ask. I went with tuna. Apparently, I was right. He dug in immediately.

I took homemade chicken broth out of the freezer to let it thaw in a pot for a hearty chicken stew so Patty would have something to eat the next day.

In the meantime, I was itching to decorate my sunroom. Years of worry about the heat drying out a live tree in that location had prompted me to capitulate and buy an artificial tree for the sunroom. It was one of the first joys of Christmas each year to decorate it with a garden and animal motif.

I couldn't help thinking of Luis when I plugged in the tree. White lights glowed, reflecting in the wall of windows that looked out over my backyard. I climbed a ladder to attach the topper, a white dove of peace my niece had made for me.

To reach the top, I had to go past the rung marked "do not stand above this point" and lean a bit. Probably not the smartest thing to do. I could see how easy it would be to fall. Happily, I didn't. But I climbed down

167

with great care. And then I examined the rungs. They were metallic. What would happen if I held a string of lights while on the metallic ladder? How many times had I unwittingly wrapped lights on metal railings?

I opened a large red box, weathered with age, that held the ornaments for the tree in the sunroom. Garlands of red berries lay on top. I pulled them out and lay them across branches, circling the tree. After that, the very best part — revisiting memories with each ornament. The cute ladybug, the blown-glass squirrel and chipmunk. The funny bird with a long feather for a tail and the kitten that looked just like Mochie. Santa had left glitzy butterflies, light as air, in my stocking last year. They sat on top of branches where other ornaments would have been too heavy. I chuckled aloud when I found the two gray mice with Christmas ribbons tied on their tails.

It didn't take long to finish the tree. Mars and I had hung a wreath on the door the day before. A classic red amaryllis sat on the coffee table next to a roughly cast angel meant to be outdoors in a garden. The battery-operated candle inside a red lantern with a heart motif had already turned itself on.

I retrieved tan and red pillows that bore images of bright red cardinals and holly berries. With only the tree and the candle glowing in the night, I plumped up the cushions and placed them on the love seat and the chair.

Pleased with the results, I returned to the kitchen to slice leftover chicken breast into bite-sized pieces for the stew. I added cooked egg noodles and sunny yellow corn to the pot and tasted it. A sprinkle of salt and a good pinch of black pepper were all it needed.

Patty returned around ten.

"Could I offer you a snack or cookies?"

"No thanks. Baxter ordered takeout, and we noshed on cookies. They were all on display on the dining room table. I never thought I'd say this, but I'm about cookied out."

She chuckled. "It was pretty funny. Baxter was worried about us eating them without permission from Gwen. Can you imagine? Gwen hides goodies from Baxter and the kids because she knows they'll devour them. Apparently, she's crazy for peanut brittle. She made it to give as gifts, but the whole family chowed through it, so she had to make another batch. This time she hid it, but the kids found her secret stash. They gobbled it up, but then they had this empty orange box. I would have just thrown it away and pretended I knew nothing about it. Luckily, Bradley found a pink box with Liza and Luis's name on it hidden way back in the pantry behind the pasta. So they used the candy meant for Luis and Liza to replenish Gwen's secret stash in the orange box and then they put the boxes back where they found them!" She laughed until tears rolled down her face. "Oh gosh! Now Gwen is going to give her neighbors a gift that looks like most of it has already been eaten! Who will be more surprised when the gift box is opened and it's almost empty? Gwen or Liza and Luis?" Patty roared with laughter and dabbed at her eyes.

"Where was Gwen during all this?"

"She refused to come downstairs and join us. How rude is that? She must hate me more than I dislike her, and that's a lot. Acting like a child is bad enough, but she's setting such a poor example for the children. Doesn't she realize they need to learn to accept people and be polite to them?"

"That's a shame. Would you like a drink? A glass of wine? How about a Cranberry Jingle? I'm in the mood for one."

"Okay. Thanks."

I pulled two tall glasses out of the cabinet.

"At least you spent some time with your children."

"I did! That part was wonderful." She smiled wistfully. "They're growing up so fast. I hate that I've missed so much of their lives." Tears ran down her cheeks again, and she buried her head in her hands. "How did it ever come to this? How could they have been taken from me by that evil woman? Gwen robbed me. I didn't do anything wrong. I was a good mother!"

I handed her a tissue and patted her shoulder.

She blew her nose. "Just yesterday Bethany was playing with dolls and Bradley wanted a bike for his birthday. Now she's talking about boys and college, and he wants a *car*!" She broke into sobs again.

I hurried to the counter, scooped ice into the glasses, poured in vodka for a kick and peach schnapps for sweetness, and topped it off with cranberry juice. I brought them to the table with red napkins and a platter of cookies from the swap. I was going to eat one of the Scotcheroos, whether she wanted one or not.

"Have you considered moving here?" I asked.

Patty wiped her nose and gripped her glass. "I'm not trained for anything. How would I live?" She took a long swig of her drink. "But I have to do something. I can't go on this way. For their sakes, I have to be here for them."

"I hope you can work something out."

"Gwen has been a thorn in my side for years." Patty inhaled deeply. "The air there tonight was so thick and uncomfortable. Everyone was on edge. I bet they were all afraid that Gwen would make a scene. I anticipate that she'll object to anything I want."

"She can't prevent you from moving here."

"No. But she can sure keep me from seeing the kids."

"Aren't they too big for that? I would think it's easy with small children, but your kids are old enough to make excuses and go to your house. Gwen would never be the wiser."

"I'm pulling Bethany out of school for a half day tomorrow. We're going to her favorite mall for lunch and window-shopping. And I'm picking up Bradley in the afternoon. I hope Gwen won't call the school and tell them not to release the kids to me."

Patty finished her drink. "I want to thank you again for putting me up. And for putting up with me!" She laughed at her own little twist on the words. "You're very kind to listen to my troubles."

"I wish I could help in some way. I have a date scheduled with a lawyer at the annual bar association dinner dance. Maybe he can introduce me to someone who could take your case."

She stood up and stretched. "If only I had the money to pay a lawyer. Good-night, Sophie. And thanks again."

As I made sure the fire was out and the doors were locked, Edith Scroggins suddenly came to mind. I hoped she was safe and had locked up her house. It was too late to call her. She was probably fine. At least I hoped so.

I headed up the stairs. A light shone underneath the door to my guest room. After the long drive and the emotional reunion with her daughter and son, Patty had to be exhausted.

Mochie and I hit the sack, too. From the warmth of my bed, I could see the candle glowing in the window, and I drifted off.

In the middle of the night, Mochie jumped on top of my chest, waking me. He leaped to the edge of the bed, alert and listening.

"It's okay. It's just Patty," I assured him. I turned over and closed my eyes.

But there was no mistaking the creaking of my ancient stairs, or the loud *click* of the latch when she unlocked the front door.

I slid from my bed and peered out the window.

Chapter Thirteen

Dear Sophie,
We're on a very tight budget this year. How can I make my old holiday decorations look fresh on a shoestring?

Miserly Mom in Peartree, Tennessee

Dear Miserly Mom,
Use inexpensive pushpins adorned with pearls, sequins, and charms to dress up pillar candles. Fill everyday items like vases and glass bowls with simple round ornaments of the same color and they'll bring a whole new look to your décor. Cut evergreens that grow in your yard, and arrange them with your cherished decorations.

Sophie

Dressed in black, Patty scurried along the sidewalk. It wasn't long before she blended into the shroud of darkness.

I wanted to imagine that she had a good reason to be out and about when everyone slept. Maybe she left the house for a smoke? That would be considerate of her since I didn't smoke. But why was she awake at all? Maybe she couldn't sleep from all the stress?

I crawled back into bed, but sat up wondering what was going on. Maybe she needed something and hadn't wanted to wake me. Or — there weren't many good reasons for hustling around in the middle of the night.

Patty didn't return shortly like I hoped she might. I finally drifted off to sleep.

In the morning, after a shower, I pulled on a cashmere sweater with a V-neck in a deep wine red. Black trousers, gold hoop earrings, and a bold necklace of twisted garnet beads completed the outfit.

I made coffee and fed Mochie shredded chicken in sauce for breakfast. Patty hadn't risen yet, so I snagged a pineapple square to tide me over until breakfast. An hour later Patty still wasn't stirring.

I preheated the oven, figuring that muffins would be good any time she rose. I hauled out two bowls. In one I placed flour, sugar, salt, baking powder, heady cinnamon, nutmeg, and a pinch of cloves. I whisked the eggs in the other bowl then added rich melted butter and tart cranberries. Folding the ingredients with a spoonula, I combined them, careful not to overmix. I spooned the batter into muffin tins lined with cupcake papers and slid them into the oven.

In the meantime, I fried an egg for myself. If Patty wanted eggs, I would be happy to make some for her. In a tiny pot, I melted butter and set it aside. I mixed cinnamon with sugar in a small bowl and set it next to the butter. When the muffins were done, I dipped the top of each into the butter and rolled it in the cinnamon sugar. The sugar on top of the muffins glistened like crystals. I arranged them on a cake stand that had been hand-painted with green polka dots around the edge and three red Christmas stockings on the top.

A quick call to Nina confirmed that we were still on for lunch with Liza at Bernie's restaurant, The Laughing Hound. Determined to check on Edith, I left a note for Patty, in case she woke while I was out, slung on a warm jacket, and walked over to Horace and Edith's house. It looked exactly as it had the day before.

I lifted the handle of the huge knocker and banged it three times. If Edith was home, she would certainly hear it. No one opened the door this time. I leaned to the right and the left to peek inside, but sheer drapes prevented me from seeing anything.

Just in case she had fallen, I walked around to the garden behind the house and knocked on a back door. I didn't hear anything. If Edith was there, she didn't moan or cry out. What appeared to be a kitchen window looked out over the garden. I would need a ladder to see into the house, though. On the other side, a much larger window offered hope. A white pergola with bare wisteria vines looping through it formed an outdoor room. I stepped on the limestone floor. Cupping my hands around my eyes and leaning against the window, I peered inside.

An oriental rug, red on the interior with a blue border, dominated the dining room. A colonial-style brass chandelier hung over a large walnut table on massive pedestal legs. The walls had been painted a soft golden hue. Nothing seemed amiss.

I walked through the garden and looked back at the house. No one peered out the windows. Nothing moved. I let myself out the back gate, into the alley. Hadn't the housekeeper said Edith left a key over the back door? I stopped to consider whether I should let myself in.

If Edith weren't prone to fits of screaming fury, I might. But I suspected she was a very private person, and I felt the need to respect that.

Elvin walked around the side of his camper. "Oh! Hi. I didn't expect to see anyone back here in the alley. I'm Elvin Babineaux, Baxter's brother." He held out a fleshy hand to shake.

I introduced myself. "I saw you up on the roof helping Baxter decorate."

His face flushed when he laughed. "I love this neighborhood competition. If you ask me, there's no such thing as too many Christmas lights. Is your house done yet?"

"I think Mars and Bernie might finish up tonight or tomorrow. Have you seen Luis this morning?"

"He's fine. He ran by here a few times this morning. Looks like nothing happened to him. Baxter and I are going to give him a hand later on today."

I waved good-bye and walked past Natasha and Mars's garage.

When I strolled by the front of the Babineaux house, I saw Baxter draping lights on the bushes. "Baxter, have you heard anything about Horace or Edith?" I asked.

Baxter untangled a string of lights. "Horace is coming along very slowly. You know

179

doctors, they don't tell you much. And Edith acts as though my interest in Horace is offensive. She, uh" — he released such a deep breath that I thought he deflated a little — "she fired me."

"Why?" I was shocked.

"We . . . The employees still can't get into the office. It's a nightmare. I told her what I thought, and she didn't care to hear it. She seems to think she's in charge."

"Why would she lock them out? Surely she understands that business must continue?"

"Because she's an old crab. I've talked about it with some of the other employees. She's asserting her dominance because she can. Like an old alpha horse trying to make it known that she's still in control."

"Is she a Realtor?"

"Only technically. I'd be surprised if she ever worked a day in her life. She certainly isn't actively involved in selling real estate."

I asked if he had Horace's home phone number.

"He's still laid up in the hospital."

"I thought I should check on Edith."

Baxter roared with laughter. "I had no idea you were so humorous. That's a good one."

"I'm not joking."

"Oh?" He pulled a cell phone from his wallet, looked up the number, and read it to me.

"Thanks."

"Uh, Sophie? Have you seen Gwen today?"

"Can't say that I have. Did you lose her?" I teased.

"She didn't come home last night. I pretended she was upstairs because I didn't want the kids to worry." He focused on the lights, but his fingers didn't work at untangling them. "I . . . Did she ever say anything about another man?"

Oh no. Poor Baxter. "I'm afraid you're asking the wrong person. I don't think that's the kind of thing she would have confided in me. We aren't that close. If you're talking about the Christmas letter, I think the reference to her affair was a joke."

He nodded his head very slowly, like he was deep in thought.

I said good-bye but suspected he didn't hear me. I hustled home to write the number down before I forgot it.

When I opened the door, it didn't sound like Patty had risen yet. Mochie was the only one padding around the house. He accompanied me to my study, where I called Edith. An answering machine picked up. I worked at my desk until I heard the shower running upstairs.

Patty stumbled into the kitchen in a hurry. "Goodness! I haven't slept this late since before I had Bethany." She rubbed her eyes. "I'm a little groggy. Oh! Coffee. Thank you."

She helped herself to a muffin and checked the time. "I'm going to be late picking her up. I hope you don't mind if I eat on the run." She collected her coat and purse and rushed out the door.

Maybe she would tell me about her midnight escapade later. Or maybe not. I cleaned up the kitchen and prepared to leave for lunch. I pulled on a black winter coat, wrapped a long red and white scarf around my neck, and slung my handbag over my shoulder.

Walking in Old Town was always fun because of the fascinating architecture and the colonial atmosphere. But at Christmas, everyone dressed their houses for the season, making even a simple walk a special occasion. A few flakes of snow drifted in the air.

I admired the wreaths on doors and windows, loaded with pinecones and berries and bright ribbons. I marveled at some of the pineapples, wondering how they stayed in place. Topiaries had been transformed with greenery, fruit, birds, and Christmas ornaments of every description. Bernie had gone all out on The Laughing Hound, too. Boughs of pine sparkled with twinkling white lights. He'd even hung mistletoe over the entrance.

The hostess showed me to the garden room that reminded me of an English conservatory because of all the windows. Through the glass ceiling, I could see huge snowflakes floating gently outside. Enormous Christmas wreaths of multi-colored glass balls hung on the windows. Colorful lights in the wreaths twinkled merrily. A tree so large that it very nearly hit the high ceiling added to the festive décor.

Nina and Liza had just taken their seats when I walked in.

"How's Luis?" I asked.

Liza almost glowered when she said, "As though nothing ever happened. He got up early, went for a run, and by the time I dragged my lazy bones out of bed, he had made breakfast, dressed for work, and was reading the paper."

"That's great. I'm so relieved that it wasn't serious." I unfolded the napkin and placed it in my lap.

The waitress arrived to run through the daily specials. I ordered immediately, practically drooling at the thought of crab-stuffed ravioli with a fresh lobster sauce.

When the waitress left, Liza glanced around. "But get this. When Luis was out running he saw Baxter, who said Gwen didn't come home last night!"

Nina's forehead wrinkled. "Because of her argument with Natasha at the cookie swap? That's nuts."

I felt a little guilty about gossiping, but I said, "Baxter asked me if Gwen could be having an affair."

Nina groaned and swiped a hand through the air. "I knew that letter would be trouble. Who says that, even in jest? First she scared all the wives, and now it's only natural that Baxter would think she's seeing someone. She put the idea in his head."

"It's odd that she didn't come home," said Liza, wiggling her eyebrows. "Poor Baxter. Do you think she left him for good?"

I didn't like gossiping, but this might be my chance to find out more about that suspicious ladder. "You and Luis know Gwen and Baxter pretty well, don't you, Liza?"

"You'd think so after reading her Christmas letter, wouldn't you? Can I tell you how many people have asked me about our trip to Paris? That Gwen is a pip! We went to

Paris, *Virginia*! It's a sleepy little town with one very good restaurant in an inn. And Kenny G?" She laughed aloud. "He was our waiter! Kenny Graham! Can you believe how she twisted that story? Technically it's all true, it's just not what anyone thinks when they read it."

Nina sputtered, "Baxter and Gwen didn't go to France?"

"No! And did you notice the lie about their mountain cabin? She wants people to think they bought it. It's a rental. They didn't even stay there. Luis took that picture the day we went to *Paris*."

"So you're not close?" asked Nina.

"We've done a few things together," said Liza, "but we're not nearly the bosom buddies she implied in her letter. I know her like a person knows a neighbor. I'll say this, though, she has to be the center of attention all the time. People say I'm dramatic" — she touched the base of her throat — "but Gwen is consumed with herself." She lowered her voice to a whisper. "Luis says that's called histrionic personality disorder."

"That's so sad." I sipped my tea. "The Babineauxs have so much to be proud of anyway. Why would Gwen feel the need to exaggerate like that? Or is there trouble brewing underneath?" I didn't say it but wanted to blurt out, *Would she have sawed the rung on her husband's ladder?*

"Baxter seems quite fond of Gwen. I usually think of a trophy wife as younger than the first one. Gwen certainly isn't young, but she's flashy and works at being seductive. Patty seems more timid, like a little mouse." Liza had them pegged. "They're totally different types."

"Does Luis think Gwen has this disorder thing for real?" asked Nina.

Liza flipped her palms up dramatically. "You're married to a doctor. I'm sure he's just like Luis. He hates it when I repeat his on-the-fly diagnoses. I told him all about Edith Scroggins, but he wouldn't even venture a guess at *her* problem!"

The waitress delivered our lunches. Although Nina's truffle burger appeared juicy, and the scent of bacon in Liza's Tagliatelle Carbonara made me take note to try it sometime, my square ravioli with chunks of crab in a salmon-colored sauce was by far the most alluring. Heavenly! The sauce accompanied the crab perfectly without overwhelming it.

Liza groaned when she sampled her dish. "Oh, this is fabulous!" She leaned toward us as though she hoped no one else would overhear.

"I truly do not know what possessed me when I allowed Luis to choose a house by himself." Liza's large eyes opened wider. "We had such a nice place in Manhattan. It was gorgeous. Everything was taken care of. We had a doorman and a dog walker. The whole thing had been redone and had all the latest fixtures. The kitchen was stainless with those cute glass tiles as a backsplash. The bathroom, oh my! I think it's the only thing Luis misses. It had pulsating jets that massage. The place was perfect. But no, Luis had to move down here for the history."

Nina nodded knowingly. "A lot of people love living here for that reason. After all, how many places can you live where George Washington walked the streets?"

"I could deal with that, but what made him buy a huge house? I want to rip everything out, but he goes on and on about colonial this and historic that. Meanwhile, I'm gagging. I don't want to insult you. I know everyone around here loves their old homes, but this Williamsburg style just isn't for me. Thank goodness Luis came through with the grand piano he promised me." Liza lowered her voice to a mere whisper. "But the basement! I won't go down there for anything." She studied us, her eyes so huge the whites showed on the top and bottom.

"Ghosts?" I asked.

Liza's eyes grew huge. "I don't want you to think I'm a complete loon."

Nina laughed. "We think the ghost of the previous owner of Sophie's house lives in her kitchen."

Liza's face contorted in confusion.

I was fairly sure she thought *we* were the loony ones. "She doesn't moan or rattle chains or anything. There's really no proof."

Liza placed her hands on the table. "At least I have someone to talk with about this. My mother and sister thought I was out of my mind. Do you have stone basements? Ours has stone walls, a slate floor, and beamed ceilings. And there's an old stone fireplace that's black with the soot of the ages. It's one of the creepiest places I've ever been." Her voice grew shrill when she said, "And it's *in my house!*" She whispered, "Sometimes I hear noises. Luis says it's just the house settling. It's a couple hundred years old — how much more is it going to settle?"

Nina nodded. "I had our basement drywalled."

"I suggested that we drywall it, but noooo, Luis won't hear of it. He says people lived there during the Civil War, and he thinks it's cozy. I told him it's his man cave. It's only fair, right?" She snickered. "I have my lovely piano, and he's stuck puttering around in that awful basement with a huge sofa, a big-screen TV, and his wine collection. I call it the dungeon."

"You don't sound very happy," I said.

Liza sagged. "To tell you the truth, I wanted Luis to take the position he was offered in Miami. My mother and sister moved there, and I feel like a fish out of water here, flopping around with nowhere to go. Give me a condo in a building with an elevator, a view of the water, one bedroom, and a kitchen big enough for only a microwave, and I'll be happy. I have the perfect place picked out."

"Only one bedroom?" asked Nina.

"Not even with a den! I don't want any room for company or for cooking. In New York, Luis was perfectly content to eat out or order in. The corner coffee shop delivered our coffee and breakfast every morning. When we moved here, Luis suddenly thought I was supposed to be a domestic goddess, and that he's some kind of macho handyman. I have no idea where that came from. The man didn't even own a toolbox! Now he likes to buy used stuff from old men at yard sales." Her upper lip curled in disgust.

The hostess showed Baxter, Elvin, and Sugar to a table across the room. We waved at them and they politely waved back at us.

"So, what's the story with Sugar?" asked Liza.

I looked at Nina, who looked back at me with a blank expression.

"Oh, puleeze!" Liza dabbed at her mouth with her napkin. "She's been coming on to Luis like a locomotive. And, I'm sorry, but ballerinas don't come with surgically enhanced ta-tas. She might be a dancer, but I suspect it involves poles, not tutus. Hasn't she been after your husband, Nina?"

"He's been away." Nina frowned at her. "Maybe that's why Gwen doesn't like her. Do you think Sugar would have had the nerve to put the moves on Baxter? Did you notice that Gwen treated Sugar a little bit like hired help yesterday at the cookie swap?"

"I didn't notice that. I did catch Sugar listening in very closely when Gwen hustled Patty off to the kitchen."

The conversation moved on to Liza's interest in music and the Christmas decorating competition.

Liza's phone rang a couple of times. She

finally pulled it out of her purse. "Pesky thing. I hate it when phones ring during meals. Oh! It's Luis. Would it be terribly rude to talk to him? It's not like him to keep calling. It must be an emergency."

She took the call and blanched. Her eyes nearly bulged and the fingers of her free hand clutched the handle of her knife as though she planned to plunge it into someone.

CHAPTER FOURTEEN

Dear Natasha,
Last year my crazy girlfriend gave me a
gold reindeer that's almost two feet tall.
I have no idea what to do with it.

> Needs New Friends in Dasher,
> Georgia

Dear Needs New Friends,
Make it a focal point on a shelf, buffet,
or a console table behind your sofa.
Cluster shorter objects around it, perhaps a white candle with gold accents
and a gold picture frame.

> Natasha

Liza Simon's face paled. "No!" she breathed
into her cell phone.

Liza was prone to being dramatic, but the
horror on her face was unmistakable. My
eyes met those of Nina, across the table.

I hoped the phone call wasn't bad news.

Especially not at Christmas. But the chatty woman had been rendered speechless, and she looked like someone had died.

She hung up and Nina asked, "Is everything okay?"

Still holding the knife, Liza leaned toward us. "Batten down the hatches and lock your doors. Lizzie Borden is coming for Christmas. How's that for advance notice? The kid is supposed to be with her mother for the holidays this year!" Her eyes narrowed to slits. "She probably waited until the last minute because she knew I would find a way to wiggle out of it."

Nina signaled the waiter. "Another round of coffee, please, and we have an emergency situation, so do you think we could have three slices of chocolate raspberry cheesecake?"

Liza perked up for a moment. "Dessert? I *love* you guys."

The waiter poured more coffee as I asked, "Who is this person?"

"Luis's only child, Pandooooora." Liza's eyes looked up while her mouth turned down. "Who names a child Pandora? Seriously, don't you think that's asking for trouble? She's fourteen, thinks she knows everything, has already pierced body parts you don't even want to know about, and unleashes evil on the world everywhere she goes."

We had barely doctored our coffees with cream and sugar when the cheesecake arrived. "Three cheesecakes aux framboise," announced the waitress. She set a slice of dark velvety chocolate in front of me. A thin layer of raspberry gelée glistened on the top. Raspberry sauce circled the cake in the shape of hearts, and fresh raspberries sat next to the cake in a dollop of whipped cream.

"You're not big on kids?" Nina asked.

Liza bounced in her seat in surprise. "I *love* kids! That little Katrina Babineaux next door is adorable. She's always coming over to see my Yorkshire terrier. Luis's daughter is . . . different." Her tone dipped down an octave. "She calls herself the Darling of Darkness."

"Goth?" I savored a bite of the creamy cheesecake.

"I can deal with Goth. I don't mind the black clothes or the effort to be different. If she wants to wear a nose ring like an old bull, I don't care. I wasn't exactly the perky blond cheerleader type myself. I was the tubby girl with braces, and hair that kinked and frizzed when straight hair was all the rage. I would have loved to scare the cool kids that picked on me."

"So what's the problem?" Nina speared a fresh raspberry.

"Pandora is out of control. Luis and her mother say she wasn't like that before the divorce, but I don't believe it. The kid knows how to make them feel guilty, and she works it for everything it's worth. If she wants a burger at three in the morning, Luis will find a burger at three in the morning. It's insane. And his ex-wife just will not co-operate. Poor Luis spends more time on the phone with that woman now than he did before the divorce. She calls about every little thing, and" — Liza waved her hands in a big circle — "everything in the world is his fault. I despise the entire situation. So he bends over backward to make them happy. Whatever the ex-wife and Pandora want, they get."

"Sounds like the problem is with Luis," I observed. "Maybe he feels guilty for not being there for her all the time anymore."

"There's no convincing him that he's creating a monster. Doesn't everyone know that children need parameters? He's afraid his ex won't let him see Pandora if he doesn't comply with their every whim. But I'm not permitted to express an opinion because I have been cast in the role of the wicked stepmother." She cackled and splayed her fingers in a witchy way. She heaved a great sigh. "This is going to be the worst Christmas ever."

In the late afternoon, staple guns hammered on my roof again as I zipped up the velvet dress I had bought. Daisy had come over with Mars, and now watched carefully while I dressed for my date.

I skipped the high heels that were worthy of the dress and went with navy blue satin sling backs with peep toes and modest heels, which were more comfortable. A pair of simple diamond stud earrings and a rhinestone bracelet, and I was set. I let my hair tumble down on my shoulders in loose curls. After all, this had the potential to be a romantic evening. I had seen Alex a few times since we met, but he still lived a dual life, part-time in Old Town and part-time in North Carolina.

Feeling giddy as a young girl, I sashayed down the stairs. The phone rang in the kitchen.

"Soph?" said Mars. "Could you do a big favor for Bernie and me?"

"Where are you?" I'd thought he was on my roof trying to get the lights to work.

"On your roof. Would you go over to my

garage and bring back a box of staples? There are two on the middle of my workbench. It's a hassle going up and down, and we're just in the middle of something. You can bring them up to the third floor and hand them to us through the window."

He knew I had a date. Was this some kind of ruse to get me out of the house? "Maybe Natasha could bring it over. I'm all dressed to go out."

"Are you kidding me? You know she wouldn't do anything to help us."

I checked the time. Alex wouldn't pick me up for at least forty-five minutes. "Okay. But it better not be dirty in your garage." What was I saying? Natasha probably dusted it daily.

I hung up the phone, pulled on a coat long enough to cover my tea length dress, and hitched Daisy's leash onto her collar so she could get in a short walk before I left.

We crossed the street and stopped to look up at my roof. No lights glowed yet. I suspected that many of the Clark Griswold contestants hadn't finished their lighting schemes either, but most of the houses sparkled at least a little bit in the wintery night.

Luis had made enormous progress. In true Griswold style, he dropped lines of lights from the roof down to the ground. The lights seemed to run up and down them, making me slightly seasick. They probably looked better from a distance.

Baxter and his brother had outlined the dormer windows on the Babineauxs' roof with bright white lights. Giant letters between them glowed orange and pink, spelling out *NOEL*.

Natasha was working on her front door when we walked by.

I stopped and called out, "I thought you were done with decorating."

She trotted down the stairs and glanced next door. Speaking in a hushed voice she said, "I will not be outdone by someone who copies my color scheme. I'm switching everything over to black and silver."

"You're decorating twice in one season?"

"This is why you're not at the top of the domestic diva game, Sophie. You don't understand the importance of originality and being first with trends."

"I seem to recall silver Christmas trees a long, long time ago."

"Exactly. They're fashionable again! Think about it. Everyone is in love with stainless steel and clean lines." She *tsk*ed at me. "Or hadn't you noticed that? Black and silver is so chic. It's the ultimate elegance."

I hoped she would go heavy on the silver so it wouldn't look like Halloween. "Mars asked me to bring him staples from your garage."

"Carriage house," she corrected me. "Just as long as I don't have to do it." She gasped. "Is that your house?"

I turned to look. Mars and Bernie had plugged in their Santa, sleigh, and reindeer. The reindeer appeared animated, as though they were leaping into flight. "Wow. Who knew Mars could do anything like *that*?"

Natasha choked and hacked. "Must be Bernie's handiwork. I don't much care for him, but he's very clever at that sort of thing."

I said good-bye and rounded the corner of her house. Daisy kept her nose to the ground in the alley, undoubtedly smelling other dogs who had walked there.

The VW bus lurked in the darkness like a hulk. A bright blaze hit my eyes as the carriage house lights flicked on. I staggered backward, blinking. Jonah had added a ton of lights to the gingerbread house motif.

Daisy must not have appreciated the lights quite as much as I did. She wanted to follow a scent away from the carriage house. I had to tug her to the door. I knocked as a formality, because I knew that it led to Natasha's workshop. The entrance to Jonah and Twiggy's apartment was inside the building.

I flicked on the light. Ribbons, ornaments, and wrapping paper cluttered the huge table in the center of Natasha's craft room. I couldn't believe she was redoing her entire holiday décor.

The door to the upstairs apartment bore a wreath that could only have been hand-crafted by Twiggy. A foot-high iced gingerbread-house-shaped cookie sat in the middle of a traditional fir wreath, sur-rounded by red and white gingham ribbon, gaily wrapped candies, and iced gingerbread boys and girls.

I opened the door to the garage and flicked the light switch. Immaculate, as expected. No ordinary garage lights for Na-tasha. Overhead can lights gleamed on the glossy gray floor.

Daisy whined and pulled at her leash, eager to inspect the garage.

"Honey, Alex is coming to pick me up soon. We don't have time for lots of sniff-ing." She led the way to the workbench. I picked up the two boxes of staples and turned to leave.

Daisy stood her ground, though.

"Come on, already." I tugged at her leash gently.

Daisy ignored me. Her nose led her around Natasha's car to a wall of white storage cabinets. I had a brand-new garage, but I envied the tall cabinets, big enough for brooms and buckets and patio umbrellas. They could tuck everything away so neatly. Daisy propelled me forward, and I stumbled.

Chapter Fifteen

Dear Natasha,
My persnickety mother-in-law is coming for the holidays this year. She always makes comments about my simplistic decorating style. What's the one over-looked item that I can wow her with?
Grumpy Daughter-in-Law
in Angeltown, Tennessee

Dear Grumpy,
Everyone forgets the hanging light fix-tures. Especially in the foyer and the kitchen. Drape the chain and arms with a short garland of pine, and add a lavish wire ribbon and berries, or even better, long feathers! You'll knock her socks off.
Natasha

I regained my footing. I should have worn sneakers.

Daisy pawed at one of the storage doors.

"Daisy! No!" I didn't want her to scratch it.

I gathered up my voluminous skirt and crouched to examine the door. "Aw, Daisy!" I fingered three perpendicular scratches. They didn't run deep, but they marred the perfect door.

Daisy didn't seem to care and scratched the door again. "Daisy!" I pulled her back, dropping the boxes of staples. Bars of the sharp things skidded all over the glossy painted floor. This was *not* what I had intended to do in my new dress. "Daisy, sit. Stop scratching that door."

I released her leash and for a few minutes, she stayed perfectly still while I collected the staples. All I needed was for Mars or Natasha to drive over the stupid things and get them lodged in a tire.

When I thought I had them all, I turned back to Daisy. She was still sitting but had scooted over to the cabinet and was in the process of opening it with her nose.

Someone had hidden a Christmas gift there.

Gold stars glimmered on pink paper that had been wrapped around a box taller than me. Undoubtedly one of those nightmarish items that was hard to wrap. The top of the package gave it away. There was no mistaking the shape of a lampshade. It had to be from Natasha to Mars. Maybe a standing lamp for his study? A gold ribbon circled the middle of the tall package, ending in a big fancy bow with six loops, definitely handmade.

I hadn't worn a watch, but I was fairly certain I needed to head home. It would be awful if Alex arrived to pick me up, and I wasn't there.

I reached past Daisy to close the cabinet when, to my horror, she slammed a heavy paw on the package, piercing the wrapping paper.

"No!" I shrieked. "Oh, Daisy! What have you done?" I couldn't just patch it with tape. I would simply have to apologize and rewrap the whole thing. There wasn't anything else I could do.

I leaned over to grip her collar. There would be no more pawing at the gift. I hoped she hadn't broken anything.

But when I leaned over, I realized something was very, very wrong. And it wasn't just torn gift wrap.

The box hadn't fit around the lamp perfectly. Someone, probably Natasha, had slit a box up the side to wrap it around the base of the lamp. Daisy's claw had torn the tape holding the box closed. I thought I saw a shoe.

I looked closer. Definitely a woman's shoe. Bending as close as I could without toppling over, I realized it must be a gag gift. Undoubtedly a joke similar to the sexy leg lamp in *A Christmas Story*. Didn't seem like something Natasha would give anyone, though. Her sense of humor didn't run in that direction.

Daisy worried me. If it was a gag gift, why was Daisy so interested in it?

I reached up to the lampshade and pried loose two pieces of tape. A curl tumbled out and lay atop the wrapping paper.

I screamed and jumped back, falling over Daisy.

No! It couldn't be a real person. It just couldn't. Maybe it was a gag gift from Mars to Bernie. That sounded more like it. I blew air out in relief, and clambered to my feet. That made perfect sense. Mars bought Bernie a silly "woman" lamp. Natasha had probably wrapped it for him, and they'd hidden it in the garage.

I took a deep breath to calm my nerves and picked up the curl to jam it inside. I was no authority on wigs but it certainly felt like real hair. I stared at the package. If it was Mars's, he'd get a big laugh out of

205

giving me a fright. But just to be sure, I tore open the box — and found myself staring up into Gwen Babineaux's dead eyes.

The scream that shuddered out of my throat could have curdled milk.

My heart thudded. I checked her neck for a pulse. Her skin felt incredibly cold. I ran for Natasha's workshop in search of a telephone to call for help. Black and silver ornaments crowded the counters, near orange and pink ones. A stack of pink gift boxes almost hid the wall phone. I punched in 911 and gave them the location.

The dispatcher tried to keep me on the line. I stepped on something soft and backed up. On the floor lay a five-inch-tall gray felt mouse. Unless I was mistaken, it looked a lot like the one Edith Scroggins had made such a fuss over at Rocking Horse Toys. I picked it up to examine it more closely. It wore a Santa hat, but the glasses were missing.

Stray thoughts about Edith passed through my head. Gwen invaded them, and I hung up the phone.

Breathing heavily, I hurried back to Gwen. I had little hope that she might be alive, but I checked her pulse again. Did I feel something? I wasn't sure. I was using my forefinger and middle finger so I wouldn't mistake my own pulse for hers.

What was taking them so long? I wished there was something I could do for Gwen.

An ambulance siren howled briefly.

I ran outside to guide the paramedics who disembarked with amazing calmness.

A police car had arrived as well. Officer Wong strode toward me purposefully, her uniform straining against her curvy figure. Her expression grim, she uttered one word: "Scroggins?"

I glanced at the mouse that I still carried in my hand. Where was Edith? And why was her mouse in Natasha and Mars's garage? "No. It's Gwen Babineaux from next door."

They all followed me through Natasha's workshop and into the garage. I jammed the mouse into my pocket.

Wong flicked a strong flashlight beam over Gwen and the wrapping paper. "Whoa! If she's not alive, then don't move her."

I watched them, vaguely conscious that I held my breath. Maybe she *was* alive. Maybe they would find a heartbeat that I couldn't feel.

They didn't. Officer Wong called in on her radio and I overheard the words, *crime scene.*

"What happened here?" she asked.

I explained how Daisy had torn the wrapping paper.

"That's really creepy." Wong shuddered. "It's like a message from the mafia or something to wrap someone up as a gift."

I peered at her. She wasn't kidding. I hadn't taken the time to consider why Gwen was wrapped. If someone had done this to Gwen as a threat to Baxter, then it was the cruelest, most horrible thing imaginable. "Her husband sells real estate. That doesn't seem likely."

"Then why wrap her up?"

Good question. I had no answers.

At that moment, Baxter emerged through the door that led to the workroom. He squinted like he'd run in from the dark and the lights hurt his eyes. "Everything okay here?"

Wong said, "Baxter, let's step outside."

Baxter ignored her, his eyes fixed on the cabinet. He walked closer in haste. "Gwen?" It was barely a whisper. "Gwen!" He shouted her name in panic. Baxter lunged toward her between two of the paramedics. Wong stepped forward to restrain him.

"What happened to her? What's going on?" shouted Baxter. "Is she okay? Gwen!" Baxter screamed her name as though he hoped she would respond.

Wong said calmly, "I'm very sorry, Mr.

Babineaux."

Baxter's Adam's apple bobbed. He held the back of his wrist to his nose and closed his eyes. His head fell forward and his shoulders began to shake.

One of the first responders gently escorted him outside. Baxter shuffled along without protesting, like an empty shell of a person.

We heard a little tussle, and Sugar burst into the garage. Like a ballerina on light feet, she crept forward, assessing the situation, and then cried out, "Mom!"

CHAPTER SIXTEEN

Dear Natasha,
Each year my mother raves about my crafty sister's Christmas wrap, which she makes herself. I can't compete with homemade paper. How can I make my gift wrap special?

> The Other Daughter in Gift,
> Mississippi

Dear The Other Daughter,
Find sturdy boxes with tops and bottoms. Wrap them in luxurious fabric, using a glue stick and a glue gun as necessary to adhere it. Use the glue stick to wrap a bit of velvet ribbon around the sides of the top pieces. Adorn the tops with bouquets of fresh berries and pine.

> Natasha

"What happened?" Sugar croaked. She shook off the gentle hand of a paramedic.

"Why aren't you helping her?"

"I'm very sorry," said Wong.

I was still reeling from the facts that Gwen was dead and Sugar had called her *Mom.*

Sugar's forehead furrowed. "She . . . she's dead? She can't be. Mom! Nooo! Mooooom!"

And then she collapsed in a sobbing heap. It broke my heart. I couldn't imagine what she must be going through. I helped her to her feet. We shuffled slowly. Sugar bent over as though she had no strength left in her. I kept her walking through the workshop and out the door into the cold night air. Next door, Bethany and Katrina rushed out the back gate.

Sugar's head jerked up at the sound of their voices. She wrested her arm from my grip and breathed, "They must never see her like that." With a burst of newfound strength, she rushed toward the girls, turned them around, and ushered them quickly into their own backyard.

Neighbors and additional police cars arrived in the alley. A man stepped out of a car and strode toward me. I knew who he was before I could make out his face. I knew from the way he carried himself. I knew his gait and how he held his shoulders. Wolf Fleishman. The detective I had dated for many years. I always suspected I would run into him again someday, just not tonight.

"Hello, Sophie." His voice was low, somber, soft. I remembered it all too well. Daisy strained at her leash to reach him. He strode closer and patted her. "In there?" he asked.

I nodded and showed him the way. Wolf looked good. He had always carried a few extra pounds. Both of us liked to eat, but he was tall enough to pull off the extra weight.

Wolf's eyebrows jumped when he caught sight of Gwen wrapped up like a present. He said nothing, but I could see that he was taking in every little detail.

"How are you involved in this?" he asked.

"I found Gwen. Actually, Daisy did."

He frowned. "You're not exactly dressed for walking Daisy in an alley."

I gasped. I'd forgotten all about Alex! "I have to go!"

"I'm not through with you yet, Sophie."

"Look, I've told Wong everything I know. Okay?" I turned and started to jog away.

"Sophie!" Wolf charged after me. "You can't just leave the scene of the crime. You know better than that."

"Wolf! You know where I live. I'll answer any questions you have. Look, I'll come back. Okay? Just let me go home for a few minutes to make a phone call."

I didn't wait for his response. If he hadn't known me so well, I imagined he might have chased after me. I hurried Daisy along the alley and out to the street. I had to slow down to catch my breath. Ugh. Having to talk with Wolf would be uncomfortable at best.

When I reached my house, Mars yelled to me, "Where have you been? My house isn't that far away. Come up to the third floor and hand me the staples. We've been waiting."

Aargh. In the commotion about Gwen, I'd forgotten all about the staples. They lay in the workshop, where I had made the call to the police. "Has Alex been here?" I shouted.

"Not yet. What's with the flashing lights over my way?"

I rushed into the house and checked the clock. Alex would surely be there any minute. I hurried up the stairs. Mochie and Daisy sprang ahead with more energy than I could muster. I made it up to the dormer window and opened it, huffing and puffing.

Mars reached out his hand.

"I'm sorry. I left them in Natasha's crafting room. Gwen Babineaux is dead."

"What?! We heard the sirens."

"Mars, you might want to head home. I

found her in your garage."

His boot slipped on the roof shingles. "*My garage?* Bernie! We have to go. Come on."

Mars climbed through the window. "What was Gwen doing in my garage?"

"Beats me." I gave Bernie a hand as he crawled through the window. "She was wrapped in pink and gold Christmas paper."

The color drained from Mars's face. "Natasha," he whispered. He gazed at Bernie and me with fear in his eyes. "What am I saying? She couldn't do something like that. I never said that. There has to be a reasonable explanation."

I stopped short of saying what I thought. There simply was no reasonable explanation for a person to be wrapped up like a gift. None whatsoever.

Bernie shook his head. "Sorry, old chap. Looks like Natasha finally went over the edge."

Mars shot him an annoyed look. "No, no. It can't be. I better get over there." Mars rushed out of the room and scrambled down the stairs.

"Wrapped in Christmas paper?" Bernie snorted. "That smacks of Natasha in every imaginable way. I believe she's gone 'round the bend this time."

Bernie accompanied me down the stairs.

The phone rang before we reached the bottom. I raced into the kitchen to answer it.

"Hi, Sophie."

I recognized Alex's voice.

"I'm so sorry to cancel on you, especially this late, but I have an unexpected work emergency."

"Oh." I hated that he could hear the disappointment in my tone. I cleared my throat. "That's okay," I said brightly, as though I didn't care. "We'll get together another time."

"Thanks for being so understanding. I'll call you, okay?"

What could I say? "Okay." And that was that.

Bernie slung a comforting arm around my shoulders. "He called it off?"

"I'm afraid so."

"Well, we can't have you all dressed up with no place to go." He offered me his arm. "Would you care to accompany an English bloke to his restaurant?"

"I think that would be lovely. Oh, good heavens! How could I have forgotten about Gwen even for a second? I can't go anywhere. I promised Wolf I would come right back."

"Wolf?" Bernie shook his head. "Be careful, Sophie."

"About what?"

"Don't fall for him again. It's no good being in love with someone who isn't available."

"Dana." I'd forgotten all about his relationship with Dana. One Halloween, Bernie had met a very lovely woman and dated her. Unfortunately, she had an equally charming former husband and a young son who wanted nothing more in the world than to reunite his parents. "Did she go back to her ex-husband?"

Bernie avoided my question. "I just don't want you to be hurt. You did a huge favor for Wolf, and he owes you. Don't mistake that for romance. I'll walk you back over to Natasha's garage."

When we stepped outside, a blaze of lights surrounded us. I locked the front door. At the sidewalk, we turned to admire my house.

A red sleigh glowed atop the roof. Golden reindeer appeared to be lifting off in flight and then landing, and then taking off again. Icicle lights ran along my roofline and accented the dormer windows. Bright lights lined every angle on my house. They graced the limbs of the tree in front of the house, too. On the other side, Bernie and Mars had created a tree out of lights by drawing them to a peak at one of my chimneys and somehow planting a star on top of it. Smaller trees lined my short walkway.

It was over-the-top but beautiful. "Bernie, it's amazing! Clark Griswold would be proud."

"We still have some work to do on it, but we're almost there."

"I can't imagine what else you could do. Natasha and Gwen . . . I can't believe Gwen is dead."

"I was joking about Natasha," he said. "She didn't really have a quarrel with Gwen, did she?"

"I heard they had a bit of a tiff yesterday when Gwen threatened to put unflattering pictures of Natasha on the Internet. You know how Natasha takes pride in her appearance. And she accused Gwen of stealing her Christmas colors."

Bernie cast a sideways look at me. "You have to be kidding. Even Natasha wouldn't kill over that. Would she?"

He accompanied me around Mars and Natasha's house to the alley. The lights on the police cars strobed in the night, and I couldn't help thinking that unlike the Christmas lights, which were so cheerful, the police lights pulsed an ominous note.

Everyone in the neighborhood had come out to watch.

Wolf spotted me right away.

"Want me to stick around?" asked Bernie.

"I'm okay. Wolf's a decent guy."

"I'm standing by if you get into trouble." Bernie joined Nina, Liza, Mars, and Daisy.

Wolf made a beeline for me, took me by the elbow, and propelled me to a calm spot beside the garage. "Are you out of your mind? I know we have a history, but you can't just go running off like that. I could have you arrested."

"You knew I would come back."

"Sophie! This woman was clearly murdered. How do I know you didn't hide something? The murder weapon, for instance? It's bad enough that you and Daisy contaminated the crime scene." He sucked in a deep breath. "No matter what went on between us before, I'm in charge here."

I pulled the little mouse out of my pocket and held it out to him.

"What's this?"

"It might be a clue. I think it belongs to Edith Scroggins. I found it on Natasha's crafting island."

Wolf was not amused. He didn't take it. "Now you're jerking me around. Don't change the subject. Look, I'm sorry about the way things worked out between us. It wasn't fair to you." He mashed his lips together and stared at the ground for a moment. "I don't think I ever thanked you personally for what you did for me."

"Yes, you did. The flowers you sent were beautiful. I think we should just try to move past that part of our lives."

Wolf smiled at me and snorted. "Same old Sophie. Tell me how you found Gwen."

"Sophie!" In the eerie lights of the gingerbread decorations, a man ran toward us.

CHAPTER SEVENTEEN

Dear Natasha,
I am one of your biggest fans. Your robin's-egg blue signature color has inspired me to decorate my house in blue this holiday. Any advice?
Having a Happy Blue Christmas in
Bluefield, West Virginia

Dear Having a Happy Blue Christmas,
Silver and white go beautifully with blue for decorating. Make a blue skirt for your tree, use a blue tablecloth, wrap all your gifts in blue, white, and silver, and go nuts with blue ribbon everywhere!
Natasha

"Stop, Sophie!" Alex jogged up to me and placed his hand on my arm. He had left the military years ago, but the ramrod-straight back and authoritative bearing was part of him.

I couldn't help grinning just a bit. After all, it's not a bad thing when your ex-boyfriend happens to see your new and extremely good-looking boyfriend being protective. His brow furrowed, creasing in between his dark eyebrows. Square jaw, great chin, kind eyes — I still couldn't believe he was interested in *me.* "You should have legal counsel before you talk to the police."

Wolf's head snapped toward me. "That's why you left? You called a lawyer? Whoa." He held up his hand and regarded me while shaking his head in disbelief.

"It's not like that, Wolf." I introduced them. "Alex was supposed to be my date tonight." He must have planned to pick me up. Dressed in an elegant suit with a burgundy tie, he held his chin high.

Wolf stared at Alex. "And now you're representing her?"

"Could I have a word with Sophie?"

Alex drew me away. "Hire me as your lawyer?"

"You don't understand. I didn't kill Gwen. I found the body. I have nothing to hide."

"You're sure?"

"Oh, please! I think I would know if I had killed someone and wrapped her in Christmas paper!"

"Eww. Okay, if you insist, you can tell him what happened, but if I think you're incriminating yourself, I'm going to stop you."

Alex was adorable. He would probably hate knowing how cute I thought he was to try to come to my rescue. A wrinkle had formed between his eyebrows, and his eyes were so earnest and sweet that I wanted to kiss him. Instead, I walked back to Wolf and told him exactly how it was that I had found Gwen.

He nodded. "That accounts for the staples we found on the floor. That's the cleanest garage I've ever seen. How well did you know Gwen Babineaux? Anybody have a beef with her?"

"I barely knew her at all. I didn't even know Sugar was her daughter."

Wolf's eyebrows raised. Someone called his name. Wolf paused for a second more. "Now could I have a minute with Sophie, Counselor?"

Alex turned to me with concern. "That's up to you. Remember, you don't have to say anything."

"Go on. I'll be all right."

Alex backed away, keeping us in his line of sight.

Wolf scratched his neck. "Your date, huh? Seems very protective. Should I be worried that you're more involved in this case than I think?"

"No. I've told you everything. I even offered you the mouse."

"Are we going to be okay, then?" he asked.

Aha. He meant us, as in Wolf and Sophie, who used to date. "We are." We would be okay. I had made my peace with the end of our relationship.

"You look great. Stick around awhile in case anything comes up. Okay?" He ambled away, a figure of calm authority in a sea of bright lights and hysteria.

Maybe it was lucky that I had been wearing a beautiful dress tonight, even if I wasn't going to the ball.

Alex stood at my elbow in a second. "What did he want?"

"Uh, this is a little awkward. We used to date."

His mouth twitched to the side. "Good to know. Might complicate things for me."

"It's over. Has been for quite a while."

"That wasn't what I meant. He might try to make things difficult for me as an attorney. Don't be so sure he's over you, either. He's still looking at you."

Wolf was speaking with a police officer, but Alex was right — Wolf was watching us.

"What are you doing here, anyway?" I asked.

"I came to see a client."

"Me?" That didn't make sense. How could he have known?

"Someone else. That was why I canceled our date. I hope you understand."

"Who?" I squinted at Alex. Who would have been so panicked that they called a lawyer within an hour of the discovery of the corpse? "Natasha?"

"I can't divulge that." He wrapped an arm around my shoulders.

For my benefit or for Wolf's? Either way, I didn't mind. I snuggled a little closer to him.

"It's actually a relief that you don't need a lawyer. I wouldn't have been able to represent both of you."

Wolf had moved on to Natasha, yet Alex didn't race to her side. She wasn't the client.

"I'm sorry about tonight." Alex's fingers closed over mine. "I promise I'll make it up to you."

"I told Wolf I would come right back to tell him what I knew. At best, we would have been embarrassingly late."

"Are you all right? I know you've found some bodies before, but this one sounds particularly disturbing, wrapped up and all."

"I'm just devastated for the Babineauxs. They had plans for a very special holiday and, well, it doesn't get any worse than this. I can't imagine what they're going through. They have a sweet little girl who is only six. This will shatter her world."

"I need to get back to my client. Is there someone who can walk you home?"

I tried not to laugh. He was too sweet! "I live on the other side of these houses. I think I can get there on my own."

He kissed me lightly on the lips and strolled away. I was dying to know who had called him. I strayed toward Bernie, Nina, and Mars, but kept my eyes on Alex. He walked straight through the Babineauxs' gate.

"So what's the scoop?" asked Nina.

"I've got nothing." I jammed my hands into my pockets and felt the mouse. I turned to gaze at Edith's house. From the alley, I could see only the second and third floors. The windows were black as pitch, as though no one was home. Suddenly, the little mouse scared me. What if Gwen's killer had knocked off Edith, too?

"Anybody want to come with me to check on Edith Scroggins?"

Mars and Bernie snickered like I was joking, but Nina said, "Sure, I'm game."

We left the busy alley and walked around to the front of Edith's house on the next street over.

Christmas lights sparkled around the door imparting a charming glow. I banged the knocker on the front door. No one answered.

"I'm getting worried about her. She was afraid, and she hasn't answered her phone or her door for two days now."

Nina reached over and tried the door handle. "Locked."

"Let's look around back. The housekeeper said there's a key over the ledge."

Nina followed me in the dark. "They really ought to have spotlights or something along here."

I knocked on the back door. "Mrs. Scroggins? Mrs. Scroggins?"

I tried the door handle. It turned, and I opened the door but remained outside. "Mrs. Scroggins? It's Sophie Winston! Hello?"

My heart sank. "Maybe she's not home." *Or maybe she's dead.*

"She could have taken your advice and moved to a hotel."

"Then why was her mouse in Natasha and Mars's garage?"

"I'll take the second floor," said Nina.

226

"Hello? Mrs. Scroggins?" I flicked on light switches as I went.

I was in the living room when I heard screams.

"Nina?" I dashed up the stairs.

More screams. I ran into the bedroom in time to see Edith and Nina screaming, aghast at the sight of each other.

"Why are *you* screaming?" I asked Nina.

"She scared me. She was in here with the lights off."

"La Traviata" played softly in the background. "Out! Out of my home!"

"You're alive!" I said.

"Of course I'm alive," snarled Edith. "When did it become socially acceptable to barge into a person's home?"

"You haven't been answering your phone or your door." I spoke calmly, hoping she would understand.

Edith stood amazingly erect, her head held high. "That is my option. One isn't always receiving. One has special times and days of the week when one receives."

"This is a beautiful bedroom," said Nina.

Edith became momentarily gracious. "Thank you."

Soft blue walls offered a calm backdrop to a bed with a bold blue canopy built into the ceiling. A cream fabric ran in folds behind the headboard up along the wall and over top of the bed. Swags of cream fabric printed with a colonial pattern in the bold blue and edged with blue pom-poms draped from the canopy. The same material covered a curved headboard with a border of blue fabric accenting the curves. Cream throw rugs and chairs upholstered in blue continued the stunning theme.

Edith's scowl returned quickly. "You needn't bother trying to flatter me. Leave my home this instant."

Nina tilted her head suspiciously. "What were you doing with the lights off?"

"How dare you? It's none of your business what I was doing in my own bedroom. Get out, you impertinent imbecile!"

Binoculars lay on one of the blue chairs near the window. "Spying?" I asked.

"There's nothing wrong with looking out the window when the police are practically in one's own backyard."

"Gwen Babineaux is dead." I watched her reaction. I thought I saw a momentary flicker of discomfort.

"That's too bad. It's of no consequence to me, I'm sure."

How could anyone be so cold?

"Have any other odd things happened in this house since we last spoke?" I asked.

228

She assessed me. "If I tell you, will you leave?"

"Yes. We will."

"Very well. I shall hold you to your promise. Nothing has happened. Now kindly see yourselves to the door and don't pinch any of the silver on your way out."

I pulled the mouse out of my pocket and held it in my open hand without saying a word.

Horror crept over her face. "Where did you get that?" she whispered.

Chapter Eighteen

Dear Sophie,
We have a breakfast nook with built-in shelving that screams for Christmas decorations. I've tried adding cards and candles, but nothing seems to do the trick.

Clueless in Shepherd, Texas

Dear Clueless,
Start by placing pine branches on the shelves. Add red candles, jars, plates, mugs, and ribbon, then add a few Christmas items that your family loves, like a toy, a Santa, angels, or a nutcracker.

Sophie

"Suppose you tell me what happened?" I suggested. I wasn't going to give her a chance to create a story by telling her where I'd found the mouse.

The corners of her mouth still turned down, but I sensed a change in her attitude. She had lost her angry edge.

"Very well. Perhaps we should speak in the library."

She sailed past us and led the way down the stairs. I flicked off the bedroom light on my way out.

The library featured a white marble fireplace against paneled walls of bookshelves. A painting of an attractive young woman hung over the fireplace, flanked by sconces. It took a moment for me to realize that it captured Edith in her youth. The young woman beamed. Hair the color of pecans cascaded around her shoulders. She sat with one shoulder forward, in a form-fitting pale green gown that showed off a tiny waist. From the shimmer, I guessed it might have been silk or satin. Most amazing, her face didn't harbor any bitterness. No hostility. I couldn't imagine that happy young woman screaming at anyone.

"May I offer you cognac or sherry?" she asked, her hand resting on a crystal decanter.

She poured three glasses. I noticed that she wasn't afraid of the sherry, even though she'd told me she was afraid to eat anything in the house.

She handed each of us a small crystal glass in the shape of a thistle. The stems supported small rounded cut-crystal bowls with tops that flared out. "Scottish?" I asked.

"Yes. Horace is particularly fond of them."

She took a seat in a burgundy wingback chair, arranging her long legs side by side. "Where did you find the mouse?"

"Where did you lose it?"

Edith took the mouse into her hands. "Didn't it have glasses?"

I thought it had.

"I did not *lose* it. I placed it on a shelf in a built-in cabinet in my breakfast room. Yesterday evening it was gone." Her nostrils flared, and she closed her eyes briefly. "I had hoped that the torment had ended. That with Horace in the hospital and incapacitated, there would be no other strange occurrences."

"So now you know conclusively that it's not Horace who is playing tricks on you." I sipped the sweet, rich sherry.

"Unless he has an accomplice."

Nina flashed a look at me. I knew she was thinking about Brown-Eyed Girl. I hoped she wouldn't spill the beans.

"Do you have any reason to think Horace is having an affair?" I asked.

"I shouldn't be surprised if he had. He

stays with me out of guilt and promises he made to my father. But, no, I am not aware of any philandering on his part."

"Then why haven't you been to the hospital to see him?" blurted Nina.

I expected to be summarily tossed out on our keisters.

Edith said simply, "I don't do hospitals."

"You don't *do* hospitals?" Nina repeated incredulously.

"Pardon me, I'll try to speak up so you can hear. That's right. I do not visit hospitals."

Nina shook her head in disbelief and held out her hands as if she were pleading. "But . . . but he's your husband. Don't you think he needs you?"

"He knows why I'm not there. And I know there's nothing I can do for him. I don't relish the thought of watching him die. He is aware of my reasons."

Horace might understand, but we were at a loss. I sipped the sherry wondering what I could say to get Edith to tell us more. "How did you meet Horace? I bet it's a lovely story."

"He worked for my father. There was nothing lovely about it. I married Horace under pressure from my parents."

Ouch! So much for the theory that everyone likes to tell the story about how they met.

While I was wondering how to get her to talk and Nina was sending me messages with her eyes, Edith surprised us both by opening up.

"I was planning a wedding." She paused, swallowed hard, and studied the floor. "My parents took me to New York to shop for my trousseau. A whole new wardrobe. Ohhhh, the dress was beautiful. Sleeveless with a scooped-out back and an empire waist. The top was hand-beaded with pearls and the floor-length skirt was tailored satin. It even had a matching coat. We were going to be married here in Old Town." She stroked her eyebrow gently. "But exactly two weeks before the wedding, my fiancé was killed in Vietnam."

I hadn't expected that. Poor Edith! "I'm so sorry. What a tragedy."

"That must have been very hard on you," said Nina. "Is that why you won't go to hospitals? Because of your fiancé?"

Edith glared at her. "Why do you persist in questioning me about my personal history? It's none of your business."

I didn't know what to do. She had never recovered from losing her fiancé. I sought something positive to say. "You were lucky to find Horace."

She stared at me like I was daft and shook her head, snorting his name. "Horace. When I made no effort to procure a suitable husband, my parents chose one for me. Horace had come to work for my father's real estate company. He was from the wrong side of the tracks, eager to please my father and claw his way up in the world. I didn't love him, but Horace understood the deal as well as I did. Marry the boss's daughter and inherit the business."

I had always liked Horace so much. This was a side of him I didn't know.

"Oh, don't be so appalled, Sophie," said Edith. "It's not the first time a dowry has been offered. Horace and my parents got what they wanted. Almost." She rubbed her hands together in her lap as though she were washing them. "Horace and I had a son, Samuel, after my father." She stopped talking and gazed at the fireplace, her lips drawn tight.

Nina looked over at me. I moved my hand ever so slightly in a signal to wait.

"When Sammy was five, Horace took him along to look at a house in Old Town. Sammy was so excited." She smiled at the memory. "He loved going to work with Horace and running around empty houses. I remember thinking he would surely be an architect. That particular day, they visited an exceptionally old building. Sammy raced ahead of Horace and climbed the stairs to the attic." She paused and seemed to be gathering strength. "A beam collapsed on him. For thirty-eight days and nights, I never left his side. But my poor, sweet Sammy died."

The only sound in the room was a ticking clock.

My heart broke for Edith.

"I had everything anyone could want. More money than I needed. A lovely home. Beautiful clothes. Good health. But the one thing that mattered to me was gone forever."

I choked out, "I'm so sorry, Edith. I had no idea."

"Why should you? It happened a long time ago. Horace says I have allowed it to ruin my life. Don't dislike Horace. He's basically a decent sort. He stepped up and married me at my parents' request. And he put up with me after Sammy was gone."

"But you blame him for Sammy's death, don't you?" asked Nina.

"It was Horace's fault." She stated it as fact.

"Now you think Horace is trying to gaslight you," I reminded her.

"That's the only way he can have the entire business for himself, isn't it? Who else would want to be rid of me? Only Horace, or, perhaps, his paramour."

Nina tilted her head. "If you're afraid, why aren't you locking your back door?"

"Are you criticizing me?" Edith folded her arms across her chest and gripped her upper arms. "I have lived in this house since the day after I was born." She bowed her head slightly. "But this is the first time I have lived here alone. Horace took care of locking the doors at night. I will be more vigilant from now on."

For the first time, I thought I saw a softer side in Edith's expression. A gentleness that the young woman in the portrait had lost through tragedy.

"Will you answer the phone when I call?" I asked.

"Yes. It was kind of you to be concerned. Though I shan't forgive you for bursting into my house uninvited. The only other person who checked on my welfare was Horace's secretary, Phyllis . . ."

I could feel Nina sending me vibes.

". . . but I suspect her visit had more to do with the paycheck she inquired about."

We said good-night, and she acted very much the hostess when she saw us to the front door.

When we turned the corner to head back to the alley, I asked, "Think Brown-Eyed Girl is the one tormenting Edith?"

"No. But I want to find her more than ever. Horace lost a child, too, but he didn't turn into a sour recluse. He's spent most of his life with a woman who still thinks of him as less than her, as being from the wrong side of the tracks."

"He married her so he would get the business."

"The truth is that he made something of himself. He worked hard or Scroggins Realty wouldn't be what it is today. I think Horace deserves a shot at happiness with Brown-Eyed Girl."

My thoughts had turned back to the mouse. Either Natasha had bought one or the person gaslighting Edith had deposited it in Natasha's workroom.

The alley still teemed with police and neighbors.

Patty ran up to us, her skin oddly pale in the strange combination of Christmas lights and car lights. "There you are! Alex told me you were out here." She wiggled her eyebrows. "And let me just say that you have got one adorable guy on the hook, Sophie. Good looking and smart, too!"

My breath caught in my throat. Patty? Could she be his client? "He's very nice."

"But watch Sugar around him." She *tsk*ed. "I just wanted to let you know that I'll be sleeping over with the kids tonight. They're taking Gwen's death pretty well, but you know how teenagers are. They try to act cool and then they fall apart because they're not equipped to handle the situation. Your neighbor Luis has been wonderful with the kids. Really amazing. He suggested I pick up some sleeping pills for Baxter and told me what to get."

"Baxter must be inconsolable," said Nina.

"Hmm." Patty closed her eyes briefly as if gathering herself. "They all are. I may not have liked Gwen, but even I'm horrified. I never saw this coming. That's why I think I should stay over. Sugar is a blubbering mess. Elvin doesn't know what to do, and Baxter is a basket case. I've been trying to get the kids to help me cook dinner just to distract them and create a sense of normalcy, but that's really impossible with the police questioning everyone."

"How's little Katrina?" I asked.

"I don't think she understands yet. Twiggy's packing her up right now. She and Jonah are taking her for the night just to get her out of the house. Heaven knows where

239

they're going, because the cops won't let them into their apartment. I don't think they've —" Patty's head turned fast. "Oh no, you don't! There goes Bradley. Excuse me." Patty ran toward her son, turned him around, and steered him past Twiggy and Kat, back through the gate that led to the Babineaux home.

Twiggy gazed around somewhat hopelessly. Where would I go if I couldn't stay in my own home? They would have to check into a hotel. That would cost them!

"C'mon," I said to Nina.

We approached Twiggy and Kat. In as happy a voice as I could muster, I asked, "How would you like to stay with me tonight? I have a kitty cat who would love to play with you."

Kat nodded eagerly, but never let go of Twiggy's hand.

I smiled at Twiggy. "You and Jonah, too, of course. And his mom. She's living with you?"

"I can't let you do that. It's too much of an imposition."

"Nonsense. Come on." I steered them down the alley away from the commotion. "We can cut through Nina's yard. And I have a fun bedroom upstairs where my niece likes to stay. Maybe Kat would like that room."

Nina accompanied us across the street to my house and within ten seconds of unlocking the door, Kat carried Mochie in her arms.

"Are you sure about this?" asked Twiggy.

"Absolutely." I led the way up to the third floor. Making a big deal out of it, I swung my arms and sang, "Ta da!"

Kat entered timidly. "The cover on the bed is purple!" She climbed onto it, still clutching Mochie. As though Mochie knew she needed extra love, he purred so loud that I could hear him.

I showed Twiggy to the room next door. "Sorry, the bathroom is down a flight."

"Are you kidding? Don't you dare apologize! I don't know how we'll ever repay you for this."

"No need. It's what neighbors do. I'm going to change clothes, then I'll start dinner. Are you sure Kat won't have an allergic reaction to Mochie?"

"I can't guarantee it, but she hasn't appeared to be allergic to cats yet. Frankly, I suspect it's a lie. Gwen concocted that story so she wouldn't have to take care of pets. We'll watch Kat for sniffling or congestion."

I trotted down the stairs to my bedroom on the second floor. In a way, I hated to take off the beautiful dress and turn back into a pumpkin again. But hopefully there would be loads of other occasions to wear it. I pulled on a lightweight pink V-neck sweater and comfortable elastic-waisted navy blue pants, but kept the rhinestone bracelet on for fun.

I hurried down the stairs to see what I could whip up for dinner. To my surprise, Liza sat at my kitchen table holding her Yorkshire terrier. She clutched him to her like a child would hold a stuffed animal for comfort. Her strawberry blond hair jutted in wild directions. Her usual grin had vanished, replaced by the tense mouth of a frightened woman.

"You can set your dog down, Liza. How does he feel about cats?"

Nina had poured four glasses of wine and handed me one. By my calculations, we would be seven for dinner.

"He was always fine with my mom's cat." She set him on the floor and removed the green Christmas sweater he wore. "There you go, Oscar."

He shook rapidly from nose to tail as if glad to be rid of the sweater, then nose to floor, he explored every corner.

I tossed kindling into the fireplace and strategically placed a couple of nice-sized logs over it.

"I hope you don't mind that I brought him over here," said Liza. "Luis is at the Babineauxs', and I'm a little rattled. I've never known anyone who was murdered."

CHAPTER NINETEEN

Dear Natasha,
I have elegant china for our formal Christmas dinner. But breakfast always looks too much like it does every other day. How can I spark up my white plates to make it feel like Christmas?
Plain Jane in Spruce, Michigan

Dear Plain Jane,
Sew chair wraps with each person's name machine-embroidered on the back. Add matching napkins, and tie ribbons of a coordinating color on the handles of all the breakfast mugs.
Natasha

I located three pork tenderloins in the fridge. They didn't take long to cook and were always soft and juicy. I had bought cranberries on a whim, but they would make a great sauce. In minutes, I had potatoes boiling in a pot, and the pork tenderloins browning in a pan.

I had baked three Linzer tortes in anticipation of my family visiting for Christmas. I pulled one out of the freezer to let it thaw for dessert.

When Twiggy came downstairs, I asked, "What veggies will Kat eat? Peas? Carrots?"

"She loves peas." Twiggy bit the corner of her lip. "I don't mean to offend you, but plain. No seasonings."

"Not a problem. How's she doing?"

"I've told her that her mom went to sing with the angels. That might not have been the best thing to say. She seems to think her mom is going to be in a Christmas choir. I think Baxter is the one who should explain it to her, but he's in no shape to do it now. Maybe in a day or two."

"That poor little girl. My heart just bleeds for her." Liza sniffled. "Imagine losing your mother so young. It's lucky you're close to her and can comfort her."

Twiggy glanced at the stairs, her forehead furrowed. She whispered, "Gwen wasn't a very attentive mother. Half the time she didn't even brush Kat's hair. Jonah and I love Kat, but honestly, Gwen used us as free babysitters. We said we'd watch her one day, and then she brought her by another day,

245

and before we knew it, Kat was with us every afternoon."

"Free day care. That sounds like Gwen," Liza sighed. "Everything was all about her. Wonder what she was doing while you were taking care of Kat."

The kitchen door opened. Patty gazed at us in surprise. "Oh! I hope I'm not interrupting anything. Gosh, it smells good in here. And the blazing fire and Christmas lights. Aww, I wish I could be over here with you guys. I came to get my glasses so I can see when I take out my contact lenses."

"We were just talking about Gwen," said Twiggy. "How are your children coping?"

"It's so hard to tell with teens. Bradley wanted to go out with friends. This is the first time someone close to them has died, you know? Sooner or later, it's going to hit them that she's not coming back. They know it, but I don't think it has sunk in completely with Bradley yet."

Nina handed her a glass of wine.

"Thanks! I'm furious with Gwen." Patty gasped and clapped her hand over her mouth. "What a terrible thing to say when she's gone!"

I placed the tenderloins in a fresh pan and slid them into the oven to roast. With a splash of water, I deglazed the pan in which

I had browned them, then added creamy butter, shallots, and robust sage. The scent of the sage sizzled up to me.

"Don't feel guilty," said Nina. "We were just talking about the fact that she was something of an absentee mom for little Kat. How was she with your kids?"

Patty sat down. "You know that Christmas letter she sent out? As soon as I read it, I knew something was wrong. I love my kids. There is nothing in this world that I love more. But I'm not stupid. My Bethany is smart. She's always been a straight-B student because she doesn't apply herself. I knew there was no way she was so advanced that she needed homeschooling. And Bradley! He's out of control." She buried her head in her hands for a moment. "Yesterday I went to pick up Bethany at school. Hah! Imagine my embarrassment when I found out that she's been kicked out. That's why they have to homeschool her."

"What did she do?" I asked.

"She used extremely foul language with a teacher. I'd like to blame that on Gwen because she sure didn't learn those words from me, but Bethany probably picked them up from friends or movies. But then she was stupid enough to tweet them, and the school booted her out."

"Wow." Liza blinked at her. "They're tough today. I would have been kicked out of school for sure!"

"It gets worse. All those lovely civic improvement projects Bradley 'spearheaded'?" She nodded her head, her lips in a smirk. "Community service for smashing pumpkins on people's doorsteps at Halloween. And I knew nothing about this. Not a thing! That idiot lawyer they hired convinced the judge that *I* was a raving lunatic and that Baxter and Gwen would give the kids a secure family unit. Baloney! I guess they've proven him wrong. And at whose expense? The kids', that's who." Patty banged her fist on the table, frightening Oscar.

She frightened me a little bit, too. Gwen's death might have beneficial consequences for Patty if Baxter relinquished custody of the children.

Patty stood up. "There are going to be big changes. Things will be different now that Gwen is gone. Patty is back in charge." She walked through the kitchen and up the stairs.

Twiggy bit her upper lip and gazed at the fireplace with frightened eyes. She didn't have to tell me what she was thinking. Exactly the same thing weighed on my mind. Gwen's death was a windfall to Patty. She probably had more motive to do Gwen in than anyone else did.

I tossed the cranberries into the sage mixture, along with a cup of orange juice and a little sugar, and placed a glass top on the pot to speed it along to a simmer.

Claudine, Twiggy's mother-in-law, arrived toting an overnight bag. The first words out of her mouth were, "I feel just awful imposing on you like this."

"It's my pleasure, really." I poured the water off the potatoes and popped them into my KitchenAid mixer to mash them.

Nina carried Claudine's bag upstairs for her while Liza poured Claudine a glass of wine.

"I love the fireplace in your kitchen, Sophie," she said. "I think I'd bake and cook a lot, too, if I had a kitchen like this." Claudine pushed a lock of silver hair behind her ear. "I didn't really know Gwen, but the rest of you must be shaken to have such a horrible thing happen to your friend."

Liza's eyes nearly bugged out. "There's a killer loose in our neighborhood! I hadn't thought about it that way before." She gazed toward the foyer and whispered. "It could be Patty!"

I plopped softened butter and cream

cheese into the mixer and let it whirl.

"Or Baxter," said Nina. "They always suspect the husband first."

Patty came through again at that moment. I took a stab at finding out who might be Alex's client. "Give my best to Alex, Patty."

"Oh, be still my heart. He's a keeper, Sophie."

"You know, he broke off his date with me for a *client* tonight."

"What rotten luck. Not many men would choose Baxter over you!"

So it was Baxter who called a lawyer within an hour of the discovery of Gwen's body. That was telling. Did he expect them to blame him or was he protecting someone else in the family?

Patty left and little Kat finally joined us.

Oscar barked madly at the sight of Mochie in her arms, but Mochie kept his cool in spite of the red velvet Christmas cape Kat had tied on him.

"That's quite an outfit, Kat. Does Mochie like wearing it?" I asked.

"I think so. It belongs to my doll, but she doesn't mind sharing." She pulled a pair of doll-sized glasses from her pocket and plopped them on Mochie's face. "The glasses won't stay on, though. His ears aren't in the right place."

I squatted next to Kat. "Could I see the glasses?"

She readily handed them to me. I swallowed hard. They were the right size for Edith's mouse. Hoping she would tell me they belonged to one of her dolls, I asked, "Where did you get these?"

"In the living room. Uncle Elvin said I could have them."

Oscar grabbed the cape in his mouth and pulled, which prompted Mochie to hiss and smack him.

I rescued Mochie and placed him on a chair by the fireplace so he would be higher than Oscar. Kat immediately scolded and hugged Oscar. He focused on Kat, who engaged him in a dog game while Mochie took a much deserved break, without glasses. But they weighed heavily on me.

"Could I keep these for a day or two?" I asked.

"Sure." Kat giggled at Oscar, who barked at the door.

We heard a tap on the door. Twiggy opened it.

"Can we come in?" asked Jonah. "Look who I brought with me."

Alex stepped inside. "I'm not in the habit of inviting myself to dinner."

"We have plenty. The more the merrier."

Oddly enough, the presence of Kat, Jonah, and Alex changed the climate in the room. No one mentioned murder, Gwen, or Christmas wrapping paper. It felt like old friends had gathered together.

They protested when I tried to move everyone to the larger dining room table. The guys brought some extra chairs into the kitchen, I popped Christmas CDs on at a volume that allowed for easy conversing, and we sat down to savory pork tenderloin with sweet shallot cranberry sauce, peas, and as Kat called them, *smashed potatoes* with butter.

Jonah was every bit as charming as he was at Rocking Horse Toys. Apparently, he didn't put on an act just for his customers. I envied the way he looked at Twiggy, as though the two of them could communicate without words. He had his mother's wavy hair. I could imagine it turning the same beautiful silver one day.

"Mom used to live in Old Town a long time ago," said Jonah.

Nina's fork skidded across her plate. She leaned forward. Turning to me, she mouthed *brown eyes.*

CHAPTER TWENTY

Dear Sophie,
I like a more natural Christmas look for my cottage — not so much glitter. Plus, I'm trying to teach my children that things don't have to be shiny and from a store to be pretty. Where do I start?

> Emma and Bella's Mom in
> Tannenbaum, Arkansas

Dear Emma and Bella's Mom,
Look outside. Collect pine, holly, nuts, and berries for decorating. Teach Emma and Bella how to string popcorn and cranberries, and make a paper-ring garland for the tree. Buy four or five colors of felt, and get out the button box. Help them sew hearts, stars, cottages, and angels for the tree.

> Sophie

"Everything has changed so much," said

Claudine. "Not in the center of town, of course. I mean all the condos on the outskirts. Back then, I think there was only one stoplight between King Street and Tyson's Corner! The house I lived in is still there. I've walked by a few times, but I haven't gotten up the nerve to knock on the door yet."

Nina cleared her throat. "Did you know anyone by the name of Horace?"

That got Claudine's attention. Twiggy's and Jonah's, too.

"I did! Why do you ask?"

Nina turned the color of the cranberries. Clearly she hadn't thought past asking the question.

I jumped in. "We have a friend, Horace Scroggins, who is in the hospital."

"I heard about that. What a terrible accident." Claudine dabbed a napkin on the corner of her mouth. "I was very excited when I heard his first name. There aren't that many Horaces around. The name isn't very popular anymore. But my Horace's last name was Maccrindle. I'm sure he moved away long ago."

"Has anyone heard how Scroggins is doing?" Jonah accepted a second helping of the pork.

A tuckered-out Kat leaned against his

shoulder half-asleep. Oscar sat happily beside her with bright eyes, waiting for a morsel of food to come his way.

"Luis went to see him this morning," said Liza. "They're worried about his lack of progress."

"Horace helped me find the location for Rocking Horse Toys. Such a nice guy. I'm hoping we can afford to buy the building one day."

"Were you at his party?" asked Nina. "I don't remember seeing you there."

"This is the busy season for us. I don't get much time off. We begged mom to move here to help us out. I don't know what we would have done without her."

"My husband died two years ago," Claudine confided. "I knew it was time to sell that big old house. One day at work, I thought, *Why am I still doing this? Going to work every day at a job I don't even like. Meanwhile, my only child is halfway across the country!*" Claudine's shoulders lifted in a happy little movement. "I sold the house, quit my job, and moved here to be closer to Jonah and Twiggy. I need to find another place to live, though. That tiny apartment might be a little bit too close sometimes."

Twiggy and Jonah protested, but Claudine smiled knowingly.

Alex hadn't said much during dinner. He helped me clear the table while Jonah carried Kat up to bed. Twiggy went along to tuck her in, though I suspected Kat wouldn't wake up. She'd had a long and horrific day.

"Coffee or tea with dessert? I have decaf."

"Does Irish coffee go with an Austrian dessert?" asked Nina.

"I don't see why not."

Alex helped Nina take tall glass Irish coffee mugs off a high shelf. Meanwhile, I sprinkled powdered sugar over the Linzer torte, sliced it, and placed a piece for each of us on Spode Christmas tree dessert plates.

Jonah and Twiggy returned, laughing about Kat. For a few minutes, we were busy handing around Irish coffees and dessert plates.

"Have Yourself a Merry Little Christmas" played in the background. A lot of people in my neighborhood would be having the worst Christmas ever.

Now that Kat slept on the third floor, safely out of earshot, the conversation turned to Gwen again.

"Is it true that she was wrapped in Christmas paper?" Nina asked Alex.

"Far as I know. Sophie, Baxter, and Sugar

are the only ones outside of the police who saw her." Alex ate a piece of the torte. "Umm, this is good!"

I dredged up the horrid memory. "Pink wrapping paper with stars on it." I tried a bite of the torte. The rich, nutty pastry melted in my mouth, punched up by the contrast of the sweet raspberry filling.

"Pink!" Nina set her coffee down with a clunk. "Natasha. It had to be Natasha. I can't believe it. She finally flipped her lid!"

"I'm not following. Does Natasha have a thing for pink?" asked Alex.

"Natasha always has to do things differently. Never mind that red and green are traditional Christmas colors, she always has to use other colors. This year she and Gwen both decorated with orange and pink."

"Pardon me," said Liza, "but that's tangerine and magenta."

Everyone grinned.

Jonah sighed. "I saw that wrapping paper in her workroom. But anyone could have gotten in there. It's not connected to Natasha and Mars's house, so they don't lock up. I usually go downstairs before we head to bed to make sure it's locked."

Alex didn't say a word but he listened to Jonah, and I suspected that Jonah had just landed on Alex's list of suspects.

We hadn't finished our desserts when someone hammered on my front door. I rushed to answer it, lest the sound of the door knocker wake Kat.

Sugar burst into my house. "Where is Kat?"

CHAPTER TWENTY-ONE

Dear Natasha,
I'm hosting my first cookie swap this year and can use all the advice I can get!
Love Cookies in Christmas Cove,
Maine

Dear Love Cookies,
The most important thing is to assign a specific type of cookie to each participant. That way you won't end up with half a dozen of the same type of cookie, and it will be harder for cheaters to buy them at the store.
Natasha

Twiggy and Jonah ran into my foyer. Alex watched from the kitchen doorway.

A red dress clung to Sugar's ample curves, barely covering her bottom. She breathed heavily, her bosom heaving. Her eyes met Jonah's and lingered a beat too long.

"Shh, Kat's asleep," said Twiggy. "Has something else happened?"

Sugar squeezed her forehead with both hands. "In all the commotion, I thought she'd been lost. Patty said she was with you, but the police wouldn't let me into your place, and I didn't know where she was."

Jonah rested his hand on her back. "Kat is fine." He spoke soothingly in a low voice, almost as if the two of them were in private. "We thought it would be better if she wasn't in the middle of the sadness at Baxter's house tonight. Come on upstairs with me and have a peek at her."

"She really ought to be home in her own bed," said Sugar. "I know *I* would sleep better."

"This way." Jonah took Sugar's hand into his, gave it a squeeze, and led her up the stairs.

Twiggy's face blazed. Instead of being her usual kind self, she clenched her fists, hunched over, and tiptoed up the creaky stairs behind them. If she meant to surprise them, she wouldn't. They would hear her coming.

Alex's eyes met mine. "Trouble brewing there?" he whispered.

I wrinkled my nose. "I'm afraid so."

The three of them returned shortly, without Kat. Sugar decided not to wake her, apologized for bursting in on us, and went home.

Twiggy relaxed, but she didn't take her eyes off Jonah.

Alex lingered after Jonah, Twiggy, and Claudine went up to bed, and Liza and Nina headed home.

"You were awfully quiet tonight." I tucked the last plate into the dishwater.

"Just trying to figure this thing out." He wrapped his arms around me from behind and spoke softly into my ear. "Sophie, was Gwen wrapped sloppy, like I would have done it? Or neatly? Ends nicely folded and taped?"

"You're thinking of Natasha?"

"So it *was* a tidy job. That doesn't mean it was Natasha. You could have wrapped Gwen neatly, I'm sure."

I recognized teasing in his tone of voice.

"Or Jonah," Alex mused. "He must wrap packages at the store all the time."

"Jonah?" I whispered. "But he didn't have a motive."

"We don't know that. Anyone who lived upstairs in the apartment over the garage had super-easy access to Natasha's wrapping stuff."

261

"So you don't think it was Natasha."

"I didn't say that. How did you get into the garage?"

I shrugged. "Easy. The door to Natasha's workshop was unlocked, and I just walked in."

"That doesn't exactly limit the possibilities."

I turned to face him. "So you think you have to pin it on someone else to get your client off the hook?"

He chuckled. "I don't plan to *pin* it on anyone. Are you afraid?"

"Of what?"

"Maybe you haven't heard. There's a killer loose in your neighborhood."

My thoughts flew to Patty. *If* she had murdered Gwen, and that was a very big *if* in my mind, then the rest of us, with the possible exception of Baxter, were safe. She just wanted her children.

"No, this was a targeted killing. Gwen appears to have aggravated a good number of people. Someone planned it, don't you think? The killer knew he had time to wrap her without being interrupted."

"It always comes back to Natasha. How's Mars at wrapping?"

"He avoids it at all costs. He's very big on asking stores to gift wrap."

Alex took a deep breath. "Mmm, you smell nice."

"I had a big date tonight."

"Anyone I know?"

"Nope. Some guy I met last summer. He's out of town a lot. Probably a drug dealer."

"You sure know how to pick losers." He leaned in to kiss me. "See you tomorrow?"

"I'll probably be serving breakfast here at the boardinghouse in the morning if you want to stop by."

"Maybe. If I get my drug shipment tonight."

I locked the door behind him when he left. He had a good point about the wrapping paper being neat. Neither Nina nor Mars could have wrapped Gwen so perfectly. Not that they were suspects. How well could Baxter or Patty wrap? Patty hadn't been here for very long. Would she know about Natasha's craft room? Maybe her daughter, Bethany, had told her about it. After tamping out the fire, Mochie and I went up to bed.

Mochie pawed at my head, waking me out of a deep sleep. I groaned and rolled over, ignoring him. He crept around to the top of my head and tried again, batting a soft paw on my forehead. I opened one eye. Three in the morning. I pulled the covers over my head.

Mochie squirmed underneath the feather comforter and bumped his head against my chin.

I sat up. "You're not going to let me sleep unless I feed you, are you?"

He scampered to the bedroom door, his tail twitching impatiently while I pulled on a fuzzy green bathrobe. Bleary-eyed, I followed him down the stairs and staggered into the kitchen.

I was reaching into a cabinet for a can of cat food when someone spoke. I shrieked, suddenly wide awake, and hit the light switch.

Twiggy said, "I'm so sorry! I didn't mean to scare you. I hope I didn't wake you."

"No problem. Mochie was hungry." Though from the way he circled Twiggy's ankles, I had a feeling he'd woken me because he heard her go downstairs. The sound of the can being opened didn't get his attention, confirming my suspicions.

"Having trouble sleeping?" I asked.

"A little." She sniffled and wiped her nose with a tissue. Twiggy seemed tiny and frail in her flimsy white robe. A nose as red as Rudolph's marred her face.

I took milk out of the fridge and poured

enough for two mugs into a pot. "Gwen or Jonah?" I asked.

"Probably both." Claudine spoke from the doorway. "Do you have enough milk for one more, Sophie?"

"Of course." I added milk to the pot. "Would you like hot chocolate or a splash of Amaretto or Baileys Irish Cream in your milk?"

Simultaneously, they said, "Baileys!"

Claudine ran her hand across Twiggy's hunched shoulders and hugged her. "I'm so sorry, honey."

"I didn't think anyone else had noticed."

Claudine sat down at the table. "Sugar isn't exactly meek. She and Gwen are nothing short of brazen when it comes to men."

I poured the hot milk into three chunky red Waechtersbach mugs adorned with Christmas trees and white stars and brought them to the table, along with a bottle of Baileys and a platter of assorted cookies from the swap.

As I sat down, Twiggy asked, "Did Jonah's father have affairs?"

"No, sweetheart. He was a very good man. Better than I deserved, probably."

I doubted it. In her powder blue bathrobe, silver hair curling around her ears, Claudine was the picture of a perfect grandmother.

I wanted to tell Twiggy she must be mistaken. Jonah seemed like a nice guy. But I had seen him in the alley with Sugar. "Are you sure?" I asked. "Maybe nothing has happened yet."

"After the cookie swap yesterday, Jonah went to make some deliveries. I left Claudine in charge of the store and followed him. He didn't take the van — he walked. And he wasn't carrying anything to deliver." Twiggy poured a double dose of Baileys into her mug. "He met Sugar at a bar on King Street. They talked in a cozy little niche in the back, where I'm sure they sat so they wouldn't be noticed." Her shoulders curled forward. "I can't compete with someone like Sugar. She's voluptuous and seductive, and I'm such a skinny little squirt."

"Hey, don't put yourself down," I said. "Do you know how many of us would love to be skinny? You're adorable."

"I don't know what to do. Do I talk to him and tell him that I see what's happening? Or do I just ignore it?" She moaned. "Oh, I know I can't close my eyes and just hope for the best."

Claudine pursed her lips. "When Jonah was born, I promised myself that I would never interfere with the life decisions he made for himself. I didn't want to be like my parents, the kind who hover over a child trying to steer him where *they* want him to go. But I think I should make an exception. Whatever he feels for Sugar won't be lasting. I don't want him ruining his life over a silly temporary infatuation."

"Do you think that's what it is? An infatuation? I could deal with that. I think." Twiggy bit into one of Natasha's cookies. "Ugh. What are these? They taste like dirty shoes covered in chocolate." She gasped. "Gosh, I hope they're not your cookies, Sophie!"

"Natasha baked those," I assured her.

Claudine tried a corner of the cookie. "Do you think she baked them to annoy Gwen?"

Anything was possible, but I doubted that was Natasha's intent. "Natasha thinks she has a superior palate to the rest of us. We don't know what's good."

Claudine laughed so hard that she clapped her hand over her mouth. "How do people get these inflated notions about themselves? That's hysterical. The next time I cook something for dinner that none of us like, I'll trot it right over to Natasha and tell her it's haute cuisine."

"Try one of Gwen's bars," I suggested.

Twiggy cut one in half, tasted it, and offered the other half to Claudine. "These are great!"

In a second she sagged again. "I hate confrontations. Jonah is leaving me no other choice, though. I thought this would be such a wonderful Christmas, with the store doing so well, and with Claudine here — instead it's going to be the worst Christmas ever." Twiggy choked and coughed. "What a horrible person I am. Gwen is dead, and I'm carrying on about my husband being interested in another woman. I can still try to save my marriage, but Gwen . . . She'll never see Kat grown up. And Kat won't have a mom. I can't imagine anything more sad."

"Who would have done such a heinous thing?" Claudine wrapped both her hands around her mug. "I heard about the argument between Gwen and Natasha, but it's impossible to imagine Natasha being that crazy. She might be obnoxious —"

"And opinionated," added Twiggy. "And nosy, and pretend to be better than the rest of us, but down deep, I think Natasha has a good heart."

"Gwen must have done something to anger somebody big-time." Claudine sat back. "I'm just grateful Edith Scroggins didn't go online and badmouth Rocking

Horse Toys like she said she would. The Internet can be dangerous. It's too easy to make accusations and say ugly things in the heat of the moment. People need to learn to take a breath and understand the ramifications of what they put out for public consumption."

Claudine was as sweet as my Baileys-infused hot milk. Yet when she mentioned Edith, I had to think of the mouse that disappeared from Edith's house and reappeared in the garage where I had found Gwen. Claudine had been angry and had rightfully stood up to Edith. Surely she hadn't entered Edith's house and stolen the mouse from her. And if so, why had it wound up in Natasha's workroom? Suddenly, I felt a little bit wary of the sweet lady with the charming smile.

"How long did you say you've been in town?" I asked.

"About a month."

Long enough to play some tricks on Edith. "Did you know Edith when you lived here as a child?"

"Gracious, no. It seems as if everyone I knew has moved away. It's all so different now. After the holidays, when things slow down at the store, I'll try looking up some friends. But so far, Jonah and Twiggy have been keeping me busy! And now we have to take care of this little matter with Sugar . . ."

I hoped that wasn't as sinister as it sounded.

In the morning, I woke to the smell of coffee. Mochie was nowhere to be seen. Since I had company in the house, I threw on a white turtleneck and stretchy jeans, and ran a brush through my hair before going downstairs.

Someone knocked on the door before I made it to the kitchen. Alex already? I glanced in the hall mirror. No makeup, but my hair still looked fairly decent from the night before.

I swung open the front door wearing a big grin — only to see Wolf. "You're out early."

He sniffed the air. "Coffee. At least I didn't wake you. I understand all the Lawrences are staying here?"

I nodded. "Come on in."

He followed me into the kitchen. Claudine and Twiggy greeted us cheerfully.

"I hope you don't mind," said Claudine. "We thought making breakfast was the least we could do to repay you for letting us bunk here. Do you like banana pancakes?"

Twiggy handed me a mug of coffee. "Jonah left already to receive an early delivery." She pulled me aside and whispered, "Mom and I have been discussing whether it's better to send Kat to school today or to take her to the store."

I spooned sugar into my coffee and offered Wolf milk for his. "School might keep her busy. As long as none of the other kids say anything about her mom."

"That's what worries us. There's no telling what they might have overheard from their parents."

Little Kat sat at the table, eating pancakes with Mochie next to her.

"The pancakes smell delicious," said Wolf. "I'd love some if you're sure you have enough."

"I'm guessing this isn't a social visit," Claudine said politely. "Perhaps you could wait until the little one is upstairs before you mention the recent event?"

Wolf nodded in agreement. "Of course." He ventured to the table. "How are you, Kat? Do you remember meeting me yesterday?"

She seemed like a normal child, not a bereaved one, when she said, "Wolf. Grrr."

"I see Mochie likes you."

"All kitties like me, but my mom won't let me have one." Her face fell.

"That's too bad. Do you have a stuffed

kitty cat?"

"Uh-huh. Four of them."

Twiggy swooped down on her. "Time to clean up and get dressed. I brought your tiara for you to wear today!"

Kat raced up the stairs almost as fast as Mochie. Twiggy followed at a slower pace.

Wolf and I sat down at the table, our plates heaped with pancakes and turkey sausages that smelled divine.

Claudine joined us. "These have been Jonah's favorite breakfast since he was a little boy."

"Thank you for cooking, Claudine. This is such a treat. My mother is the only one who ever makes breakfast for me anymore." I sipped the rich coffee, savoring the warmth.

"Claudine, would you mind if I asked you a few questions while we eat?" asked Wolf.

"Sure, that's okay. I don't know much. I just arrived a month ago so I didn't really know Gwen — just to say hi, that kind of thing."

"Did you ever notice anyone hanging around the garage?"

"Mars and Natasha were in and out. Honestly, though, it's been so busy at the store that we leave early and come home late. This is the kids' first Christmas at the store. It's kind of make-or-break time for them, you know? They're working so hard to make a go of Rocking Horse Toys. That's why I was upset with Mrs. Scroggins when she didn't want to pay full price for that little mouse. Like two extra dollars mean that much to her?"

"Horace's wife?" asked Wolf.

"She's quite an unpleasant person, I must say."

I glanced at Wolf and guessed I shouldn't mention the mouse in front of Claudine.

"Were any of you home in the late afternoon or early evening day before yesterday?"

I enjoyed my pancakes quietly. Instead of slicing cold bananas over the pancakes, Claudine had cooked the pancakes with banana slices inside them. The warm bananas with a bit of pancake and sweet maple syrup over top were delicious.

"The day of the cookie swap?"

"Yes," said Wolf.

"That was a crazy day. Twiggy went to the cookie swap. She was back at the store earlier than expected. I understand the swap fell apart when there was a squabble between Natasha and Gwen. Since Twiggy was back early, Jonah left to make some deliveries, and when he came back, I took a break and did a little shopping before picking up takeout for us to eat at the store."

273

"Did you go home during your break?"

"No."

"I guess you wrap a lot of gifts at the store?"

"Oh yes! Lots of folks want their presents wrapped before they take them home so their children won't know what's in them. Jonah is so clever. On Christmas Eve, he's going to be open until one in the morning so people can stop by to pick up bicycles they bought and other big gifts like that beautiful sailboat in the window. Have you seen it? A dad purchased it for his son but asked us to leave it in the window because his little boy goes by every day to see if it has been bought yet! Won't he be surprised?"

Wolf's poker face broke into a sunny smile. "I like that. What a great dad."

Twiggy returned and poured herself a cup of coffee. "Kat is so in love with Mochie! And I think it's mutual. She's pulling a string along the floor, and he's chasing it." She joined us at the table.

Wolf asked her the same questions.

"I took the cookies home after the cookie swap broke up. No point in lugging them to the store." She bit her lower lip. "Natasha was in her workroom having a hissy fit." Twiggy shrank back and frowned. "I'm sorry. I hate to rat on her like this, but it's true. She was so upset with Gwen. She was in and out, hauling out black and silver stuff, racing around in a big huff."

"What time was that?"

"It was dark. Jonah set the lights on the outside of the carriage house to turn on at six, and they were on when I left, so definitely after six."

"Did you see Gwen or anyone else in the alley after that?"

Twiggy thought for a moment. "No. Gwen had taken to letting Sugar pick up Kat at the store, and Sugar ran late that night. When do you think we can get back into our apartment?" She paled. "Not that it isn't wonderful here with you, Sophie! I didn't mean to sound unappreciative."

"Don't apologize. We all know there's no place like home."

"Gwen's body was taken to the medical examiner's late last night. I suspect they'll be through with the rest in a couple of days."

"Days!" Twiggy winced.

"There isn't an outside entrance to your place, is there?" asked Wolf.

"No. Couldn't you rope off a little entryway for us to get in and out? We'll keep the doors locked, and there's no reason for us to go into the garage at all."

I finally spoke up. "Do you know how Gwen died yet?"

Wolf shot a sidelong glance at me. "If I don't tell you, your pal Humphrey will weasel it out of someone at the medical examiner's office. It's not official, but it looks like a nasty blow to the head. I've seen enough of them in my career to bet on it."

Claudine and Twiggy looked slightly sick at the thought.

The front door knocker sounded. I excused myself and hurried to the foyer to open the door.

Alex and Nina stood outside.

Nina winked at me as she entered. "I smell breakfast! Need coffee now!"

Alex bent to give me a kiss. "Good morning. Does that breakfast invitation still stand?"

"Absolutely."

But the moment we stepped into my kitchen, the air grew unbearably thick. Everyone greeted one another.

Wolf uttered a terse, "Counselor."

Alex responded with an equally cold, "Sergeant."

Wolf stood to take his leave, and thanked Claudine for breakfast.

"Did I miss something?" she asked. "You don't have to rush off. Maybe you'd like another cup of coffee?"

Nina was pouring coffee. She set down the coffeepot, chuckling. "Sophie used to date him" — she pointed at Wolf with the forefinger of her right hand — "and now she's dating him." She pointed at Alex with the forefinger of her left hand and an expression of amusement.

"Oh dear," said Claudine. "I didn't realize."

I wanted to fall through the floor. The tension was silly and unnecessary, but the awkwardness made me itch all over.

I saw Wolf to the door.

"Thanks for not mentioning the mouse. Do you still have it?"

"No. I returned it to Mrs. Scroggins. Someone has been pinching things from her house."

Wolf's head snapped up. "And you didn't think that was important enough to mention to me?"

"You didn't care about the mouse! You can ask Wong. She knows all about it. I'm sure it has nothing to do with Gwen's murder." Maybe.

By the time I returned to the kitchen, Claudine had started another batch of pancakes. "The trick," she said, "is to make the pancakes thick and fluffy and slice the

277

banana thin. After you pour the batter, you quickly press the bananas into each pancake before the top starts setting up. Then you flip, cook, and" — she slipped a spatula underneath a pancake — "voilà! They're done!"

About the time Nina and Alex started to eat, Twiggy left to take Kat to school, and Claudine disappeared upstairs. I sipped a second cup of coffee and nearly spewed it when Alex asked, "What was Wolf doing here?"

"He came by to ask questions of Claudine and Twiggy."

"What kind of questions?"

"Nothing fancy — did they notice anyone hanging around the garage? Where were they after the cookie swap?"

Nina leaned forward. "Rumor has it Gwen was bludgeoned."

"Amazing how fast news spreads. That's what I understand, too." I gazed at Alex but, like Wolf, his face didn't register anything. How did I always end up with men who could hide their reactions so well? "Have you seen Baxter yet this morning?"

"I stopped by the house," said Alex. "Patty told me he left early for the mortuary to make funeral arrangements. What do you know about Patty?"

A chill ran over my arms. "Not much. She seems nice. Are you implying that she might have killed Gwen?"

Alex nodded casually. "Ex-wives aren't always happy with new wives. Wouldn't be the first time an ex-wife murdered her replacement."

"I need to bring Baxter and the kids some food. Mac and cheese? Everyone likes mac and cheese, don't they?" I asked.

"They don't need cookies. That's for sure." Nina swirled the last bit of pancake through the maple syrup on her plate. "I'm having Bernie make them a cold-cut platter for sandwiches."

Patty banged on the kitchen door yelling something garbled. I unlocked the door and opened it.

She nearly fell into the house. "Alex, help! The police arrived with a search warrant. Baxter's not home, and I don't know what to do!"

CHAPTER TWENTY-TWO

Dear Sophie,
I would love to have a cookie swap. But most of my friends are on diets or will be going away for the holidays and don't need a hundred cookies. Still, it seems like so much fun.

> Cruising for the Holiday in
> North Pole, Idaho

Dear Cruising,
Bake the cookies and have a lovely evening or afternoon sharing them. Then pack up the rest and take them to a homeless shelter or a senior center where they will be much appreciated.

> Sophie

Alex loped out the door and the rest of us followed.

Unlike Patty, who flitted like a nervous bee, Alex was the consummate professional.

He walked into the Babineaux house the picture of composure.

Patty watched with us. "I bet they're going to kick him out!"

"Does anyone else think he's sexy when he's in control like that?" asked Nina. "I think it's the military stance with the shoulders back and chin up."

"The kids are still asleep!" Patty flung her hands back and forth when she talked. "They'll be terrified when the cops barge into their rooms."

"Patty!" I exclaimed. "Go tell Alex that right now."

Nina and I hung back on the sidewalk.

"It's cold out here." My turtleneck was far too thin for hanging around outside. I was about to suggest we go home when someone screamed.

Nina and I flew to the doorstep in a flash. Wearing what appeared to be a man's pajama top with a cartoonish moose print on it, Sugar ran past us from the living room to the dining room. When we heard a second scream, Nina and I ventured inside.

Sugar held clenched fists in midair and stared at the table, still decorated with the orange tablecloth.

Wolf bounded in. "Who's screaming?" His

gaze flicked my way. "What are you doing here?"

Alex raced into the dining room and came to a halt.

"It's gone!" Sugar's voice quavered. "The sterling silver sleigh is gone. And the reindeer candleholders are missing, too."

"When did you see them last?" asked Wolf.

"I don't know." Tears ran down Sugar's face. "I don't remember! With everything that happened, I didn't notice them until just now."

Alex stepped over to Sugar and placed an arm around her. "It's okay. Take a few minutes to think about it."

She turned and buried her face in his suit.

Nina elbowed me. What did she expect me to do? It wasn't like I could separate them. Though I was a little annoyed by the sight of those long, bare legs. At least the shirt covered her derriere.

Sugar sniffled. "Someone must have stolen them. They were worth a lot of money! I bet that's why Mom was murdered. She was so proud of them. I mean, they were sterling and everything." Sugar gazed toward Nina and me. "You were here for the cookie swap. Weren't they beautiful?"

Wolf eyed me. "You saw them?"

I nodded. "They were amazing. Very detailed."

Alex gently pried Sugar off his suit. "Think back to last night. Do you remember seeing them then?"

Sugar leaned her head against Alex's chest and placed one hand on his suit jacket. "It's all such a muddle. We were in the kitchen mostly. Patty . . ." Sugar screeched. "Do you think Patty took them? You know, out of jealousy? For the money?"

Patty emerged from the kitchen. "Oh, very nice, Sugar. After all I've done for you guys? You can search my car. That sleigh was huge. It's not like I could have slipped it under my coat and snuck it out of here."

"Patty has a good point," I said. "Someone would have had to make a couple of trips to carry all the pieces out."

Patty flashed me a grateful smile.

I looked around. Baxter and Elvin were noticeably absent from a house in which so much was happening.

Alex stepped away from Sugar and sidled over to me. "Did anyone take pictures of this incredible sleigh?"

Sugar turned toward him. "You're so smart! I bet Gwen put them up on Facebook. Or has pictures in her camera."

Wolf frowned. "Camera? Where is it?" He

283

followed Sugar and Patty toward the kitchen.

"I owe you dinner," said Alex. "Several, in fact. Lunch today?"

"Sure."

"I'll call you." He hurried off to the kitchen.

Nina and I showed ourselves out. The front door closed with a snap behind us.

Nina said, "Elvin's sleigh could hold the big silver one."

"Bet it's not in the alley anymore."

"Me, too. We should check."

We dashed down the street and through Nina's yard to her gate. One look told the story. It wasn't as though Elvin could hide his big camper anywhere. It was gone.

"I'm freezing." Nina shuddered, and we headed back to my house.

In the kitchen, I pulled macaroni out of the cupboard and put on a large pot of salted water to boil.

"Where are your cookies?" asked Nina.

"In the dining room."

She returned with an orange box tied with a pink ribbon. A tiny silver sleigh ornament hung on it. "Double Chocolate Caramel Bars," she read. "That would hit the spot with a second cup of coffee."

She slid off the ribbon and sampled one.

"These are to die for. Seriously. Who made these?" She examined the box.

"Gwen."

Nina choked. Coughing, she reached for her coffee. "That's not funny," she croaked.

"It's an orange box with a pink ribbon, Nina. There are only two people with that strange Christmas color combo going — Natasha and Gwen. And Natasha made an herb cookie dipped in chocolate."

Nina stared at the rest of the bar. "There's something gross about eating a cookie that a dead person baked."

I opened the fridge to look in my cheese drawer. Luckily I had an assortment of cheeses. A lovely triple cream, extra sharp cheddar, and Gouda. I set them on the counter in time to see Nina swallow the last bite of Gwen's Christmas bar.

She gave me an innocent look. "What? They're very good. Gwen wouldn't want to see them go to waste!" She helped herself to another one while I poured the pasta into the boiling water and heated the milk. "Why would the police need a search warrant to see the victim's home?"

"Because Alex told them they couldn't go inside and look around."

"Exactly. And why would he do that?"

We both said it at the exact same time,

"Because that's where the killer lives."

"Baxter," I said.

"Or Elvin."

"Why would Elvin kill Gwen?"

"Probably for the same reasons as Baxter. Maybe he thinks he's helping his brother by getting rid of her."

"Yesterday, Sugar ran into the garage and, Nina, when she saw Gwen, I swear she screamed, 'Mom'!"

"I thought I misunderstood her when we were over there a few minutes ago. You're just telling me this now?"

"Hey, a lot has happened in the past twelve hours or so. It slipped my mind that you weren't there. Do you think it's possible?"

"Sugar must be right around thirty, don't you think?" asked Nina. "A thirty-year-old daughter and a six-year-old daughter? I guess it could happen. Gwen met Baxter, already had an adult daughter from her first marriage, and then had Kat with Baxter."

"So that would put Gwen at fifty-ish?"

"Something like that. If Sugar was her daughter, I hardly think she'd kill her. Maybe Gwen didn't like her being with Elvin." Nina wrinkled her nose. "That *is* kind of creepy. Imagine your husband's brother sleeping with your daughter." She stuck out her tongue. "Ick!"

I poured the macaroni into a colander and shook it to drain. While it cooled, I stirred the cheese, watching the colors melt into the hot milk. "I guess Natasha is glad she's off the hook."

"Are you kidding? They don't eliminate anyone until they have the perpetrator. They could decide that it wasn't a family member who killed Gwen."

I poured the macaroni into the cheese, stirred it all together nicely, and dumped it into a long casserole dish. I preheated the oven and mixed panko bread crumbs with Parmesan cheese for a crusty crunch on top.

Minutes after I slid it into the oven, Nina took off for home. I spent the next fifty minutes taking care of work in my study, glad things were slow at the moment. When the timer dinged in the kitchen, I withdrew the golden cheesy wonder from the oven. The police might still be at the Babineaux house, but either way, the Babineauxs would probably appreciate something hot to eat for lunch.

I plopped a piece of aluminum foil over the top to keep the cold out, slid on a lush, white Polartec jacket, and carried the mac and cheese across the street.

Baxter opened the door, haggard and

drawn, his skin the color of gray skies.

"I'm so terribly sorry, Baxter. I brought you something for lunch."

He nodded lamely, as if he couldn't function right yet. I stepped inside and followed him to the kitchen. It wasn't as spotless as it had been when I'd seen it a few days before. The island counter brimmed with kitchen items. Foil, spoons, bowls. A few dirty dishes and an orange box like the one that held Gwen's bars for the cookie swap. But the house was still. The police must have left.

I located a dish towel that I could use as a trivet and set the hot casserole atop it on the island. "Is there anything I can do for you?"

He rubbed his forehead with a fleshy hand in an odd jerking motion. "I don't know what needs to be done. I'm just trying to get my footing."

"Well, don't worry about Kat. Twiggy and Jonah are taking good care of her."

His eyes flicked. "Kat! How could I have forgotten about Kat? I don't know what will happen to her now."

"I don't understand."

He licked his lips. "I'm not her father."

CHAPTER TWENTY-THREE

Dear Natasha,
You are my idol. I'm always asking myself, "What would Natasha do?" I've been hand-stamping my wrapping paper for years. Now I'm wondering how to make my Christmas letter special.

Crafter in Garland, Pennsylvania

Dear Crafter,
Each person should receive a personal handwritten card. Surprise them with a little pop-up. Write your Christmas greetings on the inside of folded craft paper. Adorn the front of the card. Use a glue gun to attach the ends of a short string on opposite sides inside. Cover the glue with a bead. Attach a tiny round or rectangular photograph of each family member to the string, and you have a spectacular Christmas card!

Natasha

I almost lost my own footing at that revelation. "Who *is* Kat's father?"

"I don't know." He scratched the back of his neck. "Kat was about three months old when I met Gwen. I wanted to adopt Kat, but somehow we never got around to making it official and, after a while, it just didn't seem to matter. Her biological father never came around or called or anything. I didn't give it any thought in recent years."

His head fell forward. "I don't know if they would even let me adopt her now. My world is falling apart," he sobbed. "It's over. There's nothing left. My wife is dead. I don't have a job. The kids' college funds are gone. I'm out of money, so broke I'm going to have to sell this house." He crumpled to the floor and sat with his head in his hands, his entire body shaking.

I knelt next to him and wrapped my arms around him. There was nothing to do but hold him and let him cry.

"I wish I had died instead of Gwen. She was the strong one. I have nothing to live for anymore."

"Don't say that! You have something very important to live for — Bethany and Bradley. You have the one thing no one else can give them, Baxter — a father's love. They need you now more than ever before."

He clutched my hand. "I'm of no use to anyone."

"Then you have to pull yourself together for them. You have to be the strong one now. You know you can."

"I can, can't I?"

"You'll pull through this together. You and Bradley and Bethany." I omitted Kat's name on purpose. Poor baby. She had no idea how her life would change.

He sucked in a deep breath. His chest heaved. I stood up and handed him a tissue. He took my hand and rose slowly, like a very old man. "I apologize. I've never had a meltdown like that before."

He hugged me to him, still sniffling. "You're so right. I have to figure it all out for my children. I owe them that. Life might not be as sterling as it was, but, actually, that might be good for them. Elvin and I had summer jobs at their age."

"See? Everything will work out."

He released a long, shuddering breath. "I guess it's lucky that Patty's here, huh? At least they didn't lose their mom."

It probably wasn't the time to ask, but I went for it anyway. "Did I understand correctly that Gwen is *Sugar's* mother?"

Baxter huffed. "I didn't know that myself until yesterday." He winced and massaged the back of his neck. "I'm discovering that Gwen had quite a few secrets, and I don't mean the guess-what-I-got-you-for-Christmas kind. Now that she's gone, the truth is slithering out. I wonder if I knew her at all. Maybe . . . maybe Gwen didn't mention Sugar because she wanted everyone to think she was young. The cops are telling me she lied about her age. Gwen told everyone she was forty when she was really fifty."

"She looked great. I know she worked out a lot."

"She wanted to go to Paris," he said sadly. "The one in France. We couldn't afford it. I promised her we would go for our tenth anniversary. And now she's died without ever seeing Paris."

"Don't beat yourself up. You couldn't have predicted that."

He placed his hands on my shoulders. "Sophie, don't put off your dreams."

He turned and walked away.

I wandered out through the living room, pausing only long enough to notice that the shade from a floor lamp was missing. A pang ripped through me. It must have been the one atop Gwen's head.

I let myself out of the house, shaken by Baxter's deep depression. What had I expected? Of course he was sad and probably numb, too. I'd had no idea there were money issues. Poor Baxter.

While I was out, I went next door to check on Natasha. Mars and Daisy answered the door. The big tail-wagging hug from Daisy was just the canine therapy I needed to cheer me up.

"How's Natasha?" I asked Mars.

"Indignant. Gwen really pushed her buttons."

"Sounds like our Natasha."

He led me to their kitchen. Not a single item lay on the spotless stainless steel countertops. A huge square wreath of glistening silver ornaments hung in the window, adorned by an airy black bow. It was striking in a high-tech sort of way.

Natasha stood on a ladder, holding a long garland of silver stars. "At least it's not the police again. I hate your Wolf, Sophie."

"He's not *my* Wolf."

"I hate him anyway."

Mars sighed. "Why don't you tell Sophie what happened?"

Natasha turned. "Mars thinks you can help me."

I shot him a doubtful look. "Was it your wrapping paper that covered Gwen?"

"Of course it was! There's not any point

in denying it because I make it myself. You can't find paper like that in stores."

"You make the paper?" asked Mars.

"No! I *have* made paper before, but I usually buy the paper and then hand stamp it with something appropriate for the recipient."

"Like what?"

Natasha gazed down at me. "Didn't you teach Mars anything when you were married to him? I might stamp it with a French horn or a note for a musician, or trains for a little boy."

"Must have taken quite a bit of paper to wrap a whole person," I said.

"Doesn't matter. I changed my color scheme, so I didn't need it anyway."

I hoped she hadn't said it that way to Wolf! He might think she had used it instead of throwing it out. "Why do you think Gwen was wrapped?"

"Mars, I told you Sophie couldn't help." Natasha sighed. "Isn't it obvious that the killer wanted to pin it on me?"

A reasonable assumption.

"Tell her what you did." Mars was insistent.

Natasha tilted her head upward, her chin jutting forward. "It was a natural reaction. I didn't know she would be killed!"

Mars left the kitchen for a few seconds and returned with an iPad. He flicked to a page and showed it to me. Gwen had posted a photo of Natasha on her website. Natasha's almost black hair stuck out from her head. If she had placed her finger in an electrical outlet she wouldn't have managed as much static in her hair. It must have been from the pantyhose and balloon game. Even worse, Natasha's chin was tucked in, and she looked up, with an absolutely devilish expression. I had never seen her like that before. If I hadn't known Natasha, I would have been terrified of her.

Mars flicked the page up. In the next photo, Natasha wore the balloon antlers on her head. The pantyhose bottom smashed her hair tight to her head and the balloon-filled antlers curled like ram's horns. I bit my lip as hard as I could to keep from laughing. "Well, let's hope that Gwen doesn't have a big following on her website."

Natasha glared at me. "Oh, that's right. No one will go to that page now that she's dead."

Oof. Of course they would.

"Not to mention that she posted the same charming pictures on her Facebook page!"

Mars flicked the screen a couple of times.

"And there they are again." He flicked it one more time. "And here's what Natasha did."

"I had to retaliate! I wasn't going to stand by and watch her grind all my hard work to dust!"

Mars zeroed in on a message from Natasha. *Heaven help me not to kill the woman whose deranged jealousy of me led her to post such unflattering photos, which were clearly Photoshopped to present me in a way I have never looked. It's a shame that liars and untalented copycats have access to worldwide audiences who have no knowledge of their true character and believe the trash they post.*

I was stunned. "Why would you do anything so incredibly juvenile?"

"What was I supposed to do?"

"The mature thing would have been to say nothing and let it slide. This is a direct threat! No wonder the police are looking at you. They had opportunity, and you handed them motive. Why didn't you just leave your signature on her corpse? Oh, I'm sorry. You did! You wrapped her in your personal private stash of wrapping paper."

"You think I killed her."

"No, I don't think that at all." I really didn't. "I know you better than that." At least I thought I did. "But this does not look good for you."

Natasha finally climbed down the ladder. In a very small voice, she asked, "Will you help me?"

"I'll do what I can. But you have to promise never to be so incredibly stupid and hotheaded again."

I watched Natasha carefully for her reaction. "Wouldn't you have noticed someone in your workshop?"

She didn't flinch. "Carriage house. It's a *carriage* house. I was out front, changing the decorations, and then I had to sew a black tree skirt and black stockings in my upstairs sewing room."

Horrified, I looked to Mars.

He closed his eyes briefly, as though resigned to the black décor, and nodded his head. "What do we do first?"

"We'll have to do some poking around to see if we can figure out who really killed Gwen. And you" — I pointed at Natasha — "stay home and finish decorating. No more posts on the Internet of any kind."

"Oh, I know who killed her," Natasha said casually. "Claudine. I saw her sneaking around the carriage house when she should have been at work."

Chapter Twenty-Four

Dear Sophie,

As much as I would love to pour a glass of wine and spend some time having fun with my friends at a cookie swap, my husband always complains about being "thrown out of the house." Is there a way to include husbands that wouldn't be a lot more work?

Harried Mom in Christmasville,
Tennessee

Dear Harried Mom,

Make it a family affair. Invite your friends, their spouses, and their kids. Instead of asking everyone to share a dozen cookies that day, maybe they can all bring two dozen. Set up two tables, one with cookies and drinks for children and one for the adults. Be smart and hire a couple of high school kids to entertain the children!

Sophie

"Why would Claudine want to murder Gwen?" I asked.

Natasha gave me a look like she thought I was too stupid to live. "Obviously, Gwen was a despicable person. The fact that she posted those hateful photos proves that. She thought nothing of ruining the career I've worked so hard to establish. And, by the way, I'm a little miffed at you because you're the one who told me to play nice." She shifted her focus to Mars. "And you, too! You nagged me until I went to that cookie swap." She switched to a nasty little tone of voice. "*You must be nice to the neighbors or they'll think you're a snob.* Look where that got me!"

It got *me* out of their house about as fast as I could go. Mars barreled after me, attaching Daisy's leash as they went. "Where to, Sherlock?" He handed me the leash and pulled on a brown leather jacket as we walked.

"Mars, what possesses you to stay with her?"

"That's what we're going to talk about now? Don't you think that's better suited to a glass of wine by the fire?"

Actually, I didn't think so at all. In fact, it sounded too cozy and romantic for me. Like a complete chicken, I changed the subject. "Yesterday morning, Baxter asked me if Gwen was having an affair."

"Whoa-ho!" Mars chuckled. "Why am I not surprised? Gwen liked attention."

"Oh?"

"Don't look at me that way. If she was seeing someone, it wasn't me. But she liked to dress to show off her figure. You know what I mean. And she was good at flirting and being seductive. Sugar is like that, too. The Babineaux men must like that type."

"Like mother, like daughter."

"Huh?" He stopped walking. "You're kidding!"

"I wish I were. I don't know why they kept it quiet. Turns out Baxter is broke, too. There was a lot going on under their roof that no one knew about."

"How can he be broke? They bought that house less than a year ago."

"I guess they overextended. Didn't Gwen do a lot of renovating?"

"I know they redid the kitchen, because Natasha was so jealous that she wanted to rip ours out again."

"Why? Natasha acts like she has the perfect kitchen."

"She says stainless steel is out."

"Then what's the new trend?"

"Please," Mars groaned. "Like I listened to her that long? I said no more renovating. She chose what she put in our house and now she has to live with it."

"Natasha and Gwen were a little bit alike. I have a feeling that Gwen might have been extravagant. She bought some incredible candleholders and the most amazing sleigh. They're sterling silver. They would have cost a bundle."

"Living beyond their means, eh? So what do we do next? Interview Claudine?"

I shot Mars a skeptical glance as we walked. "Seems like there could be other, more likely candidates. What do we know for sure? Gwen was killed after the cookie swap and before the next evening. It would help if we knew exactly when. It seemed to me that Wolf was most interested in the evening before I found her. Who had a motive?"

"Baxter, for one." We paused so Daisy could sniff a gate. "If Gwen was running through their money, it's a good bet they had some major fights. Maybe one got out of hand. What about Baxter's ex-wife, Patty?"

We walked again, and I drew in a deep

breath. "She seems very nice. But if anyone was angry with Gwen, it was Patty. She feels like Gwen stole her children. Apparently Gwen wasn't very generous about sharing them. And there's one other thing." It pained me to say it. "Patty slipped out of the house that night. I have no idea where she went, but it doesn't look good for her."

Mars stopped dead in the middle of the sidewalk. "That's it! You're brilliant! It was Patty. Let's call Wolf and tell him."

"Slow down, Mars. We don't know that. Besides, I'm sure he interviewed her. After all, she spent the night at Baxter's . . ."

"That ties it up even tighter. Maybe they killed her together."

There was a horrible thought that hadn't crossed my mind. "It's possible. But I think she felt everyone was in shock and she needed to help out, especially with the children."

"You don't have to make her out as a nice person, Sophie. She obviously murdered Gwen."

"Mars," I said casually, "what time did you finish working on my roof and go home that night?"

"You suspect me?" He snickered.

"No. But answer the question."

"I knew Natasha was at the cookie swap,

so I went down to The Laughing Hound with Bernie for a beer. There were loads of witnesses in the bar."

I smiled at him. He didn't realize where I was going with my questions. "What time did you get home?"

"Natasha had prepared a pumpkin, blue cheese, and radish quichelike thing for dinner, so I was in no hurry to go home. I split a pizza with Bernie, then hung around because he asked the chef to whip up crepes filled with vanilla ice cream and topped with a chocolate hazelnut sauce. Have you tried them? I could eat them every day. Why can't Natasha cook things like that? But to answer your question, I wasn't home until ten. And I can give you the names of witnesses."

Did he really think I suspected him? I was a lot more interested in knowing just how much time Natasha had in the privacy of her workshop and garage. Not that I thought Natasha would intentionally kill anyone. Still, it was worth ruling her out. The garage and workshop were detached from their house. If Natasha had been inside their home decorating for extended periods of time, anyone could have slipped into the garage or workshop to steal the wrapping paper and hide Gwen's body. Including, unfortunately, Natasha.

"Did you notice anything different in your garage? See anyone hanging out in the alley?"

"No on both counts."

"This is the store where Gwen bought the sleigh . . ." I blinked. Silver reindeer pranced before a sleigh full of glitzy round white Christmas ornaments. Either they had another one just like the one Gwen had bought or it was back. I handed the leash to Mars. "I'll just be a second."

I entered the store and approached a bald man with a precisely trimmed mustache who was polishing a deer-head candlestick exactly like the ones that had graced Gwen's mantel. "Excuse me. The sleigh in the window — did you have two of them?"

He had the nerve to look me over top to bottom. "You must have had your eye on it to notice. Someone bought it, but it was returned to the store."

"When?"

He raised an eyebrow critically. "I'm quite sure that's none of your business."

"Is it sterling?" I asked.

"Are you interested in purchasing it?"

What a pill! "Yes," I lied.

He forced a smile, showing pointy little teeth. "It is indeed sterling silver. We have these coordinating buck antler candlesticks that go with it."

"How much for the set?"

When he told me the five figure number, my knees nearly buckled. I could renovate both of my bathrooms for that kind of money. I thanked him and hurried out of the store, making a mental note not to patronize it. Not that I had that kind of excess cash anyway.

"It was returned," I said to Mars. "It costs a small fortune."

He didn't appear interested. "Guess who's next door working at Rocking Horse Toys."

"Claudine? Will you let that go? Unless we ferret out a reason for her to have wanted to kill Gwen, you're wasting your time on her."

"What about Gwen's brother-in-law, Elvin?"

"He's working at the toy store?" We edged over to the store window and peered inside.

The buttons on a Christmas red vest threatened to pop off of Elvin's tummy. He wore jaunty pointed elf ears and a green elf hat with red accents in the shapes of stars. Elvin laughed with a customer while he wrapped a gift.

"I wonder if he knew Gwen was Sugar's mom. There must be more to that story, don't you think? Why would they hide their relationship?"

"We can add Sugar to the list of suspects, too." Mars cringed. "Although I can't imagine killing a family member. How are we going to find out what the deal is with Sugar?"

"I guess we'll have to ask her. But maybe we should start with Elvin. He probably knows something about what was going on in that household."

All smiles, Elvin's customer left.

Mars started for the door.

"Wait! How are we going to bring it up?"

Mars tilted his head at me. "Sophie. I deal with slick politicians all the time. Do you really think I don't know how to weasel information out of someone?"

I was game to let him try. He must have learned something in his years as a political consultant. Mars held the door for Daisy and me. She led the way into the store.

Elvin couldn't have been more jolly if he'd been Santa himself. "You're Baxter's neighbors. Right?" He placed a pudgy finger aside of his nose. "Sophie, you helped Baxter the day he fell off the roof. And I know Mars because he lives next door. What can I help you with today?"

Mars thought he was so clever. I let him handle that question.

He let it slide. "I didn't expect to see you working here."

"Aww, I'm just a big kid. If there are two things I know about, it's kids and toys!" Elvin lowered his voice, his tone a bit less cheery. "Need to make a little money for Christmas presents. Now that Gwen is gone, Sugar and I are extending our trip to help take care of things around the house. Poor Baxter isn't himself. It's terrible to lose someone close to you, but at this time of year it's twice as hard. Everyone wants to embrace the joy of the season. Instead, poor Baxter feels like nothing will ever be right again. We thought we'd be a comfort to the kids. Make things a little merrier, so the house doesn't feel so empty without Gwen." He gazed at the floor. "I guess I should have waited until after the funeral to start working, but we don't know exactly when her body will be released."

"Such a tragedy," murmured Mars. "Do the police have any leads?"

I tried to act casual and picked up a baby doll.

Elvin's lips twisted inward. "Not that I know of. Gwen seemed like a warm and loving person to me. I can't imagine why anyone would do her in."

Was that really how he felt? Gwen had said

he couldn't stay with them and had instructed Baxter to hide Elvin's bus immediately. Hardly warm and loving.

"I heard she kicked the family out for the cookie swap." Mars laughed.

Elvin grinned. "Guess she was afraid we'd eat all the goodies. Everyone except Sugar, that is. She got to stay because she's a lady. *Just for women* is what I was told."

Sugar! Sugar was the only person left in the house with Gwen after the cookie swap. She had the best opportunity of anyone to kill Gwen. They must have been alone together once the party broke up. Then again, anyone could have slipped inside after the guests left.

Mars leaned toward Elvin like he was confiding something. "Is it true that Sugar is Gwen's daughter?"

Elvin's eyes went wide, and he slapped his thigh. "Who'd have thought *that*? Came as a surprise to everyone. Sugar lost track of her mom a few years back. Gwen married Baxter and moved, and the name Gwen Babineaux didn't mean anything to Sugar. Can you imagine their surprise when we drove up? I'm just glad they had a chance to see each other again before Gwen died." He stared at the doll in my hands. "Funny how life works out sometimes."

Lost track? Who loses touch with her mom? I chided myself immediately. Just because I was close to my mom didn't mean everyone was. I thought back to Sugar's arrival. Had Gwen and Sugar acted like long-lost mother and daughter? Gwen had hustled Sugar into the house very quickly. Why would she have done that? I tried to recall if they had hugged. I thought they had. Still, there had to be more to that story. Something didn't smell right to me.

"Must be awkward having Patty around," said Mars. "The ex-wife? Oof!"

I groaned inwardly. Mars had failed to read my mind and pursue questions about Sugar.

Elvin grinned from ear to ear. "It's not like that at all. Patty's a great gal. Baxter never should have dumped her the way he did. She's the best. True-blue, you know?"

"Sounds like you have a soft spot for your former sister-in-law." Mars winked at Elvin.

Eww! How creepy. Since when did Mars wink at people?

"It's not like that." He leaned toward Mars and whispered again. "But from what I hear, Gwen put the moves on most of the men in the neighborhood. At least Patty didn't sleep around." Elvin raised his palms. "I shouldn't be speaking ill of the dead.

Gwen's gone and Baxter sure misses her."

Mars asked him a question about a train set as though he were interested in purchasing it.

My phone rang and I stepped outside with Daisy to answer the call.

"This is Mrs. Horace Scroggins calling. May I speak with Ms. Winston?"

CHAPTER TWENTY-FIVE

Dear Natasha,
I'm throwing a Christmas tea for my visiting mother-in-law. She seems to think we should give each guest a favor. I'm at a total loss. A gift for each guest seems like overkill.

> Nothing Is Ever Enough in Blitzen,
> Oregon

Dear Nothing Is Ever Enough,
You must have favors. Make spiced sugared almonds or jalapeno nut brittle. Put them in pint-sized canning jars. Adhere festive labels and tie circles of holiday-themed cloth over the tops.

> Natasha

It had been years since I'd heard anyone speak quite so properly on the phone. I identified myself and said it was nice to hear from her.

"Would you do me the favor of coming to tea this afternoon around three?"

I assured her that I would be delighted. But what little I knew of Edith led me to believe that she wasn't simply being sociable. Something must be up.

Mars joined me on the sidewalk. "If I were a little kid, I'd be begging my mom for those trains. Did you see how cool they were?"

I rolled my eyes. "Did Gwen ever make a pass at you?"

"Not like Elvin made it sound."

"So she did!"

"Don't go imagining anything. Gwen had a habit of cozying up to people. She liked to hear that she looked good."

"Cozying up? What exactly does that mean?"

"She's just a little bit more forward than you are. More like Natasha."

"Natasha comes on to men like a Mack truck!"

Mars laughed. "She's not that bad. Gwen didn't mean anything. It was just her way. She liked attention from men. Why are you surprised? She liked attention from women, too. Didn't you notice that she wanted to have the best house, the best cookies, the best party, the best clothes, that kind of thing? You never noticed that she was always trying to trump the women around her?"

I bet he had never noticed it, either. That observation probably came directly from Natasha's complaints about Gwen. He was right, of course. I just hadn't ever given it much thought. Gwen reminded me of Natasha in that way. Except that Natasha was irritating because she always thought she was right and had to correct everyone else. Gwen had never done that. At least not that I knew of. "Maybe that's the problem between Gwen and Sugar. Maybe Gwen competed with her own daughter?"

"Not a reason to kill her, is it?"

We walked toward my house. "Probably not. I'll catch up with you later."

"Sophie! Wait. What can I do to help?"

I thought for a minute. "Find out where Baxter was during the cookie swap and what time he got home."

Mars pretended to pout. "Isn't there something more important that I can do?"

I crossed my arms over my chest and faced him. "Remember the *broken* ladder that caused Baxter to fall from his roof? Maybe Gwen tried to kill *him* first." I ticked off my reasons on my fingers. "Baxter had a wife who was spending huge amounts of money even though they were broke. You admitted that she was overly friendly to men, and Baxter told me he thought she was having an affair. Gwen didn't come home the night before I found her. Either she was with her paramour, or she was already dead. I think it's important to know where everyone was, and I'm sorry to say that the situation doesn't look good for Baxter."

"How do you do that?" Mars's brow furrowed.

I shrugged. "You just have to pay attention to people."

"Sophie!" Nina yelled at me from her front door. She hustled out to the sidewalk. "You won't believe this. Baxter told the cops about falling off the roof. They're looking for that ladder, but they can't find it. Wolf wants to talk to you."

Mars shot me an amused look. "Just can't quite keep away from your Wolf, can you?"

"Why, Mars," teased Nina, "if I didn't know better" — she pretended to cough — "I would think you were jealous."

Mars groaned. "Why would Wolf want to see Sophie if he wasn't still interested in her?"

Nina batted her eyelashes at him. "Because Sophie is the only one who got a good look at the ladder. I saw it, but I wasn't paying attention."

I looked at Mars. "And whose fault is that?"

"I had nothing to do with Nina's inattention," he quipped. He drew a deep breath of air. "Okay. The next time you think someone has sawed a ladder in hopes of killing her husband, I promise I'll go look at it with you."

I ignored his sarcasm. "Is Wolf in the alley?"

Nina nodded. "You can cut through my yard."

Mars tagged along with Daisy.

Nina grabbed my arm. "Did you get an invitation to tea at Edith's house?"

"I did."

Nina opened the gate that led to the alley. "I'm almost afraid to go. Think it's some kind of trap or something?"

Wolf spotted me and walked over before I could answer. "Looks like you're the only one who got a good look at the ladder."

"It was the old wooden kind. I'm not an expert, but the second rung looked to me as though it had been sawed through on one end. It didn't splinter there like wood normally does."

Wolf frowned at me. "How do you know what wood looks like when it's sawed as opposed to broken?"

Mars snorted. "Haven't you figured out by now that Sophie observes all kinds of weird things that the rest of us don't notice?"

I shot him a look. Hadn't we just had this very discussion? But Mars smiled at me, evidently pleased with himself.

Wolf cocked his head. "Did you happen to notice what they did with the ladder after the fall?"

"Sorry. Nina and I went home. Doesn't Baxter know?"

"He seems to think it belonged to the neighbors. Gwen must have put it away. Will you be around to identify it when we find it?"

"Just call my cell phone, and I'll come right over."

Wolf thanked me, and I turned to head home. Why hadn't Alex called yet? I punched his number into my phone.

"Sophie!" he exclaimed. "I forgot all about lunch with you today. I'm sorry, something came up."

It sounded like he was already in a restaurant. And I could hear a woman in the background — one who sounded suspiciously like Sugar. I just bet something came up. "No problem. I thought I should touch base."

"Thanks for understanding. I'll call you later. Okay?"

Understanding? He sure had that wrong. I ended the call.

"Anyone for lunch?" I asked. Nina, Mars, and Daisy came with me.

"Shouldn't you check on Natasha?" I asked Mars as he shrugged off his jacket in my kitchen.

"After lunch. The food is better here. And you two are more fun anyway. Nat will drone on endlessly about Gwen putting those awful pictures of her on the Internet."

I smacked my own forehead. Why hadn't I thought of this before? "I'll whip up the lunch if you two will pull up the pages where Gwen posted the offending photos of Natasha."

While they looked for the pages on their phones, bacon sizzled in a pan. I pulled out my panini maker, the world's easiest way to make grilled cheese sandwiches. I washed spinach leaves, spun them dry, and dropped them in mounds on three white plates. I topped them with warm black-eyed peas and added a dab of cranberry sauce to each plate before drizzling it with a vinaigrette made of sweet balsamic vinegar, olive oil, honey, and a bit of the liquid from the cranberry sauce.

I didn't bother asking them what they wanted to drink. Reindeer juice was fast and easy, nonalcoholic, and both of them loved it. I poured sparkling apple cider into a pitcher and added cranberry juice. An apple slice garnished each tall glass. I poured the reindeer juice into them and carried them to the table along with the salads.

After setting them on the table, I assembled the sandwiches, first spreading creamy butter on both sides of each slice of bread. Extra sharp cheddar cheese and crumbled bacon went between two slices, and then I grilled them in the panini maker.

Meanwhile, Nina had pulled up Gwen's Facebook page, and Mars had her website on his phone.

"What time were they posted?" I asked.

They said, "Ohhh," at the same time.

"Facebook is at six forty p.m."

"Website is at six forty-five p.m."

"So we know for sure that Gwen was still alive around seven in the evening," I mused. "It would be interesting to know where Baxter, Sugar, and Elvin were at that time. I wonder if any of them have alibis."

"What time did Luis get shocked?" asked Nina. "Wasn't it Baxter who called the ambulance?"

I thought back. "What time was that?

Around eight o'clock?"

"But we don't know for sure that's when she was murdered," said Mars. "It could have been during the night or sometime the next day."

I slid the hot cheese sandwiches onto plates and served them while I grilled one more. "Do either of you really think Gwen was having an affair and was with her lover?"

Nina snorted. "Not a chance. No woman would ever allude to such a thing in a Christmas letter if she were really involved with another man. Not even in jest. It would hit too close to home. A husband who might be suspicious would flip. My husband would not find it in the least bit amusing."

Mars ran an uneasy hand through his hair. "I'm not so sure. Gwen could be very flirtatious. Some poor guy might have fallen for her advances. Maybe he killed her by accident and tried to do the right thing by bringing her body home. The Babineauxs don't have a garage. That would explain why she was in our garage."

"Really?" Nina put down her sandwich. "You really think that wrapping her like a gift was doing the right thing?"

Mars waved his hand. "No, of course not. I meant he might have killed her someplace else but instead of dumping her in the river or something, he brought her back here so her family would find her."

"Eww." But I conceded the merits of what he was saying. "I didn't see blood in the garage. Where was she killed?"

We all exchanged looks for a long silent moment.

"So we need to know where Gwen went after the cookie swap." I bit into my sandwich. The rich salty bacon meshed with the tangy cheese in my mouth. No wonder they were among Mars's and Nina's favorites.

In light of our invitation to tea at Edith's house, Nina and I skipped dessert. Mars groused about Natasha's unorthodox Christmas cookies. I packed him a bag of cookies from the swap to take with him.

"Should we dress for this?" asked Nina. "Do you suppose she expects us in hats and white gloves?"

"I don't think Edith is quite that out of tune with the times. But she cares about appearances, so maybe we should gussy up a little bit."

At a quarter of two, Nina met me on the sidewalk. I recognized the dark purple walking coat she had left at Horace's party. We walked over to Edith's house, speculating about Gwen's death. A couple of police officers still focused on something in the alley when we walked by.

Edith's housekeeper, Mabel, answered the door. "Please come in." She whispered, "I thought you might be one of her guests. In all the time I've worked here, she's never had company. Not a soul!"

Mabel took our coats. Nina wore an azure dress that skimmed her figure nicely. Subtle folds fell from the shoulders before criss-crossing at the waist.

I had opted for a shawl-collared dress in emerald green.

Mabel showed us into the library, where Edith greeted us, not exactly with warmth but with the graciousness of a proper hostess.

Much to my surprise, Officer Wong was there as well. She flashed me a questioning look when she said hello.

Edith perched on a settee in front of a coffee table bearing a silver tray. A silver teapot and matching sugar bowl and creamer were all heavily chased with flowers. Next to the tray sat a small stack of dessert plates with silver rims.

Wong eyed the lemon squares and Napoleons arranged on a platter. Beside it was a flat pink box about two inches high. A glitzy orange ribbon with a double bow lay next to it.

Edith poured tea for each of us while Mabel served the pastries. I felt like we were in the company of royalty.

When Mabel left the room, Edith said, "You must wonder why I called you here." She sat up straight but appeared uncomfortable, as though she was telling us something that pained her. "I no longer believe that Horace is trying to harm me."

"That must be a relief!" I smiled at her, glad she had realized her folly.

"I'm afraid it's no comfort at all because it means someone else is after us. When Horace fell from the balcony, I had the locks changed on the doors to his office building. I received numerous complaints about that decision, some quite rude, but I did so out of caution. I couldn't have anyone falling or injured." She paused and clenched her free fist. "I know all too well how dangerous these old buildings can be. The railing has now been repaired, and the house thoroughly inspected. It has been declared to be safe. However, during the time it was closed to employees, I did a bit of snooping in Horace's office.

I felt Nina's eyes on me. *Brown-Eyed Girl!* I'd almost forgotten about her in the commotion of Gwen's death. I held my breath.

"This box lay on Horace's desk." Edith

lifted the box and opened it to show us the contents. "It contained peanut brittle. As you can see, the better part of the contents have been consumed." She returned the box to the table and gazed at each of us in turn. "Horace has a sweet tooth. There is almost no candy he won't eat. Given the odd goings-on in our house, I took it upon myself to have the peanut brittle tested. A small piece contains the equivalent of two of Horace's doses of warfarin, which is a blood thinner that can kill you."

CHAPTER TWENTY-SIX

Dear Sophie,
I just attended my first cookie swap. It was loads of fun, but now I have to store eight dozen cookies. Help!
Cookie Monster in Silver Bell,
Arizona

Dear Cookie Monster,
Store moist cookies separately from dry cookies. The important thing is that they be in airtight containers in the refrigerator. If you don't plan to eat them in the next week or so, store them in the freezer.

Sophie

"Warfarin?" asked Nina. "Isn't that what they put in rat poison?"

Liza! She bought rat poison the day we were shopping for wreaths and pine roping.

"It's an odd medicine," said Edith. "In

small doses it keeps you alive. Eat more and it kills you like vermin. The warfarin in the peanut brittle accounts for the problem the doctors discovered when Horace fell from the balcony," Edith explained. "He might have died from an overdose had he not fallen and been brought to the hospital."

None of us said a word. I was having trouble reconciling everything Edith said with what we knew. Someone had murdered Gwen. Had the same person tried to murder Horace? Was there some connection between the two events or were they totally unrelated? And why did peanut brittle sound familiar? Where had I heard about peanut brittle recently? Had it been Liza?

Wong spoke up first. "Have you reported this to the police?"

Edith rose and handed Wong an envelope. "These are the results of the tests I requested. I trust you will know how to proceed."

"You said your medicine was moved to the shelf where Horace's medicine was stored," said Wong. "Would you know if warfarin was missing from his bottle?"

"Yes. Or reasonably close at any rate. I found the receipt for the last refill, computed the number of pills he should have taken, and then counted those that remained. He is missing nearly two weeks' supply."

I stared at the box. Gwen and Natasha were the only two people I knew who would have given someone candy in a pink box for Christmas. "Fingerprints," I breathed. Edith had handled the box, probably numerous times. She had probably ruined any fingerprints.

Wong knew exactly what I meant. Very politely, she said, "Mabel, would you bring me a fresh food storage bag?"

Edith's housekeeper must have been listening to everything from another room. She appeared in a moment with the requested bag.

Turning the plastic bag over her wrist like an inside-out mitten, Wong picked up the box and the bow, and slid the bag over them.

Edith spoke calmly. "How thoughtless of me. I hope I have not ruined evidence."

Nina blurted. "Are you kidding? You don't need fingerprints. It had to be Natasha or Gwen! A quick look in their homes will tell you who this stuff belongs to. Did either of them have a beef with Horace?"

Gwen! Of course. It was Gwen. She had made peanut brittle.

Edith raised her eyebrows. "How can you know it was Gwen or Natasha?"

Nina explained about their Christmas colors.

"I've never heard of such a moronic thing," said Edith. "Christmas colors are red and green, and everyone knows it." She eyed the box in Wong's hand. "Foolish, too. If I planned to kill someone, I hardly think I would use such distinctive colors to package the poisonous apple, so to speak."

"Unless you wanted to shift the attention to someone else," observed Nina. "In which case, you might intentionally use a very obvious color, like pink."

Natasha had a stack of pink boxes in her workroom. I couldn't help wondering if Gwen had pinched some to throw suspicion on Natasha. Was that the reason she copied Natasha's color scheme?

With shaking hands, Edith poured herself another cup of tea and drank it rapidly.

"Edith," Wong said gently, "is there anyone who might want to murder Horace?"

Nina's head turned toward me fast. I knew she was still thinking about Brown-Eyed Girl, but so far Edith had given no indication that she knew anything about her.

For a long moment, I feared Edith would scream at us and throw us out of her house. But Edith leaned back against the sofa as though she was drained. "Unless Horace was up to some sort of business shenanigans that I know nothing about, I can't imagine that anyone would harbor such hatred toward him." Her gaze fell to the Oriental carpet on the floor. "Except perhaps for me. I . . . I have never forgiven him for the death of our son." She inhaled deeply and released a long breath. "But killing him would not bring my little boy back. There would be no sense in that."

Wong shot me a quizzical look. I would have to fill her in on the tragedies of Edith's life.

But I now knew two things for sure. Edith hadn't lost her senses. She knew right from wrong. She closed Horace's real estate building in an abominable manner, but for the best of reasons. How would any of us react to a spouse who'd fallen from a broken balcony, especially after losing a child in a similar incident? It wasn't mean or stubborn or unreasonable of her to have locked people out of the building until she knew it was safe for them to enter. She just hadn't handled it well. And the sleuthing she had done with his medicine wouldn't have occurred to someone who had gone senile. Edith might be bitter and caustic, but she was still sharp as a tack.

And I knew Gwen was the one who had

tried to kill Horace. "What about you?" I asked. "Is there any reason Gwen would have come into your home to move your items around?"

"Of course not!" Edith spoke with indignation. "I keep to myself. I don't butt into other people's affairs."

It would have been easy for Gwen to slip out her back gate, cross the alley, and sneak into Edith's back door. Unfortunately, I could imagine Natasha doing that, too. She would have changed the location of a mirror without giving it any thought. I bit back a smile. In my mind I could hear Natasha defending herself — *It was in the wrong spot!*

But there was no doubt about the peanut brittle. "It was Gwen."

They all stared at me. "Natasha would never make anything as ordinary as peanut brittle. She would make macadamia brittle with chipotle and shallots, or some other weird combination that she thinks is haute cuisine. And there's one other thing. The night that Patty arrived, she had dinner at the Babineauxs' house. Gwen had gone missing by then. Patty said they ate peanut brittle that Gwen had made."

Edith gasped. "Why would Gwen want to hurt Horace? Or me, for that matter?"

Wong jumped to her feet. "I'll get this

down to the lab right away and see if we can get any prints off it. In the meantime, Mrs. Scroggins, I recommend that you take great care. Don't open your door to anyone. I'll make sure we keep an eye on your street. If you notice anything out of the ordinary, I want you to call 911 right away."

Something was bothering me. Patty had said the kids had found a pink box of peanut brittle hidden behind pasta and they'd used most of the contents to refill an orange box. Why the two colors? Unless . . . they were Gwen's own code. She could safely eat from the orange box but knew that the pink boxes contained the poison!

"Wait, Wong. Shouldn't we go to the Babineauxs' first? Patty said there was another box, a gift for Luis and Liza, that contained peanut brittle, and they used the contents to refill the box they had emptied. If memory serves, she said the box for Luis and Liza was pink."

Edith blurted, "No! What if the children eat it?"

Wong started for the door. "Don't panic. We'll check on their peanut brittle. I'm sure Gwen wouldn't have harmed the children."

"You don't understand. Gwen had a hidden stash and the kids were raiding it and refilling it from tainted boxes."

Edith rose and pointed. "Use the back door, it's faster." Wong, Nina, and I were out the door in a flash. No one bothered to stop for coats, we simply ran. Right past Wolf and a gaggle of police officers. We rushed up the back stairs to Gwen's kitchen.

Baxter opened the door. "What's going on?"

"The peanut brittle," Wong wheezed. "Where is it?"

Baxter's brow wrinkled. He pointed at the cluttered island. "Right there, somewhere."

I spotted the corner of an orange box under a jumble of cupcake boxes, a loaf of bread, and something wrapped in aluminum foil. I reached for it but stopped myself in the nick of time. "I don't want to mess up fingerprints."

Wolf had followed us into the kitchen. He handed Wong gloves. "What's going on?"

"Where's the other box?" I asked Baxter. "The one for Liza and Luis?"

Baxter opened a pantry door. "Behind the pasta."

Wong searched the shelf. "I don't see it. Sophie, you have a look."

I searched the entire pantry. "It's gone."

CHAPTER TWENTY-SEVEN

Dear Sophie,
In the winter, my beautiful garden is dormant and gray, except for a few lovely red berries. When there's no snow, it's a pretty bleak view from the great room. How can I dress it up for the holiday?

Avid Gardener in Swans Point,
Maryland

Dear Avid Gardener,
Hang a wreath on the garden gate or a bench. Cluster pinecones and unbreakable ornaments on a table or in an empty birdbath. Pop a Santa hat on a little garden statue or place a couple of battery-operated lanterns where you can see them at night.

Sophie

"Baxter, you don't think your children ate

it?" I asked.

"It wouldn't be the first time they snitched a snack. What's the problem? There's nothing wrong with that candy."

We explained that it might contain blood-thinning medicine.

"Good heavens! Bethany? Bradley?" He hurried up the stairs with more life in him than he'd had since Gwen died.

Wong's eyes met mine. "I'd bet anything Gwen gave it to Liza and Luis."

Wolf leaned against the kitchen counter. "Maybe you'd like to tell me what's going on?"

While Wong filled him in, I looked through the pantry again and discovered the box smashed behind big cereal boxes. "Found it! Wong, I'll let you recover it." I backed out of the pantry, my heart pounding.

Baxter returned to the kitchen. "The kids deny any involvement. That's a relief! What could have possessed Gwen to do such a thing?"

I slipped out the back door by myself. Something must have happened between Gwen and the Scrogginses, and between Gwen and Liza and Luis. I couldn't imagine why she wanted to kill any one of them. How could she have been so cheerful and happy at the cookie swap when she was waiting for Horace to die? I shuddered at the thought.

I couldn't prove that she had moved the mirror in Edith's house or that she had taken the cash meant for the housekeeper, but unless she had thrown it out, which was a possibility, I might find the little garden statue that was taken from Edith.

The Babineauxs had a concrete parking pad instead of a garage. But inside their back fence was a little storage shed, not unlike my own potting shed. The door creaked when I pulled it open. It was packed. Loaded to the very top with yard equipment, holiday items, beach gear, paint cans, rakes, snow shovels, buckets, and heaven knew what else.

I was about to give up when it dawned on me that Gwen had taken the statuette recently. It had to be near the front. I stood back and searched visually from left to right.

At the exact moment that I saw what might be a tiny head, someone behind me said, "You look pretty in green. Aren't you cold?"

I turned around to see Baxter. "Thank you." What could I say to him? He'd caught me looking in their shed. I could feel the hot flush of embarrassment rising in my face.

"What are you doing out here?"

There was no avoiding it. I told him about the strange things going on at the Scroggins home. "Someone took a statuette from their garden. I think it's a little boy. I'm sorry, Baxter, but I suspect that Gwen was the one pulling those stunts on Edith, though I can't imagine why. I thought if I found the little statue here, it would confirm that Gwen was the culprit."

"A couple of days ago, I would have been offended. But I'm learning a lot that I never knew about Gwen. I think you're in luck. Is that it?" Baxter pointed where I had been looking.

It was too high for me to reach without toppling other items, but Baxter was able to lift it out.

Edith was right. It wasn't anything valuable. Just a little boy with angel wings, and a bird perched on his hand. "Do you suppose they need this as evidence?"

"It's going to be pretty hard to prosecute Gwen. What do you say? Shall we return it to Edith?"

While we walked across the alley and through Edith's garden, I told Baxter about the son Edith and Horace lost.

I knocked on her back door. She opened it, and for one moment she gazed at Baxter with horror. But when she saw what he held, she placed her hands on her cheeks.

"Gwen took it?" Edith asked.

I nodded. "It appears that way."

"Where would you like me to place it?" asked Baxter.

Edith hustled outside and pointed to a circle of dead grass. "Right there, please."

She thanked us. "I cannot imagine what we did to Gwen to induce such animus toward us. I had no idea Gwen harbored hatred toward Horace and me. Why would she try to poison Horace and trick me into thinking I'd lost my mind?"

A small commotion in the alley caught our attention.

Baxter and I hurried out to the alley and over to Liza and Luis's backyard.

Nina and Wolf stood by the ladder, looking down at it.

Old and wooden, with years of paint drippings, it seemed like the same ladder. The second rung still hung on to it at a rakish angle. I bent to peer at it more closely. "I'm pretty sure it's the same one. See how the end of this rung starts out smooth, like someone sawed it? But the bottom part of the rung splintered when Baxter put his weight on it." I straightened up and stepped aside so Wolf could examine it.

Luis came running toward us from his house, with Liza chugging behind him.

"What's going on?" asked Luis, breathless.

Wolf faced him. "Your wife gave us permission to search your shed. We found this ladder. Do you know to whom it belongs?"

Luis shrugged when he said, "Yeah. It's mine."

"I assume you're aware that Baxter took a bad fall off the ladder?"

Luis held up his hands. "I'm just glad it wasn't worse. I teased him about landing on his feet like a cat."

"When did you use the ladder last?"

"About a week ago, I think." Luis looked to Liza. "Yeah. I hung Christmas lights around the front door."

"And it was okay then?"

Luis nodded. "No problem. I don't understand. What's the big deal with the ladder?"

Wolf didn't answer him. "Did Baxter ask to borrow your ladder?"

Luis's mouth twisted to the left. "I don't remember. But we're friends. He knows he's welcome to anything in the shed that he needs. It's not a biggie."

"You didn't notice the ladder missing?"

"No. We have another one. Shorter, but lighter to carry around. I bought the wooden one at a garage sale. If I'd realized how heavy wooden ladders are, I never would have bought it." Luis crossed his arms over his chest. "This is what you were looking for? Gosh, if you had told me, I would have brought it straight to you. You think the ladder is somehow involved in Gwen's death?"

Wolf deftly slid right over that question, too. "Could I come in for a moment? I'd like to ask you a few questions."

"Sure. You're welcome to take the ladder if you need it as evidence or anything."

"Thank you." Wolf spoke to Luis, but looked past him at Liza, who trembled, with her hands cupped over her nose and mouth.

I hurried to her side. "Are you okay?"

She nodded, but I could see that something was wrong. Her eyes were huge with fear. I wrapped an arm around her. "Could I make you a cup of tea?"

She grasped my hand. "You and Nina come inside with me."

We followed her to her kitchen. She motioned us into a little huddle. "I have to hear what he's going to ask Luis." Liza grabbed our sleeves. "I'm in big trouble."

Chapter Twenty-Eight

Dear Sophie,
Every year my husband turns into Clark Griswold and goes crazy with lights on the house. I'm always a nervous wreck, afraid he'll be shocked or start a fire. He says I'm silly. What do you think?

Nervous Nellie in Evergreen,
Montana

Dear Nervous Nellie,
Christmas lights can spark fires. Be sure to keep your tree watered. Never connect more than three strands of lights. And use the touch test. Extension cords and light cords should never be hot.

Sophie

We knew we shouldn't listen to Wolf's conversation with Luis, but we did anyway.

I'd been interrogated by Wolf once and could imagine his earnest expression. He didn't give away much of what he was thinking.

"I'm told that you are — were — Gwen Babineaux's psychiatrist," said Wolf.

Luis sounded incredulous. "Me? No. That sounds like something Gwen would claim, though. Look, I'll save you some time here, okay? It's my guess that Gwen suffered from histrionic personality disorder. She tended to be dramatic and act in ways that drew attention to her."

"Would this disorder predispose her to being violent?"

"You think she attacked the person who killed her? Interesting. But no, she would not have been more violent than anyone else. She had low self-esteem and sought the approval of other people. They tend to be overly dramatic. For instance, she was prone to being flirtatious. She did things that made people focus on her."

"It was all about her, huh?"

Luis smiled. "Yes, that's a good way of putting it. But more so than for most people."

"So, for instance, that might prompt her to mention a love affair in her Christmas letter?"

"An excellent example. She knew that would interest people and start them talking about her."

"Do *you* think she was having an affair?"

"That, I don't know. Making up an affair would be consistent with her condition."

"Where were you between six thirty in the afternoon yesterday and six thirty in the morning today?"

"At home, with my wife. She can confirm that." A wry grin crossed his face. "In fact, I, uh, almost electrocuted myself putting up Christmas lights. The rescue squad probably made note of the time."

"You went to the hospital?"

"I didn't think that was necessary, but Baxter called them, and they came to the house."

Wolf didn't say anything for a long moment. "Thanks. I assume you'll be around if I need to ask you anything else?"

"Sure. Anytime."

Liza's face had turned the color of a ripe peach with a red flush on it. She exhaled and bent over, letting her arms hang loose and her fingertips touch the floor.

"Are you okay?" Nina asked.

Liza shook and stood up straight. "We've got to talk. Not here. Too many ears around this place."

The three of us marched across the street to my house.

We hadn't even sat down when Nina demanded, "What's up? What do you know?"

"I've done something terrible." Liza spoke in a whisper, her eyes huge. "They're going to arrest me. They're going to put me in jail! I know they will! I can't go to jail!"

I hadn't expected this. Was she going to confess to murdering Gwen?

"You know the ladder that broke causing Baxter to fall off his roof?" asked Liza.

"We were there," I said. "After he fell."

"I wanted to prove to Luis that he's not homeowner handyman material. That we need a condo. No ladders, no saws, no manly man equipment."

"*You* sawed that rung?" I was horrified.

"Don't look at me like that! It was only the second rung. I didn't want Luis to plummet from the top. How could I know Baxter would borrow it and schlep it to his roof? I figured Luis would use it on the ground, step on it, *boom,* little fall, big scare. I never thought anyone would get hurt. They're going to find my fingerprints all over that ladder! They'll think I killed Gwen!"

"Why would they think that?" I stood up and put on water for coffee. Decaf. Liza didn't need to be any more agitated than she already was.

"Obviously the ladder is tied to her death somehow. Why else would they care about a rotten old ladder? Oy! I can't go to jail. Do you think they'll go easy on me since I didn't mean to hurt anyone?"

I took out the cream and sugar. "I doubt that it will come to that. You and Luis own the ladder, Liza. They'll expect to find your fingerprints on it."

She bounced in her chair. "You're right! Why didn't I think of that? Oh, thank you!" She leaned back against her chair. "I'm so relieved. The Christmas light thing didn't work out so well, either. I'm done trying to booby-trap Luis's stuff."

It was all I could do to speak calmly. "Christmas lights? You frayed that cord on purpose?"

"Just a little bit. I didn't know you could get seriously hurt. I thought it was like a little battery jolt. I'm not the only one. Baxter said Elvin used to *wrap* himself up in lights. I thought they were harmless."

I was afraid to ask, but I did anyway. "Is there anything else you might have tampered with?"

Liza flapped her hands at me. "Goodness, Sophie, you make it sound like I'm an axe murderer or something. I just wanted to teach Luis a lesson, that's all."

I didn't know how to bring it up in a nice way, but this was as good a time as any. "I noticed that you bought rat poison the other day."

Nina coughed. "Please tell me you don't have rats!"

Liza groaned. "I swear I hear noises in our basement. It has to be mice. But Luis yelled at me for buying rat poison. He was totally right. Oscar would lap it up in a second. It's too dangerous to have around. I threw it out."

"That's good," said Nina in a most uncertain tone. "It's not like you poisoned anyone or whacked Gwen over the head or anything. Right?"

Liza laughed. "You're so funny! I haven't a reason in the world to want to kill Gwen. My money is on Baxter's ex-wife, Patty. Now, there's someone who had a motive."

"Shh!" Nina waved at Liza just as Patty knocked on the kitchen door and stepped inside.

"Is that coffee I smell? I feel like such a moocher." Patty settled into a chair by the fireplace. "I'm exhausted. I have to tell you, this is the last thing I expected when I came here. I knew something was wrong when I read Gwen's Christmas letter, but in my wildest dreams I never imagined she would be murdered."

"How are the kids?" asked Nina.

Patty tilted her head and focused on Liza. "I don't know how I can ever thank Luis. He's been there for all the Babineauxs, especially Baxter and the children. He's helping them talk through their feelings and deal with Gwen's death." She smiled. "I think Bethany might have a little crush on him. His patients must fall for him all the time. He's so comforting."

Liza beamed. "Luis is quite well regarded in his field. I'm glad he could help the children."

I poured the coffee into my Christmas mugs with the candy-cane handles and set out a platter of Scotcheroos along with paper napkins printed with huge old-fashioned Christmas lights.

When everyone sat at the table, I asked Patty about Elvin. "I understand he and Sugar will be staying through the holidays."

"Maybe longer than that. Gwen's death has brought everyone closer together. In a weird way, we all appreciate each other more. We know it could happen to any of us. Well, not murder, I hope, but you never know what life will bring. Anyway, Elvin is planning to stick around to help out Baxter.

The poor guy needs help. If Baxter argued with Gwen half as much as Bethany claims, you'd think he'd be glad to be rid of her." Patty bit into a Scotcheroo. "I always forget how wonderful these are. I really should bake them for the kids. Maybe I will now."

"Lots of fights, huh?" asked Nina.

"Mmm." Patty nodded her head. "Mostly about money, from what I can gather. Gwen refused to tighten the purse strings. She liked living lavishly. Did you know that Kat's room is set up like a little castle? Gwen paid someone to paint the walls with scenes from a fairy-tale book. That child is going to think she's a princess."

I wanted to get back to Elvin. It was a long shot that the glasses Kat had found meant anything, yet they still worried me. "Is Elvin moving in with Baxter permanently? I thought he had some kind of charity thing he does. Feeding children or something."

"He can do that anywhere. I don't know that they've decided anything yet, but Baxter would be lucky to have Elvin around."

Liza snorted. "If Baxter doesn't want him, I'll take Elvin in. He takes out their trash, helps Baxter decorate the house, and cleans their kitchen."

"That's Elvin!" said Patty. "You know how people say *nice guys finish last*? They mean

Elvin. I probably married the wrong brother. Of course, when we were young, I saw things differently than I do now. Baxter had the good job and great looks. He was athletic and had job prospects. Look at him today, living in a fancy house and broke as can be. But, you know, when I was younger, married to Baxter, and stuck on the highway with a flat tire and a van full of kids, it was Elvin I called, not Baxter. Elvin would help out anybody. That's just how he is."

My eyes met Nina's. I felt certain she was thinking along the same lines as me. Would Elvin have murdered Gwen to help Baxter out?

CHAPTER TWENTY-NINE

Dear Sophie,
I was roped into bringing one hundred cookies to a fundraiser at my child's school. Now someone has dropped out (were I only that wise!) and they expect me to bring 250 cookies. What's the easiest cookie to bake?

Overworked Dad in North Star,
Nebraska

Dear Overworked Dad,
The spritz cookie is your best choice. You can press out a lot of cookies in no time at all. They're butter cookies, which will appeal to most people, and you can make assorted shapes, which are especially festive.

Sophie

"Things are going to change now that Gwen's gone." Patty gulped coffee. "I needed this. Remember how we were talking about me moving here? I've made up my mind to stay. Bethany and Bradley only have a few more years before they're off to college. Baxter is such a mess they can't depend on him right now. I have some straightening out to do with those kids. Job number one is getting Bethany back into school." Patty sighed. "I know I'm not supposed to speak ill of the dead, but Gwen sure made a mess of things when she broke up my marriage to Baxter." Her nostrils flared. "If she hadn't come along, my children wouldn't have all these issues."

A little chill ran along my arms. I had to find out the time of death. Patty had been at my house until Luis was injured. After that, I couldn't account for her. Especially that little trip out of the house in the middle of the night.

"Sophie, you've been wonderful to put me up. I'll be out of your hair now. I'm moving into a guest room at Baxter's."

Liza tucked her head coyly and wiggled her eyebrows. "That was some quick work. How convenient of you to be there to comfort him."

"It's not like that." Patty waved her off. "If you only knew how thick the air is in that house. Trust me, there's no hanky-panky."

Nina appeared thoughtful. "Won't that look bad for Baxter? I mean, before a jury or to the police?"

Patty's eyes grew wide. "I hadn't thought about that."

Liza *tsk*ed. "It doesn't sound good to me. Ex-wife moves in one hour after new wife's corpse is found?"

"That's terrible!" Patty sat back. "Well, it's not like that, and I have witnesses. The kids, Sugar, and Elvin can see that I'm in a guest room."

"You do realize," I said, "that you're all talking about it as though you know that Baxter killed Gwen."

"Oh, Baxter didn't murder her. It was Natasha." Patty spoke matter-of-factly.

"How do you know?" Nina asked.

"I can tell from the kinds of questions the cops are asking. Everything is about Natasha's relationship with Gwen."

"I know she's your friend, but it does seem as though everything points toward Natasha." Liza brushed her hair out of her face. "Her garage, her wrapping paper, she had that column in the paper recently about how to wrap big objects, and from what I understand that was exactly how Gwen was wrapped up. Not to mention what she posted on the Internet."

Nina wasn't one of Natasha's fans, but I saw the worry on her face. It didn't look good for Natasha. But why had the mouse been in her workroom if it was Gwen who had been tormenting Edith?

Wolf knocked on the kitchen door.

"Oh no, not him again!" Patty exclaimed.

I opened the door for Wolf who said, "Sorry to interrupt —"

Patty's face turned purple. "Look, I'm telling you for the last time that I did not murder Gwen. Did I hate her? Yes! Despise her? Lie awake at night imagining horrible things would happen to her? Yes! But I did not kill her. How would you feel if someone stole your husband and then took your children, too? It was like she sucked the oxygen out of the very air I breathe and left me with nothing. But let me be clear. I did not kill her!" She pounded a fist on my kitchen table for emphasis.

Wolf had listened quietly. In a soft tone he said, "Sophie, Mrs. Scroggins asked me to bring your coats over to you." He handed me the coats Nina and I had left at Edith's house. "But thank you for clarifying that, Patty. It was most helpful." He left and shut the door.

"Nooo!" wailed Patty. "Did I say something incriminating?"

When everyone left, I pulled on my coat, slipped the toy glasses into my pocket, and took a stroll intending to visit Rocking Horse Toys. On a whim, I turned the corner and went a couple of blocks out of my way to pass by Alex's law office.

I was sorry I did. Fortunately, I was across the street when the door opened and Sugar left. But I didn't miss the way she grabbed Alex's shirt collar and planted a big smooch on his lips.

I confess I was steaming a little bit when Phyllis, Horace's secretary, tugged on my arm.

"Sophie! I'm so glad I ran into you. I go to sit with Horace every day, but he worries me so. He just doesn't seem to be getting any better. I'm not a relative, so they never tell me much about what's going on with him. When I went by Baxter's house with a casserole, he said you've been checking in on Edith. Has she told you anything?"

The door to Alex's office closed, and Sugar sashayed along the sidewalk, a little smile playing on her lips.

I shifted my focus to Phyllis. "I can ask Edith. I'm afraid you probably know more than I do."

"Thank you. Edith isn't very forthcoming. I think she's always been resentful of my relationship with Horace."

"Oh?" I gazed at her pretty brown eyes. Was she the author of the girlish love letter?

"Horace and I have worked together so many years. I think today they call it an office spouse. My ex-husband used to hate that term. But it applies to Horace and me. He knows everything about me" — her gaze drifted sadly downward — "except how much I care about him."

"Did you know Horace before you went to work for him?"

"I sure did. Edith acts like she's the only one who was born and raised in Old Town, but I was, too. I remember her wedding — the one that didn't happen because her fiancé died? Oh my word, you would have thought she was royalty. It was the biggest wedding you can imagine. Everyone who was anyone was invited. And then the big shock when she had to bury him instead of marry him. I never understood what Horace saw in her. She was pretty once, of course. You know her parents sent her off to study art at the Sorbonne. She had everything . . ."

"And then she got Horace, too."

"Hmm, lucky girl. It's a pity she never appreciated him."

I didn't know what to do. That remark about office spouses made me wonder if their relationship went further outside of the office, too. "You're a very good friend to visit Horace every day."

"The office reopens officially on Monday. Goodness, but there's a lot to do. I hope he can come home soon. People mend so much faster at home."

Had she really said *come home*? As if he was coming home to her? As gently as I could, I said, "It sounds like you had a crush on him when you were young."

"How did you know?"

"You're obviously still extremely fond of him."

She patted my arm. "Let me know what Edith tells you. I'm quite anxious about his condition."

I watched her walk away, wishing she were Brown-Eyed Girl.

I window-shopped as I walked, but my heart wasn't in it. And then I spotted Natasha through a store window. She was perfectly coiffed and dressed in a coat and matching plaid scarf in her signature robin's-egg blue. Her chic winter boots had impossibly high heels. She seemed totally pulled together. But she held a gold star in her hands and didn't move. She simply stood there with tears streaming down her otherwise flawless makeup.

I hurried inside. "Nat?" I placed my hand against her back.

"They laughed at me, Sophie." She spoke in a bare whisper. "I'm the big joke around town."

"Who?"

"The women who work here."

I glanced toward the cash register. They were snickering all right. One even made motions like she was bashing the other one over her head.

I took the star out of Natasha's hands. "Let's go home." I placed my arm around her and guided her toward the door.

We shuffled by the women, who burst into laughter as we left. Natasha didn't say much on the way home. I didn't, either.

Safely back in my kitchen, I put on the kettle for tea and handed her a warm washcloth to clean her face. "Spiced holiday tea, or just plain black tea?"

"Plain."

She had walked home with her head bent forward and still sat that way at my kitchen table. I lit a fire and helped her out of the coat she hadn't bothered to take off.

Her hands trembled. I'd never seen her this was — beaten down and hopeless.

I doctored her tea with a little sugar and milk, which I knew she didn't take. Mars had said she wasn't eating, so I was determined to get some food into her. I found the cookies she had baked for the cookie swap and brought a few to her on a little plate. Surely she would eat her own cookies.

I sat down and watched her. "Tell me what's going on."

She didn't raise her eyes. "I work all the time. Around the clock. Every day. I try so hard to look and be professional. My house is impeccable. Do you know what I've gone through to get where I am? And in one second, Gwen wiped out all my efforts. No one remembers my fabulous recipes or my beautiful decorating tips. All they can see is those hideous pictures. I'm a laughingstock. I'm ruined."

"They say there's no such thing as bad publicity." I wasn't sure I agreed with that, but it was what she needed to hear. "Why don't you turn this around by using it to your advantage?"

"That's impossible."

"What if you went online and made a joke about having a bad hair day? You could ask people to submit pictures of their bad hair days and make a contest out of it."

Natasha sat up straighter. "And I could tell them how to fix their hair problems!"

"Noooo. You wouldn't want them telling you how to fix your hair problem in those pictures."

"They think I already have by murdering Gwen. Why did Gwen hate me so much? Why did she post those stupid pictures?"

"You often tell me that people want to be you. In this case, I think Gwen might have wished she were more like you."

"I don't know why anyone would want to be me. No one likes me. Everyone comes over to your house instead of mine. Maybe I should be more like you. I mean, look how you're dressed. You don't care what people think. You don't even have a signature color. Your house isn't fashionable, you even use red and green to decorate for Christmas, just no originality at all."

I would have protested if she hadn't looked so miserable.

"Mars says you're even cheerful in the morning."

"Not every morning."

Natasha pointed at her cookies. "Look at these pathetic cookies you baked —"

"You baked those."

She picked one up and nibbled on it. "See how distracted I am? I didn't even recognize my own cookies. They're good, too!" She ate the cookie and helped herself to two more. "I should bake more of these. I know! Gwen goofed everything up, but I'll go forward with the big block decorating party just like I planned. I'll bake cookies, you can bring mulled cider or hot chocolate. Think you could manage that? And we'll finish stringing lights on the trees along the sidewalk and on the homes of those who can't do it themselves. That will restore my holiday spirit."

She stood up but bent over to hug me. "And one day, you really must let me tell you what you should do with this kitchen."

After she left, I grabbed my coat and made my way to Rocking Horse Toys. It teemed with children and parents. I waived at Twiggy briefly. "Kat's not here?"

"Sugar is supposed to pick her up from school."

A woman sidled over to us clutching two dolls in her hands. They were identical except for the color of their dresses. "Can you set these aside for me to pick up tomorrow?" she whispered. She flicked a credit card at Twiggy and hurried back to twin girls who were admiring a dollhouse.

The busy store was perfect for what I had in mind. I wasn't sure I wanted to draw Elvin's attention just yet. I browsed through the store in search of mice like the one Edith had bought. Two of them perched on a shelf laden with stuffed animals. My heart thudded when I saw them. I reached into my pocket and pulled out the glasses Kat said she had found in the Babineaux living room. I held them up to one of the mice. They were a perfect match.

I slid the glasses back into my pocket and brought the two mice to the register to pay for them. Twiggy smiled when she took them from me. "These are so cute. They've sold very well for us."

"Did Gwen or Baxter buy one?"

"Not that I know of. Excuse me, Sophie. Elvin, would you please ring these up?" Twiggy hurried off.

Elvin looked at the mice in his hands. He paused for a long moment. Without raising his head, his eyes moved up to meet mine. A little chill shook through me. Elvin was definitely uneasy.

He forced a smile. "Cute little guys, aren't they?"

I tried to sound casual. "I thought Kat might like one. She seems to have the glasses but not the mouse." I pulled the

359

glasses out of my pocket to show him.

The genial flush in his face blanched to white. He rang up the mice and with a shaking hand, slid them into a bag.

I persisted. "Do you know where Kat found these?"

"Not a clue." He told me the price.

I handed over the cash. "That's funny. I thought you told Kat she could have them."

His Adam's apple bobbed. In a very low voice, he said, "She found them in the living room. Okay? I didn't know they belonged to a mouse."

"But you do now."

"I guess Gwen or somebody had one of those mice. Maybe the glasses broke off when she was decorating. Excuse me, Sophie. There's a line of customers behind you."

I backed away certain of one thing — Elvin knew more than he was saying. I was pondering a way to pry more information out of Elvin when I heard Twiggy scream, "No!"

Jonah did his best to calm her but there was no hope of that. Twiggy ran past me to the back of the store.

"Everything okay?" I asked Jonah.

"Kat's missing."

"Can I help?"

"Uh, sure. We're going over to her school right now. The more people searching for her, the better."

Twiggy returned with their coats, and we fled out the door before they had them on.

We arrived to a gathering of a distressed teacher, Sugar, assorted police officers, and, much to my surprise, Alex. For once, Sugar wasn't clinging to him.

The teacher was explaining that she had brought in a classroom kitten, but it turned out that one of the little boys was allergic to it. "So I informed the children that it would be Harry's last day with us. Kat wouldn't let Harry out of her arms. She just clung to him and accused me and the allergic boy of lying about his allergy. I was telling Sugar about it, and when we looked around, Kat and Harry were gone."

"Have you searched the school?" asked a police officer.

"Yes, of course."

Sugar seized Alex's arm with both of her hands. "Could social services have taken her? Is that something they would do? Sneaky like that?"

"Social services?" Twiggy appeared doubtful. "Why would they snatch her?"

"Because Baxter isn't her father. And no one knows who her dad is," I clarified.

Sugar glared at me. "I know who he is."

Everyone turned toward her. Jonah rolled his eyes and brushed a shock of hair off his forehead.

"*I'm* Kat's mother," declared Sugar.

CHAPTER THIRTY

Dear Natasha,
We have a TV over our mantel, and a fireplace under it. Our taste leans to clean, modern décor. How do we decorate it for Christmas?
    The Klauses Jr. in North Pole, Alaska

Dear The Klauses Jr.,
Leave the mantel bare. Place a narrow white Christmas tree on each side of the fireplace. Decorate it with solid-colored ornaments in rings. Red at the top, orange, yellow, green, blue, and finally violet. Festive, sparse, and modern!
                                        Natasha

I did a double take. "I thought you were Gwen's daughter and Kat's sister."

Sugar glanced at Alex, who said, "Social services is much more professional than that. And they wouldn't have taken the kitten."

Twiggy staggered backward into Jonah. "*You're* Kat's mother? Not Gwen?"

Sugar placed her hands on her hips. "I am Kat's real mother. I'm downright ashamed by what a lousy mother I was. Look, let's split up and look for her. I'll explain after we find her."

They assigned me the way back to our block. It was a long shot, but Kat might have gone home. I wished I had Daisy with me. She'd be more likely to notice a little girl with a cat if Kat were hiding somewhere.

I walked along the sidewalk, peering behind bushes. There were too many little passages leading to backyards. Kat could be anywhere. I kept walking. When I neared our block, I cut through the alley behind the Babineaux house, intending to pick up Daisy at Mars's house.

The gate to Edith's garden hung open. Would Kat have wandered in there? Anything was possible. I peeked inside. "Kat?"

I didn't see her anywhere. The chandelier glowed in Edith's dining room window. I scouted the garden, poking around a bit. When I neared the house, I made out Edith sitting at the dining room table. Across from her, little Kat drew something.

I knocked on the back door.

Edith opened it and invited me in. She was actually attractive when she smiled.

"I see you have a visitor. Everyone is in a panic about her."

"I should hope so! I've been phoning the Babineaux house, but the line is always busy. She doesn't want to go home."

"Did she hide in your yard?"

"I heard her crying. She was so sad, holding that kitten and whimpering. So I brought her inside and gave her something to eat. She told me that everyone lies about cat allergies and that she won't let them take Harry away from her. Given that she just lost her mother, I think it's extremely unreasonable to take away the cat. What are they thinking?"

I explained what had happened. "I'd better call Alex's cell phone to let them know she's safe."

When I hung up, I watched Edith with Kat. A gentleness had replaced the anger in Edith's face. The taut lines and cold eyes had softened.

Edith heaped praise on Kat's drawing. She sat in the chair next to Kat, who held Harry.

"Kat," said Edith, "your family is looking for you. They're very worried about you and Harry."

"Don't tell them I'm here. They'll take Harry away. My mommy went away. I don't want Harry to leave, too."

Edith pulled Kat onto her lap. "They love you as much as you love Harry. I'll make you a promise. If they won't let you keep Harry, he can stay here. That way you can come over to play with him any time you want."

Kat nestled her head against Edith's shoulder. I had to turn away to wipe the tears off my face.

An hour later, Kat and Harry were safely home and playing in Kat's princess bedroom. In the living room, Sugar thanked us all for helping.

Sugar clung to Alex again as she told us about Kat, which did not make me happy.

"When Kat was three months old, I left her with my mother, Gwen. I was a dancer at the time — pole, not ballet — and I left with my new boyfriend, who was in a little band that was touring the country. I'm ashamed that I did that, but I just wasn't ready to settle down with a child. When I came back, Mom was gone. I didn't know anything about Baxter or their marriage or her new name. I've spent the last five years searching for her on the Internet. When

Elvin said he was going to visit his brother, I didn't make the connection until we drove up, and there she was."

Sugar looked straight at Twiggy, who had cried when she saw Kat and appeared to be on the verge of tears again. "Mom, um, was a dancer herself, but she'd gotten too old to make any money at it. She was stuck with my baby and a job in a bar that didn't pay enough for her to make ends meet. She resented me for being young, and having my life ahead of me, and dumping my child on her. She said when she met Baxter, it was like all her dreams came true. Baxter wanted to have another baby, and Mom wanted Baxter. She told him that Kat was her daughter. She moved and changed her cell phone number, and I couldn't find her. I didn't know she had married Baxter. I walked away from Kat when she was a baby, something I will always regret. But Mom could see that I've changed and grown up. Alex, you explain the legal stuff."

"Gwen had obtained custody of Kat. When Sugar told me about Kat, we brought an emergency motion in the court. I couldn't imagine anything worse for Kat than losing the woman she thought was her mother, and then being removed from her home at Christmas."

Sugar looked at Jonah, raised her eyebrows, and gestured toward Twiggy.

Twiggy collapsed into a chair. "Oh no. I knew it. You're leaving me."

Jonah, who had been silent, kneeled on the floor, picked up Twiggy's hand, and glared at Sugar. "See what you've done now? Did I ask you to let me do this in my own time?"

Twiggy sobbed.

"Honey, don't cry. I'm not leaving you." Jonah gently wiped tears off Twiggy's face. "You see, I met Sugar once before at a convention in Vegas and — don't cry, Twiggy! I swear I'm not leaving you."

She couldn't stop. Jonah shot Sugar a look that could have fried her. "Twig, it was before I ever met you. It was just one night, but you know how that can be. It just happened. I didn't want to upset everyone until the paternity tests came back, but there's a good chance that I'm Kat's father."

Twiggy froze. Her eyes flicked between Jonah and Sugar.

"Oh, you're her father, all right," protested Sugar. "Who needs a paternity test? She's just exactly like you."

Jonah focused on Twiggy. "Honey, I swear I didn't know anything about this until Sugar came to town." He hugged Twiggy to him. "I thought you'd be upset, that's why I wanted the paternity results first."

Twiggy sobbed like she'd lost her best friend.

"Does Kat know any of this yet?" I asked.

"When we know for sure," said Jonah, "we're going to ask Luis to help us break it to her. I'm not taking any chances. It's going to be a huge shock. I can't imagine how her little mind will be able to deal with it all."

They had blown *my* mind! I sat down on the sofa, my head reeling.

I glanced up at the mantel between the two orange-flocked Christmas trees. Gwen had decorated the mantel in this room only a few days ago. At the time, no one had dreamed how many things would change in this house. Maybe she thought she was saving Kat from heartbreak by pretending to be her mother. Whatever her reasons, she had been right about the stag-head candleholders. The mantel wasn't the same without them.

I gazed around the room. "Where's the lamp that was in the corner?"

Sugar sighed. "The police took it. The killer used the lampshade to wrap Mom."

While Twiggy cried, and the others talked about Kat, I wondered about the mouse and the glasses that it had lost. Gwen had been hit over the head by something heavy. I searched the living room for an object that could have been used. Of course, the police had probably collected anything that they thought was suitable. Except for the candlesticks. I had a pair of old sterling candlesticks that had belonged to my grandmother. They were weighted in the bottom. I wished I had picked up one of Gwen's to see how heavy they were. I could well imagine someone grabbing one of them and slamming it over Gwen's head. Those antler parts could be very dangerous.

I left the chaos, walked through the kitchen, and tiptoed up the back stairway to peek in on Kat. I found Baxter watching her from her doorway. He appeared a bit disheveled, as though he hadn't bothered to comb his hair or shower. He held a finger up over his lips.

I peered into Kat's room. Sound asleep in a fancy bed, she had curled up and drifted off holding Harry, a gray tabby, in her arms. Above her, a grand crown held sheer pink and white panels that cascaded down the back of the bed and a foot or so along the sides. Exactly as Patty had described, the walls were painted with scenes depicting huge windows looking out over castles and unicorns roaming the hills.

Baxter closed the door.

"How are you doing?" I asked.

He snorted. "Every single day I learn something else that Gwen lied about. She messed up a lot of lives."

"Including yours?" It slipped out.

"I'm an old guy. Didn't think anything could surprise me anymore. But Kat . . . It breaks my heart. Mostly Gwen messed me up by spending every cent I had. The day you found Gwen, the antiques dealer called and yelled at me because Gwen's check bounced for that fancy silver sleigh and the candlesticks she bought. Wanna hear something pathetic? I couldn't cover it. I don't even have the money to pay for Gwen's casket and funeral. I had to return that silver stuff so he wouldn't call the cops. I'm living day to day, minute to minute, wondering which of Gwen's lies will be uncovered next and how I'm going to make it right."

Footsteps sounded on the stairs. Luis appeared carrying a large box wrapped in white paper printed with sheet music. A gigantic lacy silver bow clung to the top. "Would you mind if I hid this gift with you? Liza is so nosy. She always searches the house for her gifts. She would open it and rewrap it if she found it. Just this once, I'd like to surprise her."

"Ohhh," I exclaimed. "What is it?"

Luis set the package down and smiled at me. Waving his forefinger, he said, "Not a chance. This year her present will be a surprise."

Ouch. Baxter didn't need any more surprises. But he didn't show any dismay at hearing the word.

"Of course. I'll stick it in here. Come get it when you're ready, Luis."

"Thanks! What's going on downstairs?"

Baxter filled him in on what had happened.

"And how do you feel about that?" asked Luis.

"Well, let's see. I lost my job, then I lost my wife, now I've lost my little girl, and I don't know how long the bank will let us stay in this house. How do you think I'm feeling?"

Luis nodded. "Would you excuse us, Sophie?"

I gladly took my leave, grateful that Luis knew what to say to Baxter. What can you say to someone going through so many crises at once? The sun might come out tomorrow, but it would take Baxter a long time to crawl out from under all his troubles and see anything sunny. If he didn't end up in jail first for killing Gwen.

I left their house only to discover Mars and Bernie in front of my home. "What are you doing now? I thought you were finished."

"Just a final touch," said Bernie.

Mars glared at me. "Your boyfriend is a jerk!"

I suspected I would take some heat for putting it this way, but I dared ask, "Which one?"

"The lawyer. He refused to represent Natasha."

"She's getting a lawyer?"

"The police showed up again today, this time asking questions about Horace. By the way, do you know anything about peanut brittle and pink boxes?"

"They hopped on that fast!"

"So you do know about this? Natasha and I had no idea what they were talking about. They confiscated her pink boxes."

Nina yoo-hooed from the front of her house. Lights were being draped by men clambering over the roof. She jogged across the street. "I am sooo going to outdo you guys!"

"Professionals?" Bernie scowled.

Nina grinned at him and grabbed my

sleeve. "Guess what? I know who Brown-Eyed Girl is."

CHAPTER THIRTY-ONE

Dear Natasha,
I have such problems tying special bows on packages. I heard that you have an easy way to do it?
All Thumbs in Cranberry, Maryland

Dear All Thumbs,
Take a very long piece of wired ribbon. Starting on one end, tie a simple bow. Use part of the remaining length to tie another bow around the middle of the first one. Use the remainder to tie a third bow around the middle of the other two. Bend the bow parts so they look pretty.
Natasha

"Who?" I could use some good news.
"Hold it!" Mars interrupted. "I want to know about the pink boxes first."
There was so much to talk about. "I have a big pot of chicken stew —"

Bernie said, "I'll bring dessert."

Nina chimed in, "I'll pick up rustic bread and some cheeses."

They looked at Mars, who shrugged. "Okay, wine."

An hour later, we met at my house. I had already heated the stew and built a fire. I switched on the indoor Christmas lights, and the outdoor lights gleamed when I gazed through the windows. I missed the smell of something wonderful baking in the oven, but fresh pine scented the room like Christmas.

Nina sliced rustic country bread and set it on the cutting board I had placed in the middle of the table instead of a centerpiece. But I had circled it with a string of silver stars, beads, and mirrors that caught the glow from the fire.

I placed each type of cheese on a small white platter and added a cheese knife with a snowman handle. Mars carried them to the table and poured wine into fun hand-painted red, white, and green wineglasses he and Natasha had given me as a gift. With polka dots and stripes, and words like *naughty* and *nice,* they were joyous and perfect for a get-together of old friends.

Bernie refused to open the dessert box and left it on the counter as a surprise.

Daisy settled in front of the fire with Mochie, prompting Bernie to observe, "I spend all day in the restaurant, which is decorated to the hilt. But there's nothing like a dog and a cat by a crackling fire, good friends, and good food."

I ladled the stew into red soup bowls, and we sat down to eat.

"Didn't Natasha want to join us?" I asked.

Mars winced. "I didn't want her here. She's too agitated. I need to think this through with people who won't shout or pout. All she does is decorate and let me tell you, all that black is only making things worse. It's gloom and doom at our house. So tell me about the pink boxes."

Nina and I filled him in about Edith testing the contents of the pink box in Horace's office and finding peanut brittle in Gwen's kitchen.

"Edith is pretty sharp," said Bernie. "I could have told you that. She and Horace used to come to the restaurant to eat fairly regularly. In fact, she stopped by for takeout the day of the cookie swap."

"So that was where she went! I checked on her, but only her housekeeper was home. She was afraid to eat the food in her home."

Bernie helped himself to a slice of the rustic bread. "No cobwebs in that brain.

However, while it's no secret that I don't share Mars's admiration of Natasha, I can't really imagine her murdering Gwen, even if Gwen did post ugly things about her on Facebook. I must wonder, though, why the police collected pink boxes from Natasha . . ."

Mars grimaced. "Me, too. Horace and Natasha hardly have any contact. You know, this could be solved very quickly if Horace came around and confirmed that Gwen gave him the peanut brittle."

Nina was about to pop a piece of bread with Brie into her mouth. She stopped short. "I hadn't thought of that. Gwen must have been worried that he might recuperate. I wonder if he was in danger."

"If it was Gwen, then he's safe now," said Bernie. "But it begs the question whether Gwen was killed because of Horace. Did someone know she meant to kill him? Did that person murder her to prevent her from trying again?"

Nina kicked me under the table. I knew what she wanted, but I felt terrible about spreading the story of Brown-Eyed Girl and Moondoggie. Still, someone had murdered Gwen. Nina was right. Something was up. It was possible that Gwen's motivation in getting rid of Horace had nothing to do with her death. Then again, it just might.

I capitulated and relayed the story of Horace and his long-lost love.

Mars snorted. "Oh, puleeeze. Women are always excited about old love letters. Sophie probably grabbed the wrong thing, and poor Horace will be embarrassed to death when he finds out."

"Call me a romantic if you like, but I find it rather charming," said Bernie. "Imagine pining for this Brown-Eyed Girl for so many years."

Mars pretended to wipe tears away. "What a sap! You're as ridiculously sentimental as they are."

Nina leaned forward, her eyes bright. "I know who she is. It's Jill, who owns Fleur de Lis. When she was decorating my house, I very cunningly asked questions about her youth. Turns out she knew Horace! Her family moved away when she was fifteen. Isn't that a perfect fit?"

"Did you mention Moondoggie or Brown-Eyed Girl?" I asked.

Nina beamed. "I did. She said she has a friend who calls her his Brown-Eyed Girl!" Nina squealed with glee. "I think we should arrange a private meeting for them after Horace gets out of the hospital." She laced her fingers and stretched her arms proudly.

"But they already know each other." I sipped my wine. "Why wouldn't they have gotten together on their own?"

"Edith!" said Nina. "He told you she could never know."

Mars rolled his eyes. "I seriously doubt they've walked the streets in Old Town as adults without mentioning their undying love for each other. They've probably had a big laugh over it."

"Horace was Baxter's boss," I said. "Would Baxter have gained anything from his death?"

Mars sliced more bread. "He probably would have been promoted. Maybe to president of the company."

"Maybe Horace's secretary, Phyllis, did Gwen in," said Bernie. "She's been mooning over Horace since I moved here, and long before that, I'm sure. Maybe she couldn't take it anymore."

"She's been at his bedside every day." I cut a teeny piece of a creamy goat-cheese log that had been rolled in sweetly tart dried cranberries. "We should find out where she was that night and the next day."

Nina stopped eating. "What if it's Edith?"

The rest of us groaned.

"No, hear me out. Think about it. If Horace and Gwen were really having an affair, maybe Edith lost her marbles and killed her. You can't say her behavior is completely normal."

That silenced us.

I thought aloud. "So Edith confronted Gwen at Gwen's house and whacked her over the head with something. But that's where it falls apart. I don't see Edith having the strength to carry Gwen over to your garage."

"What if she lured her there and that's where she killed her?" suggested Bernie.

Mars shook his head and spoke with his mouth full, "Very little blood. She must have been killed somewhere else."

"At least we know Horace didn't kill Gwen. There are plenty of people who had motives, though." I finished the last bite of my stew.

Mars fetched a pad of paper and wrote as he spoke. "I'm making a list. There's Natasha, whom we know did not kill Gwen but had plenty of reason after Gwen posted those pictures of her. I'm only putting her on the suspect list because the three of you will complain endlessly if I don't."

"Baxter, who couldn't stop Gwen from running through their money," I added. "And Sugar, who wanted her daughter, Kat, back from her mom."

The three of them gasped.

"Oh, I didn't tell you about that? Gwen is Sugar's mother. Sugar is Kat's mother. Sugar took off, leaving baby Kat with Gwen, so Gwen pretended to be Kat's mother."

Mars wrote furiously.

"And get this," I added. "Jonah is very likely Kat's father!"

"How is that possible?" asked Nina.

"Sugar met Jonah in Las Vegas before he married Twiggy. They had a one-night stand, and Kat is the result."

"That family was so messed up!" Nina broke off a piece of bread and scooped up the remaining goat cheese. "Don't forget about Patty! She gained the most by Gwen's death. She has Bethany and Bradley back and no one fighting her for them."

"And Elvin. Patty said he would do anything for them. He might have killed Gwen for Baxter or Patty or even for the kids if he thought Gwen was a problem." I paused for a minute and looked at my friends. "Whoever killed Gwen removed a lampshade from the Babineaux house. That means the killer was in their living room at some point. I know this is going to sound odd, but Edith bought a toy mouse —"

I rose from my chair and fetched one, along with the extra glasses. "— that was stolen from her home. It looked like this. I found it without glasses on the floor near Natasha's work island. Then Kat turned up with these" — I held up the glasses to the mouse so they could see the match — "which she found in the Babineaux living room. Elvin told her she could have them. When I bought this mouse today, I mentioned it to him. You should have seen him. He knows something."

"Maybe he's the killer. How can we get him to confess?" asked Mars.

Bernie squinted at me. "I'm not sure I follow the importance of the mouse."

"Edith said it disappeared from her house the evening of the cookie swap. If Gwen was the one tormenting Edith, she must have slipped into Edith's house, taken the mouse, and then gone home to her living room, where something happened to the mouse to break off the glasses."

"You mean Gwen was holding the mouse when she was conked over the head and the mouse flew out of her hand and broke?" asked Mars. "Or someone threw the mouse?"

"And then Gwen's murderer took her to your garage, wrapped her, and for some reason also took the mouse but forgot him on the floor," Nina speculated.

"Why would the killer take the mouse?" asked Mars. "That's crazy."

Bernie sat back. "Maybe it was completely reasonable under the circumstances. The killer must have worked fast out of fear he would be discovered there with Gwen's corpse."

"But he didn't know the glasses had broken off and were still in the living room," I finished. "So who was it?"

"Well," said Nina, "if that's how it happened, then we can count out Patty and Sugar. Patty is tiny. And while Sugar is fairly tall, I don't see either of them having the strength to move Gwen to Natasha's workshop."

"Unless they had help." Bernie stacked the empty soup bowls. "Elvin or Baxter might have helped either one of them." He placed the bowls in the sink and untied the box he'd brought from his restaurant, The Laughing Hound. "I present for your enjoyment a Hazelnut-Almond Dacquoise!" He placed it on a cake stand and proudly carried it to the table.

I whisked the cutting board out of the way so he could place the cake in the center of the table. "This is worthy of the fancy Christmas dishes!" A glossy chocolate ganache covered the square cake. Whole shelled hazelnuts embellished the top edge all the way around the cake.

I brought the Spode Christmas tree dessert plates to the table, along with a cake knife and server. "Coffee or tea anyone?"

"No caffeine for me, please." Mars held up his hands. "I won't sleep if I drink it this late."

Nina laughed. "When did you turn into an old man? How about that Sleigh Ride drink with cranberries that you made last year, Sophie? Can you still stomach booze, Mars?"

They laughed and teased each other while I heated cranberry juice with a cup of dark rum, sugar, cinnamon sticks, and a hefty splash of Chambord. I poured it into tall mugs and passed them to my friends. Bernie served the cake.

I took one bite and decided it might just become my new favorite, with layers of light meringue, creamy butter cream, and more chocolate ganache inside. Pure decadence. "Is this buttercream coff—"

Nina coughed, and Bernie interrupted me. "Decaf," he whispered.

Mars shot him a look. "It's espresso. If I can't sleep, I'll come over to your place and keep you up, Bernie."

And then Mars helped himself to a second

piece, which threw us all into stitches. It was a needed relief given the tension and sadness that had invaded our lives. But it wasn't long before we came back to the subject of Gwen's murder.

"Whoever wrapped her knew how to make a large fancy bow," I mused.

"Counts me out," Nina teased.

"And a lot of men. I doubt Baxter or Elvin could do that," said Mars.

"Elvin can!" Nina ate her last bite of dacquoise. "I bought gifts for my brother's children today and everyone teased Elvin about his bow-tying skills. He doesn't even need a gizmo to do it."

Elvin again! His name kept turning up. "Where did he learn to do that?"

"Apparently he often does those charity gift-wrapping things they have at malls around the holidays. He taught himself to make fancy bows so people would increase their donations."

That didn't sound like a killer. It seemed like everything Elvin did was for other people.

"So what next?" Mars sat back and nursed his drink. "How do we figure out who the culprit is? I need Natasha off the hook before they arrest her and haul her off to the pokey."

Bernie became somber. "Are we overlooking someone obvious? What about the Lawrences? Twiggy, Jonah, and Claudine. They had all the time they needed to wrap up Gwen and stash her in the garage. They had access to Natasha's wrapping paper. And to her pink cookie boxes."

Mars gazed at me. "See? Thank you, Bernie. I've been trying to tell Sophie that they're involved. Natasha saw Claudine at their apartment when she was supposed to be at work."

"I grant you they had opportunity. And it would have been the easiest for them. But why? What would motivate them to kill Gwen?"

"Kat!" Bernie and Nina chanted her name together.

"Exactly," said Bernie. "If Gwen wasn't giving up Kat to Sugar, she sure wasn't giving her to the Lawrences."

"Either Twiggy is a remarkable actress or she didn't know a thing about it until today," I protested.

"That still leaves Claudine and Jonah. Kat's grandmother and father. Blood ties run deep." Mars raised his eyebrows as if asking me if I agreed.

"Put them on the list."

Jonah peered into the kitchen and knocked

387

on the door. Mars rose to let him in.

"Sorry to interrupt. The police are done in your garage, Mars, so we can sleep at home tonight. Thanks for putting up with us, Sophie. We're not at our best right now."

"My pleasure, Jonah. Really. It's understandable that you're going through a very tough time. How's Twiggy?"

He rubbed the side of his face and let out a stream of air. "I'm so angry with Sugar. I begged her to let me break it to Twiggy my way. She'll be okay, I guess. It will take some time, though. I'll just go upstairs and collect our stuff. Twiggy told me to ask if I should strip the beds."

I grinned. "I can't believe she even thought of that with all she's going through. Thanks, but I'll take care of the beds tomorrow."

He nodded and headed upstairs.

Mars, Nina, and Bernie were getting ready to leave when Jonah came downstairs.

Mars picked up Daisy's leash.

"Excuse me! Isn't it my turn to have Daisy again?" It wasn't so much a question as a demand.

Mars reluctantly turned the leash over to me. "I was hoping you'd forget."

"I'll walk you home. Daisy needs to go out anyway."

Mars tamped down the fire for me, and we left the house. Bernie and Nina turned toward their houses.

Mars tilted his head in that direction. "Let's go the long way."

"Trouble with Natasha?" asked Bernie.

Mars paused before responding. "Let's see, Nat wound up tighter than a spring or a calming walk in cool, crisp winter air. Which would you prefer?"

"Want to hide at my place for a bit?" offered Bernie.

Nina held out an arm to stop us. "Isn't that Natasha?"

Chapter Thirty-Two

Dear Sophie,
I love snowmen. I even collect them! But I don't have room in front of my town house to display a big snowman. Is there a way to make one to hang on my front door?
                    Snow Lover in Snowflake, Arizona

Dear Snow Lover,
Use three grapevine wreaths in graduated sizes as the head and body. Tie them together. Cut an old hat in half, and use a glue gun to attach it to the small "head" wreath. Wrap a scarf around the "throat" and, if you're really ambitious, add twig arms wearing mittens.

                                        Sophie

The Christmas lights on our street glowed so brightly that it was hard to jump from shadow to shadow and remain hidden. But Natasha appeared to be trying to do just that.

"C'mon," said Nina. "Let's see what she's up to now."

"Are you sure that's her?" asked Mars.

We skittled across the street.

"Where is she?" whispered Bernie. "I've lost her."

"See Rudolph with the glowing nose?" I asked. "She just passed him."

Mars huffed. "What's she doing?" He pulled out his cell phone and dialed.

Faint bells that sounded like a church tower on Christmas rang. Mars muttered, "Rats, that's her ringtone. It *is* her!" He held his phone to his ear.

Half a block ahead of us, Natasha reached into her pocket and dodged into a shadow.

"I can't believe it. She let it roll over to voice mail!" Mars sounded insulted.

"I bet she turned it off," whispered Nina. "She's tailing someone. Look up near the house with the lighted snowman by the door."

A second smaller figure hurried along the street, then paused behind a tree.

"Oh, this is nuts. I'm catching up to Natasha to find out what's going on."

But before Mars could jog away, Bernie

seized his arm. "Not just yet. No one is in danger or trouble. Maybe she's onto something."

"We're lucky neither of them has noticed us yet." I zipped up the collar of my jacket.

Nina said, "I'm going to walk fast on the other side of the street and try to pass Natasha to see who she's following."

Mars snagged her coat. "No, you're not. Stay safely with us, please."

We followed the darting figures for several blocks. The towering Christmas tree on Market Square glowed in the night ahead of us, illuminating a couple who paused by the tree for a long kiss.

The person Natasha was following stood across the street, arms crossed over her chest. "That's Patty!" I whispered. "Why would Natasha follow Patty?"

"We're going to find out right now. Come on." Mars marched ahead of us.

Natasha stood next to a tree as though she meant to hide from Patty, but she was totally visible to us. Mars crept up on her, and she screamed. Her nostrils flared. "You just gave me away and ruined all my hard work. You dolts!"

"Nat, what do you think you're doing?" Mars spoke like he might to a misbehaving child.

"Sophie isn't making any progress in uncovering Gwen's killer. Apparently, it's not important to her that I could go to jail. I have to take things into my own hands."

A recipe for trouble, for sure! We waited to hear more.

"Mars told me that Patty slipped out of Sophie's house in the middle of the night. So tonight, I was ready and waiting in the alley. Look at her! She's up to no good. Shh, she sees us."

Patty joined our little group. "Hi! What's everyone doing down here so late?"

Natasha spit out, "Us? What are you doing sneaking around?"

Patty stepped back. "I beg Your Highness's pardon. I wasn't aware that I needed your permission to walk about at night."

"Let's not do this in public, shall we? I'll buy a round of drinks, come on." Bernie motioned to us.

"Thanks," said Patty. "I'll have to pass. I can't leave my son."

Bernie gazed around. "Where is he?"

"See the kid under the tree with his lips locked on a girl?"

We all looked.

"That's my boy."

"Bring the two of them along."

I couldn't take Daisy inside anyplace. "I'll

head home with Daisy. You be sure to fill me in."

"No problem, Soph. Come with me."

We all followed Bernie to the alley that ran behind The Laughing Hound. He opened a gate onto a screened porch with a huge fireplace at one end. He flicked on overhead heaters and the gas fireplace. In minutes the little space was toasty in spite of the chilly weather. We clustered at a large table near the fire. Patty's son, Bradley, and his very cute redheaded girlfriend plopped themselves down in side-by-side chairs in a corner that wasn't as private as they probably would have liked.

Patty towered over them, speaking into a cell phone before she joined us. "This is such a cute place."

"Thanks! There's no place to sit outdoors in the winter with a dog, so I had this built last month." Bernie slid a platter of tiny pastries onto the coffee table in the middle of the sofa grouping. He carried a second, smaller platter over to Patty's son.

Bernie returned and asked, "I hope White Chocolate Peppermint Martinis are okay? Except for the kids, of course. I ordered hot chocolate for them."

When he sat down, Natasha was glaring at Patty.

"Did I do something wrong?" asked Patty.

"Perhaps you should tell us," Natasha spat.

Patty gazed around at us. "I feel like I missed something. Why are you so upset with me?"

Bernie snorted. "Because you obviously had a good reason for being out and about."

The bartender delivered the drinks in martini glasses. White with crushed peppermints around the rim, a candy cane graced each glass.

Patty sipped hers. "Oh, this is so wonderful." She covered her face briefly with her hands. "You can't imagine what a relief it is to be out of that house for just a few minutes, enjoying the Christmas lights, and drinking an adult drink. Thank you!"

"That's right," said Natasha. "Make us feel sorry for you."

"Nat, that's enough." Mars pressed his hand over hers.

"*You* are not the one who will go to jail if they don't find the killer. I'd like to know what Patty is doing creeping around at night."

"You think *I* killed Gwen?" Patty's eyes opened wide with horror. "Heaven knows I'd have liked to." She held up a finger. "But I didn't. I'm far too much of a wuss. You can count me out."

"Then why did you sneak out in the middle of the night?" Natasha demanded.

Patty's eyes met mine. "Oh. You knew about that? I may not be with my kids twenty-four/seven, but I still know when they're up to something."

Her face lit up with a smile. "When Bradley was eight, he discovered Elvin's girly magazines. They weren't anything awful, but to an eight-year-old boy, they were very exotic. He took to pinching one each time we went over to Elvin's. I found them neatly tucked under Bradley's mattress. Zebras and little boys don't change their stripes. The first night I was here, when I had dinner at their house, I excused myself to go to the ladies' room, but I headed straight for Bradley's room. Found one of those prepaid cell phones under his bed. Took me a few minutes, but I found the texts. I had to look up the meanings."

She grabbed a scrap of paper and wrote *420 2NTE 0200*. "420 means *let's get high,* 2NTE is *tonight,* and much to my surprise, they're using military time. 0200 is two in the morning. Bradley responded with *ILBL8,* which translates to *I'll be late.* So I got out of bed, and let me tell you, it wasn't easy because I was dead on my feet, but I was waiting for him when he slipped out of Baxter's house. I followed him because I wanted to see who he was meeting. I called their moms on the spot and took him home."

That explained a lot! I glanced at her son, who was busy making eyes at his girlfriend.

"How long have you been following me, Natasha? Isn't that against the law? Stalking or something?" asked Patty.

"Nat, cool it," cautioned Mars.

"Just so you know, Miss Nosy Pants, I have alibis because I was with people constantly. I was at Sophie's house, then I went over to Baxter's and had dinner with him and the kids, then I went back to Sophie's house, and when I went out in the middle of the night, I was with my son. So there!"

Natasha opened her mouth, but Mars clamped his hand on her arm. Natasha shot him an irritated look and said, "But she's lying!" And then she slid off the sofa in a dead faint, spilling her drink all over herself.

Fortunately, no one took a picture.

Mars kneeled over her, lightly tapping her cheeks. "Nat? Nat?"

"Should I call an ambulance?" I asked.

"Give her a minute. It's her nerves. The pressure has been too much for her. I was afraid of something like this."

Natasha came around and sat up exactly at the moment the mother of the redheaded girl arrived to pitch a major fuss. The child turned the color of a red poinsettia. I couldn't blame her. Her mother did everything except drag her off by the ear.

Patty marched her son home.

Mars and Natasha took a cab.

Bernie, Nina, Daisy, and I strolled back together.

"Is anyone else now convinced that Patty killed Gwen?" asked Nina. "She lied without so much as a nervous blink!"

"She's told me what a great guy Elvin is and that he would help anyone. Do you suppose he woke, saw what happened, and helped her clean up?" I asked. "We saw him wrapping a gift at Rocking Horse Toys. He's pretty good at it."

"Elvin seems like a decent bloke," said Bernie. "Don't you think we could get him to cough up what he knows? Maybe if we pressure him a little? Suggest it will go easier on Patty if she turns herself in?"

"Right. How are we going to pull that off?" I asked. "He's in the store all day and surrounded by people at Baxter's at night."

We passed the snooty antiques store near Rocking Horse Toys. I stopped to admire the silver sleigh. It no longer graced the window. Cupping my hands around my face, I leaned against the glass.

"Better be careful. You don't want to set off an alarm," said Bernie.

"Does anyone see the silver sleigh in the store?"

Nina pressed her nose against the window. "Nope. Maybe the police collected it as evidence."

Bernie had drifted on to Rocking Horse Toys. He backed up in a hurry, bumping into me. "Ladies, our prey awaits anon."

"Huh?" Nina bumped into me from behind when I stopped.

"Elvin is working late. How about we pay him a visit?" asked Bernie.

Poor Elvin, he had no idea what we had in mind when the three of us pounded on the door like women dying to get into a 75-percent-off sale.

"Follow my lead and play along," whispered Bernie.

Elvin unlocked the door. "What are you three up to?"

I cringed when he put it that way. "What are you doing working so late?"

"I guess you heard about Kat? There was a lot of chaos in the Lawrence family today. Half the deliveries didn't get unloaded, and we're expecting another truck in the morning, so I told Jonah to go home and get some sleep."

"Maybe we can give you a hand so it will go faster," offered Bernie.

"Sure," I said. "You guys open the boxes and, if you tell us where to put everything, Nina and I can set out the toys."

Elvin seemed wary. "You don't have to do that."

"But we want to!" Nina insisted.

I felt a little guilty about pretending to help him out when we had an ulterior motive, but a better opportunity probably wouldn't present itself.

In one hour, the four of us accomplished what would have taken Elvin until the wee hours of the morning. Bernie bantered with him good-naturedly and eventually the topic turned to murder.

"Must be tough trying to keep everyone's spirits high," said Bernie.

Elvin slit open another box. "Baxter is so torn up I'm not sure he'll ever recover."

Nina pushed a carton of stocking-stuffer games toward me. I dutifully placed them in colorful little bins. Outside the Santa's Workshop display window, snow began to fall. Surrounded by toys and Christmas displays, it started to feel like we really were in Santa's workshop. How could anyone who worked in this festive atmosphere possibly be guilty of murder?

"Do you have any theories about who killed Gwen?" asked Nina.

I thought Bernie might explode. Nina had jumped the gun with that question.

"That Natasha woman, I guess. I saw what she posted on the Internet. Baxter told me today that the police think Gwen poisoned that fellow, Horace! I don't understand what's going on at all. I don't know what to think."

I turned toward him and watched him carefully. He didn't seem upset. Then why had the mouse disturbed him so much?

"I heard the police are hot on Patty's trail," said Bernie. "She slipped out of Sophie's house in the middle of the night."

"And she sure hates Gwen," added Nina.

"No!" Elvin looked straight at Nina. "It wasn't Patty." He gazed at me. "Claudine says you used to date that Wolf fellow."

"I did."

"You gotta tell him that Patty didn't do it. She couldn't have. Gwen did Patty wrong. Real wrong. I guess you know Gwen broke up Patty and Baxter's marriage."

"It took two people to do that," I observed.

"Baxter thinks he's so smart, but he can

be as stupid as the rest of us. He never should have left Patty. I know for a fact that Patty didn't murder Gwen. You should know that, Sophie. You're her alibi."

That surprised me. "How's that?"

He nodded his head. "You gotta tell Wolf that Patty was with you the whole time before she came to the house for dinner that night. She couldn't have done it."

Chapter Thirty-Three

Dear Natasha,
Every year my husband wants to set up a train under our Christmas tree. It's a nightmare. There's no room for gifts and inevitably, something is broken, and hubby gets upset. Where can we put that thing?
Conductor's Wife in Station 15, Ohio

Dear Conductor's Wife,
The basement comes to mind. Toys belong in a playroom. However, it could be cute combined with a Christmas village in a seldom-used corner of a room like the nook under a curving stairway. Make it hubby's job.

Natasha

I should have responded to Elvin's statement right away but it took me a minute to process the meaning of what he'd said. It assumed Gwen was murdered after the cookie swap broke up and before Patty joined Baxter and the kids for dinner. How did Elvin know the exact time Gwen was murdered unless Wolf told him . . . or he was there? I stared at Elvin. Had we stupidly blundered into the killer? I'd been suspicious of him. Maybe we should make our exit as soon as we could, and pass this information along to Wolf.

Nina shoved me a box of stuffed animals, and the first one I pulled out was the Christmas mouse with glasses, like the one Edith had bought. I froze. What a stroke of bad luck. I looked at Elvin out of the corner of my eye.

He dropped the utility knife he'd been using to open boxes. It landed poorly, slicing right through the top of his running shoe. He howled and jumped backward, which flung the bloodied knife to the floor.

We surrounded him immediately. Even Daisy jumped up and ran to him.

"Are you okay?" I asked.

"Sit down," barked Bernie, "and take off that shoe."

I hurried to the back of the store in search of rubbing alcohol and bandages. Adorably outfitted for children, the bathroom provided a darling step stool under the sink.

Someone had painted happy blue walls with kittens and puppies frolicking through sunny yellow flowers. I spotted a first aid kit and hydrogen peroxide on a high shelf. That would have to do.

I used the step stool to reach them, grabbed an entire roll of paper towels, and rushed back to Elvin. His big toe bled profusely.

My face must have shown my shock, because Bernie said, "It's not as bad as it looks. Feet always bleed a lot. You know, gravity and all that."

Bernie cleaned it up with the paper towels.

I opened the hydrogen peroxide to pour it over the wound.

"Hold your breath," instructed Nina. "It only hurts for a moment."

"That's rubbing alcohol. Hydrogen peroxide fizzes but it doesn't sting." I poured it over his toe, glad the store had tile floors that would be easy to clean. It fizzed up, but in that brief moment, we saw that the cut was indeed not nearly as bad as it had seemed at first.

Bernie immediately applied pressure with the paper towels. "Have you got a bandage and some medical tape in that kit?"

Within minutes, we had Elvin patched up. Bernie had wrapped Elvin's big toe so that it seemed three times its normal size.

"Does it hurt?" I asked.

"Don't feel anything right now except that honkin' big bandage. It will probably kill me tomorrow. And I promised Jonah I would work!"

"Maybe you can sit behind the register," Nina suggested.

"How totally stupid of me." Elvin smacked his own cheek. "Seems like I've done nothing but cause trouble since I got here."

"What do you mean?" I closed the first aid kit.

"Aww, you know, Gwen being a high-society lady and all, she thought I was an embarrassment and didn't want me around."

"Well!" Nina perched on one of the boxes that hadn't been emptied. "That's just plain rude. Besides, Baxter loves having you here, and that's what's important, right?"

"I didn't want to cause trouble in his marriage."

"From what I gather, they had plenty of trouble long before you arrived," I assured him. If we were ever going to get information from Elvin, now was the time — when he was partially incapacitated. In as kind and gentle a tone as I could muster, I asked, "So, what happened with the mouse?"

"I don't know. I can't quite figure it out."

"Maybe we can help you." I had to get him to talk!

Elvin moaned. "My mama didn't raise Baxter and me to lie. It's no use. It's about to kill me what I did."

"You murdered Gwen?" shrieked Nina.

I nudged her. That wasn't going to help. If she acted hysterical he would surely shut up.

"Nah. But I found her."

"You found her?" Now I was really confused. "Was she wrapped? You took her to the garage?"

"I guess I shouldn't have done what I did, but I had to. You understand. I didn't have a choice, it was the only thing I could do." Elvin chewed on his lower lip. His eyebrows formed a V over his nose, and he appeared on the verge of tears. "Gwen kicked us all out during her cookie party. I went for a walk around town, saw some sights, stopped for a beer at that Irish bar. Hey, that's a real nice place! When I came back to the house, I wasn't for sure if all the ladies were gone, and I didn't want to upset Gwen, seeing as how she didn't like me anyway, so I kind of tiptoed in through the front door. I didn't hear anything, so I came on through to the kitchen and found Gwen lying on the floor.

Not quite facedown, kinda like she fell on her side, you know? The hair on the back of her head was sticky with blood, so I guessed somebody clobbered her." He swallowed hard. "I couldn't feel a pulse. Her eyes were open, staring at me and lifeless, and I just knew she was dead."

Elvin stopped and looked at me. "That mouse and the orange box of peanut brittle were lying beside her like she'd dropped them. I was afraid the kids would come home any minute and find her like that, so I stuck the mouse in her pocket and put the box back on the counter. Then" — he turned guilty eyes up at us — "I apologized to her, and slid one of those big black trash bags over her head and another one over her feet." Anxiety filled his voice. "I cleaned up the floor with ammonia in a big hurry, but there wasn't much blood. I remember thinking that it didn't take a big hit to the head to kill a person. Then I carried her outside to the alley." He sobbed. "Like a piece of trash!"

He squeezed his eyes shut and clenched his hands before he opened his eyes and continued. "I knew she was mean to folks. She could hardly stand having me around. It was as though I offended her by being alive. I guess I wasn't fancy enough for a woman like her. She fought like cats and dogs with Sugar, and the kids heard her yelling at Baxter every day. Still, she deserved better. She was my brother's wife, and that made her family, no matter how she felt about me."

I perched on a box, mesmerized.

"I was afraid a dog might come along and start tearing at the trash bag. Then I remembered Natasha's article about how to wrap an awkward present. I took the lampshade and was carrying it outside when I heard sirens. So I kind of flung Gwen over my shoulder and raced for the neighbor's garage. I'd seen the workroom in there, and it seemed like a private place to do right by Gwen. I found a couple big boxes and wrapping paper and got her all wrapped up nice with the lampshade on her head when I saw Natasha coming. In a big rush, I carried Gwen into the garage to hide. I was afraid Natasha might come in and see me. That storage cabinet was open, so I stuffed Gwen inside and hid behind the car."

"Eww." Nina winced at the thought.

"But then Natasha puttered around in her workroom, and I couldn't carry Gwen to my bus without her seeing me. And I knew the cops or an ambulance were around somewhere because of the siren. When Natasha left for a minute, I darted out. I remembered to take the black trash bags, but I forgot all about the mouse. It must have fallen out of her pocket when I was wrapping her. I figured I'd wait until late that night and then put Gwen in my bus and drive her out somewhere to bury her. Do it right, you know? There's lots of farmland a couple hours or so down the road from here. But when I came back in the middle of the night, the garage and workshop were locked up tight. I couldn't get in! I had to wait until morning. But you know, that alley back there is a busy place. Luis from next door must have jogged around the block about ten times that morning. Then you" — Elvin pointed at me — "came by. It was one person after another, so I figured to wait until dark. But then you found her and the jig was up. At least now she'll get a decent burial like she deserves."

We sat silently for a moment after he finished his story. Strangely enough, I believed him. He still could have been the one who'd whapped her over the head, though. It would have been easy to omit that part of what happened.

Bernie scratched his forehead. "What I'm

410

missing here is why you didn't just call 911?"

Nina gasped and clapped a hand over her mouth briefly. "You know who did it, and you were trying to protect that person."

"I don't know. I swear. I have thought and thought on it, but I don't know who done her in. I . . . I was afraid it might have been somebody in the family, you know?"

There were only a few people he would be inclined to protect that way. Baxter, Sugar, and Patty. "That's why you think it couldn't have been Patty–because of the timing. Patty, Nina, and Liza were at my house between the cookie swap and Luis getting shocked by electricity. Those must have been the sirens you heard. So it was before then," I said. That was a very narrow window of time.

"I get it now," said Nina. "You thought it was Baxter or Sugar who killed Gwen. Did you think they would get away with it if you hid the body?"

"Welllll" — Elvin licked his lips — "if there wasn't a body, there wouldn't be a murder." He wrinkled his nose. "And to be perfectly honest, I was moving pretty fast. I didn't take a whole lot of time to think on it first."

"But what about the mouse's glasses? I

thought Kat found them in the living room."

Elvin shrugged. "I didn't know they belonged to the mouse when she showed them to me. I figured they went with one of the kids' toys."

I mused aloud. "I was so sure the glasses in the living room meant that Gwen had been banged over the head with the deer-head candlestick. Did you clean up the living room?"

Elvin seemed surprised. "No. Gosh, we ate dinner and were hardly in the living room that night. It wasn't until after you found her that I spent any time in there."

"Did the police fingerprint that room or anything?"

"They came back to search, but I wasn't there, so I don't know what they did exactly."

Bernie stood up. "Is it too late to call Alex?"

Elvin certainly needed a lawyer. Even if he had told the truth and he hadn't murdered Gwen, I was fairly sure there were laws about moving corpses. Not to mention that he needed to tell the police what he had done. "I don't think Alex can represent Elvin if he's representing Baxter."

Elvin gazed up at us, desperate. "Maybe he could recommend somebody? I don't know what to do."

I phoned Alex, who gave us the number of a friend of his. Nina went out to pick up coffee for everyone, and while we waited for the lawyer, Bernie and I finished setting out the new toys.

Nina, Alex, and his lawyer friend arrived at the same time. The attorney was a pudgy guy with glasses and a friendly smile.

Nina passed out coffees, assuring us they were decaf. I was so dead tired that I would have welcomed caffeine.

Alex sipped coffee and introduced his friend as a fellow attorney. "Elvin, you're under no obligation to hire him."

Elvin appeared frantic. "No, no, no! I need help. I have to get this off my conscience! It's the worst thing I ever did in my life."

The lawyer spoke with him privately. When they were through, they emerged from the stockroom in back and the lawyer said, "Come by my office tomorrow morning, and we'll discuss your options."

Bernie called a cab for Elvin. Since Daisy was with me, Alex offered to walk me home. Nina winked at me when she and Bernie stepped into the cab.

The stroll home was beautiful. Most of the Christmas lights had been turned off, though a surprising number still sparkled gently in the night. Most of the homes followed the tradition of a single candle in each window and they warmed the night with their soft glow. Snow drifted down gently on the sleeping town. Not a single car drove by.

Alex held my hand in his very warm one. "You don't really think I have something going on with Sugar, do you?"

"Why would you say that?"

He chuckled. "I saw you across the street. And Sugar is the kind of woman who doesn't realize how much she aggravates other women. I'm glad we have a few moments together. I need to apologize for breaking off a date and then forgetting lunch." He stopped walking and kissed me gently.

"How come you can help Sugar but you can't represent Elvin?"

"First of all, they're different matters. Besides, everyone involved signed a waiver saying it was okay. Baxter loves Kat. He wants the custody straightened out, too."

"Sophie, there's something I've been wanting to discuss."

Uh-oh. My danger antennas zoomed up. So much for a romantic walk in the snow. We strolled on.

"I don't want you to be upset with me

when I take on clients. I knew that you had been, for lack of a better word, *involved* with some murder investigations, but I didn't realize that we might butt heads. You understand that I can't talk to you about my clients, right? After all, if you were a client, you wouldn't want me discussing your business with anyone else."

"I understand completely. It just surprised me that you couldn't even tell me who'd hired you." I slipped in the crucial words, "Within an hour of the corpse being found."

"You just don't miss a beat. But that doesn't mean the client is guilty. People watch all the crime shows on TV. They've wised up, and they know they need lawyers, especially when it's a family member who was murdered."

"So what you're saying is that we have to coexist on parallel planes, working toward the same goal but not sharing any information."

We reached my front door. "You can share anything you like. But I'll pick and choose. Nothing about my clients, of course, but for instance, I might tell you that I happen to know Horace's secretary, Phyllis, has been to see him every day, while his wife, Edith, didn't visit him until yesterday."

I burst out laughing. "It's a good thing

you're cute, because you are so behind! But if you tell me more about what you know, I might be inclined to share that Gwen tried to kill Horace with warfarin before she died."

The astonishment on his face was priceless. I gave him a big kiss, said good-night, and closed the door. That would teach him!

Light snow still glittered outside in the morning. It blew in the air, reminding me that Christmas would be here soon and I needed to do some shopping. But I found it difficult to think about anything other than Gwen's murder.

I let Daisy out in the fenced backyard, put on the kettle for tea, and fed Mochie shredded chicken, which he usually liked. Apparently not anymore. "I'm sorry, Your Highness, but I don't plan to open three cans of cat food every morning like a kitty smorgasbord."

He watched me, clearly confident that I would continue to offer him food until he found one with contents that suited him. Aargh. He knew me too well. I flipped back the top on a can of salmon and spooned the contents into a second dish.

He stretched his neck out to sniff it before he deigned to sample it and settle happily into his eating position to chow down.

I still wore a cozy red flannel nightshirt that came to my knees. After doctoring my tea with milk and sugar, I sat at my kitchen table to consider the events of the previous night.

If I could believe Elvin, and I thought he was telling the truth because everything fit — the fancy bow on Gwen that he knew how to make quickly, the expert wrapping he'd done, the lampshade, and the sirens he would have heard — everything except the mouse's glasses that Kat found in the living room. I still believed that Gwen must have stolen the mouse from Edith, gone home, and then something had happened to the mouse in her living room. Maybe she threw it at someone. Maybe she'd been holding it when she fell. But Elvin had found her in the kitchen. That didn't make sense. I had to rethink my theory.

Patty could be crossed off the list of suspects. Where had the Lawrences been? Twiggy went home to deposit her cookies in the carriage house. She would have had ample opportunity to go back to the Babineauxs'. She might have seen Gwen returning from Edith's house and gotten into an argument. Or perhaps Edith lied to us. Maybe she saw Gwen pinch the mouse and followed her home to confront her. Heaven knew Edith could be unpleasant. They would certainly have had an ugly encounter.

Hadn't all the Lawrences taken a break from the store after Twiggy came back earlier than expected that evening? Claudine or Jonah could have come home, killed Gwen, and gone back to work.

Baxter had shown up to help Luis. He must have been in the neighborhood. Hmm, Luis told Wolf that he had been with Liza. But she was at my house from the time she left the cookie swap until the ambulance arrived. He'd been home alone for a good period of time, but did he have a motive? And what about Sugar? When everyone left, she would have been there alone with Gwen.

We knew that Gwen had posted the photos of Natasha. Then she could have trotted across the alley to Edith's house to steal the mouse. Sugar could have been waiting for Gwen to return and then clobbered her.

I let Daisy in and made a second cup of tea and a bowl of oatmeal, perfect for a cold, snowy morning. I spooned some of the oatmeal and sliced bananas into Daisy's bowl but didn't tell her about the yummy dark brown sugar that landed in mine.

After a shower, I dressed in forest green jeans, pleased that the waist wasn't too tight, and a coral turtleneck. Simple gold hoop earrings, my brown boots, and a white parka with faux-fur trim on the hood finished my simple look.

I swapped Daisy's collar for a red one with snowflakes on it, snapped on her leash, and we were out the door. First stop, a quick check on Natasha. We crossed the street and discovered Wolf standing in front of the Babineauxs' house.

After the requisite *good morning*s, he asked, "Hey, do you know who might have bought the deer-head candleholders from the antiques store?"

CHAPTER THIRTY-FOUR

Dear Natasha,
My husband is lactose intolerant. I have all these lovely cookie recipes that call for milk or buttermilk. What can I use instead?
        Baking Elf in Cookietown, Oklahoma

Dear Baking Elf,
Soy milk is a terrific substitute. If you need buttermilk, add a little lemon or vinegar to it. Instant soy buttermilk!
                        Natasha

"I noticed they weren't in the window anymore."

"That's what the store's owner claims." Wolf lowered his voice. "Just between us, he's kind of a jerk. Says some woman came in shortly after they were returned by Baxter and paid cash for them. He doesn't have a name or address."

"Cash? That should narrow it down. Not many people have access to that kind of cash. Did she buy the sleigh, too?"

"Apparently so. You run in the same circles as some of Old Town's wealthier folks. Let me know if you hear about the pieces turning up somewhere." Wolf knelt to rub Daisy's ears.

"Did he give you a description?"

"Yeah, what's a Burberry coat? Common?"

"Fairly popular, actually. Their trench coats are classics. I have one."

"Allow me to quote him, 'Sleek black hair with bangs, makeup like a hooker, a fashionable Burberry coat, garish nail polish, and she wore a rock that belongs in the Smithsonian on her bony left hand.' "

"Doesn't sound like anyone I know."

"Can you believe it? He thinks she wasn't very young, and he did notice that she had brown eyes, which —"

I finished his sentence for him, "— only includes over half of the population. Tell me about it. So you can't check the candleholder for fingerprints."

"The store owner polished them when they were returned, so that was doubtful anyway, but we'd like to have them."

"To match them to the wound on Gwen's

head?" Maybe the killer snatched it off the mantel but conked Gwen over the head in the kitchen?

He smiled. "I'll keep after the store owner, but you might hear about it first on the grapevine. Let me know, okay?"

Daisy and I walked on toward Natasha and Mars's house. It was the holiday season, and plenty of Old Town residents would love those pieces of silver. Who was I kidding? *I* would love to have them. It wasn't outside of the realm of possibilities that someone totally unrelated to Gwen's murder had bought the set.

Still, if I had bonked Gwen over the head with one of the candlesticks and had accidentally left it behind in my haste, I might want to buy them before the cops could use them against me. Not many people could come up with that kind of cash, though.

Edith could buy just about anything she wanted. Claudine had sold her house, so she might be flush with cash at the moment. On the other hand, she was living with the kids in very tight quarters, so she maybe she didn't have much money. I didn't know anything about Natasha's finances, but I could certainly ask Mars. I knew nothing about Sugar's financial background, either. Didn't pole dancers rake in a lot of money in tips? Phyllis had worked as Horace's assistant. Hadn't she mentioned a divorce? That could have left her with some cash, depending on how they'd split things up.

We trotted up the front steps and knocked on the door.

Mars swung the door open. "Daisy!" He said hi to me as an afterthought.

"How's Natasha this morning? Is she eating yet?"

"Come see for yourself."

Mars led us to the kitchen.

Sugar and flour canisters, a bowl of chocolate chips, salt, baking powder, soy milk, balsamic vinegar, and assorted herbs in bundles sat on the stainless steel countertop. A sugar pearl silver-colored KitchenAid mixer whirred together ingredients. The scent of baking herbs wafted to me.

I waited for Natasha to shut off the mixer. "You look much better today."

Natasha grimaced. "I'm so embarrassed. Mars says no one took a picture. Is that true?"

"You've got to lighten up a little bit, Natasha. You're making yourself sick. I promise, no pictures were taken."

She adjusted her apron. The dominant fabric featured silver snowflakes on a snow white background. The straps, cinched-in belt, and flared apron skirt that layered underneath the white fabric were all black. A retro look — it brought chic to the kitchen.

"Did you sew your apron? It's beautiful."

"You like it? Really? Mars, maybe I should try marketing these. Oh! We can call the line Natasha Cooks! No. Natasha *Buon Natale*!"

"Italian? What's Italian about it?"

"Sophie, you don't understand branding and marketing. But you've given me a grand idea."

Oy, she was back all right. Back to her old self.

Natasha raised her arm toward the windows as though she were imagining billboards. "Aprons are only a small part of the business. I see pot holders and towels, wreaths and ribbons, and, oh my — wrapping papers!"

Meanwhile, I saw something else. Soy milk. "Natasha, excuse me for interrupting your grandiose dreams, but did you make your cookies for the swap with soy milk?"

"I did! It's a wonderful ingredient. With the addition of the balsamic vinegar, it becomes like buttermilk. Really, Sophie. You should know things like that."

My head spun. "Did you give any of your cookies to Liza or Luis?"

"Only at the cookie swap."

"Excuse me, I have to run. Come on, Daisy."

Mars blanched. "Don't be upset. Natasha's like that to everyone. You know that."

"See you later." Daisy and I shot out the door and down the stairs. Once we reached the sidewalk, I slowed down to think.

Luis was allergic to soy milk. The day he was shocked by the frayed Christmas lights, he'd had a rash on his chest.

I took a deep breath of the cold winter air.

But Liza and Nina came straight to my house with their cookies. Luis couldn't have eaten one of Natasha's cookies unless he had been in Gwen's house, where they were arranged on the table for everyone to see — and sample. Of course, he could have eaten soy elsewhere. It was in everything these days.

I had to keep my cool. If I told Wolf about this, he would sneer like he did about Edith's mouse. Only one person would understand — Nina. Daisy and I hustled to her house. I raised my hand to the door knocker just as Nina swung it open.

"Sophie! Perfect timing. I'm going over to Liza's. Come with me."

While we walked next door with her, I

explained my soy milk theory.

Nina tilted her head. "Oh, honey! You've been concentrating on this way too much. It's in candy bars, salad dressings, bread. He could have eaten soy so easily. I'm sorry. I really don't think that means anything."

Maybe she was right. I was back to suspecting everyone again.

Liza waited for us at her front door. Her expressive brown eyes opened wide. "Sophie, thanks for coming. There's safety in numbers, right?"

"Safety? What are you two cooking up?" Daisy loped into the house to play with Oscar.

"I'm so frustrated. This is the very first time since Luis and I have been married that I haven't been able to find my Christmas gift hidden in our house. I told you this place is too big for us."

I grinned. Luis had her pegged. She wouldn't find it this year, and it would finally be a surprise.

"It's driving me crazy. I've turned the place upside down."

"Are you sure he bought it yet?" asked Nina.

"He must have. He already bought several things for Pandoooora." Liza rolled her eyes. "It's jewelry, so it has to be in a small box.

I've been through all his trouser pockets, all his desk drawers, even the faux ones that you have to know how to open."

"We're going into the dungeon," Nina told me. "He knows Liza won't go down there."

"I don't like going by myself, so Nina agreed to come with me. Everyone ready?"

I couldn't tell her it wasn't there! I kept mum and followed them through the kitchen. A dark wood prep island with open shelving underneath dominated the kitchen. The cabinets against the wall had been painted a grayish green and rectangular coarse-textured tumbled tiles formed the backsplash.

Liza opened a roughly hewn door. Oscar and Daisy raced down ahead of us. That would take care of any mice. We crept down the stairs slowly.

I expected the worst. But Luis's private man cave turned out to be as inviting as a historic pub. The stone walls and beamed ceiled fit perfectly with plush overstuffed brown leather chairs and a sofa deep enough for a good nap with a fuzzy throw on it. A large-screen TV hung on the wall near the ancient fireplace. The opposite wall had been outfitted entirely for wine storage.

"This is charming, Liza." I gazed around. Not a single window, but one really didn't even notice. Luis had excellent taste.

She shuddered. "Ugh. Not my style at all. Now, where would he have put that thing? Aha! In a wine rack." She hurried over, stopped, and pulled her hands back in little fists.

"What's wrong?" asked Nina.

"What if there are mice in there?"

I scanned the bookshelves, impressed by the variety of reading material.

"Sophie! You have to look behind the books." Liza resorted to poking the handle of a fireplace tool into empty spots in the wine racks.

"Soph," Nina murmured my name softly. She cocked her head.

I drifted over, trying to be casual.

She lifted the fuzzy blanket from the sofa. It wasn't a blanket at all. The Grinch's face adorned a pair of green men's pajama bottoms. I'd seen the fabric somewhere before. On the morning Baxter fell from his roof. Someone wore the matching top —

Simultaneously, Nina and I whispered, "Gwen."

"Liza, where is Luis right now?" I asked.

"At work. Don't worry, he won't be home for hours."

"Watch Daisy for me," I said to Nina. "I rushed up the stairs and could hear Liza asking, "What happened? Where's she going?"

I couldn't very well tell her I was going to open her Christmas present.

CHAPTER THIRTY-FIVE

Dear Sophie,
I love sugar cookies, but my icing always looks like my kids did it. What am I doing wrong?

> Desperately Inept in St. Nickolas,
> Pennsylvania

Dear Desperately Inept,
Add a little extra powdered sugar to a portion of your royal icing. Use that to pipe on a border. Apply the runnier icing to the center with a squeeze bottle. Add a drop of water if it's too thick. Allow to dry. Now pipe on the thicker royal icing in a different color as decoration.

> Sophie

I hurried next door to the Babineauxs', my thoughts racing. Why would Luis have pajama bottoms that matched Gwen's top? Had she been truthful about having an affair with a yummy neighbor? Too many things were falling into place. They couldn't all be coincidences. I had dismissed Luis's reaction to soy. But maybe it did place him at Gwen's house after the cookie swap. Maybe he had been there and eaten one of Natasha's dreadful cookies. If I was right, then Luis had pretended to be a woman to buy the silver sleigh and candleholders incognito. I would know as soon as I ripped open Liza's Christmas present.

With any luck, Wolf would still be there. To my surprise, Claudine answered the door.

"Sophie! Guess what I'm doing."

"Babysitting?"

"Almost, but even better. Come on in out of the cold. I'm on nana duty!"

"The test results came back? You're officially Kat's grandmother?"

"It's the best Christmas ever. What a gift. Jonah and Sugar are at the courthouse now getting everything squared away. Meanwhile, Kat has a Christmas pageant tonight and no one has any idea whether Gwen made or bought a costume for her. I'm afraid Baxter is no help at all. He's in a deep funk. What can I do for you?"

"Is Wolf here?"

"I don't think so."

"Oh." How could I say this without sounding nosy? *I'm going upstairs to open Liza's Christmas present from Luis because I think he's the killer and he hid the murder weapon in her gift.* "Uh, there's something I, uh, left upstairs." That sounded incredibly stupid.

But she bought it. I chalked it up to being giddy about her new role as grandmother. I hurried up the stairs before she could change her mind.

I slipped into the room where Baxter had placed Luis's gift. I could hear Kat playing with Harry and talking to him.

I slid the bow and ribbon off the present and ripped the paper in haste. It was certainly heavy enough to contain silver. Fumbling, I lifted the lid. Nestled under white tissue paper were the sleigh with the reindeer and the two stag-head candleholders. Luis must have been the woman who'd bought them for cash. The sad thing was that I didn't think they were just a very generous gift for Liza. He wouldn't have disguised himself to buy them if they were. Wrapping them as a gift was an ingenious way to hide the murder weapon — the candleholder — from the police.

A sad sound drifted to me.

Guttural, almost like a moan, or a weak protest. As silently as I could, I tiptoed toward it. The door to the room was closed. I debated for only a few seconds before slowly turning the knob and peeking in.

Baxter lay in his bed, propped up on a pillow. Luis perched on the edge of the bed offering pills and water which Baxter feebly pushed away.

"Now Baxter," said Luis in a calm sing-song voice. "You have to take these. It's just alprazolam, a sedative. You know they'll make you feel better. They'll help you relax and sleep. All your troubles and pain will go away."

Baxter swallowed the pills.

"Just a few more," said Luis. "They'll just make you very drowsy, so you can go into a deep sleep."

A few more? That didn't sound right!

Baxter cooperated, chasing them down with the water. But when he swallowed, he gasped, like people do when they drink alcohol straight. Something definitely wasn't right.

I slid my cell phone out of my pocket and hurried back to the bedroom where the package had been stashed. I dialed 911 first and told them we needed police and an ambulance. Next I called Wolf. With any luck, he wouldn't be too far away.

But luck wasn't with me. Luis swung open

the door. He grinned at me, dimples show-ing near the corners of his mouth. "Sophie! Hi. What are you doing here?"

"How's Baxter?" My gaze drifted down to Luis's hand. He quickly tucked a pill bottle into his pocket.

"As well as can be expected. He's taking a nap. What are you up to? Opening my gift to my wife? That will land you on Santa's naughty list!"

I played along. "I was actually trying to move it. Claudine is bringing a sewing machine in here to work on a costume for Kat."

"Why don't I believe that? Come, come." He backed up and motioned to me. I didn't much like being trapped in the bedroom. Out of the corners of my eyes, I sought a weapon of some kind.

In a second we were on the upstairs land-ing. No weapons there!

"I knew that Christmas letter would get me in trouble. Gwen never should have mentioned our affair. And so publicly. Bax-ter will be dead shortly. A tragic overdose brought on by his inability to cope with hav-ing killed his wife. So very sad. It's an old story, though, the husband killing the wife over money."

"You're trying to frame him by killing him?"

"I prefer to see it as Baxter accepting the blame for Gwen's death. I might have known it would be you who would come along at an inopportune time. Well, I'm sure I'm not the only one in the neighborhood who will be glad when the nosiest neighbor is gone."

I backed up a step. "There are three of us. You'll have witnesses."

"Right. A little old lady and a distraught child." Luis tittered. "Ohhh, I'm scared."

"I think you've counted wrong. Wolf is with us." It was a big fat lie, but I needed to buy time.

"I'm not that stupid. I didn't see him come in with you."

"He's parking the car."

Luis's eyes narrowed. "Then he'll be the first to find you dead at the bottom of the stairs. Good-bye, Sophie."

Claudine appeared behind him. She held a marble rolling pin up high in her right hand. Instead of whacking him, though, she moved in close behind him. "One ought never mess with little old ladies, Luis. You never know when one of us might be packin'."

As though we were in a movie, he raised

his hands into the air.

"Sophie," said Claudine, "close the door to Kat's room and tell her to stay inside. I don't want her to see this."

"You don't have to worry about me. I have no reason to harm Kat."

I didn't believe his lie. The sparkle in his dark eyes told me he was thinking fast.

"I bet you didn't mean to kill Gwen, either."

"That's absolutely right. I never intended to hurt her."

"Like I believe that."

"It's true. I was taking out trash when I saw Gwen coming through the Scrogginses' back gate. I asked her if we could talk, and she got sassy. I followed her into her house, pleading with her to listen to me." Luis's Adam's apple bobbed. "You know Gwen. She offered me cookies like a hostess, then she turned into a sultry vixen and asked me again to leave Liza and marry her. When I said no, Gwen told me it was my fault that she had to move to plan B. She was so proud about using Horace's own warfarin meds in peanut brittle to kill him. You should have heard her talking about what a pity it was that the railing broke and the doctors discovered the overdose."

Luis's shoulders sagged. "I knew I should

rely on my training. She suffered from a disorder, but she rambled on about tricking Mrs. Scroggins so people would think she'd become senile, which would put Baxter in charge of Scroggins Realty, and they would finally see some real money with the Scrogginses out of the way. It was the babbling of a sick mind."

I had a feeling I was hearing the babbling of a sick mind.

Luis rubbed his forehead. "I should have called Baxter, or her doctor. But she turned on me and said she'd have her revenge. She would reveal our affair. She would make sure that Liza knew, and she would tell people I had been treating her privately, which would ruin my career, leaving me destitute. Don't you see? I would have been in Baxter's shoes. My life would have been over."

He snorted air like an angry bull. "I lost it." He moaned. "I just lost it. She grabbed the candlestick and came at me. I overpowered her, flipped her around, and slammed it on the back of her head."

His dark eyes glared straight at me. "I regretted it immediately. But it was too late. She fell to the floor, and I could see blood in her hair. I wanted to help her, to save her." His lips trembled, and he mashed them together. "But I did the worst thing I have ever done. I ran." He hung his head.

I didn't need to see his face to know he was crying. I could hear the tears in his voice.

"I ran away. I didn't call for help. I didn't own up to what had happened. I just ran away. I thought she was dead. But then she disappeared. Do you know the agony of those twenty-four hours? I couldn't ask anyone. I didn't know if she was playing some kind of trick on me. Why didn't they find her in the living room, where I left her?"

In a sudden rage, he lunged at me, roaring like a madman. I stepped aside just in time to watch him tumble headfirst down the stairs.

Claudine and I peered at him.

"Do you think he's alive?" she whispered.

"I'm not taking any chances. Where's your gun?"

She held out a battery-operated candle. "I took out the lightbulb. It was the only thing I could think of that was about the right size."

"Okay, give me the rolling pin. It's better than nothing. I'll watch him. You take Kat down the back stairs and out of the house. She hurried Kat and Harry down the stairs, and I heard the back door close.

At long last I heard sirens approaching. I snuck down the back way, but when I reached the foyer, Luis was gone.

I opened the front door, intending to slip out and let the cops find him, but a hand clamped over my mouth and an arm encircled my waist. He dragged me backward, into the living room.

He was simply stronger than me. My efforts to injure him were useless. I had only one choice left. I opened my mouth and chomped down on his hand as hard as I could.

He loosened his grip. I tore away and grabbed a fireplace poker. Where were the police? Why weren't they here yet?

When he laughed and barreled toward me, I whipped the poker out straight, and Luis ran right into it. He fell to the floor with the tip of the poker lodged in his abdomen, eerily reminiscent of the dagger in Horace's belly.

I had never been so happy to hear footsteps. "In here!"

Wolf didn't often show much emotion, but this time, he winced. "Eww."

The emergency medical technicians rushed in. I pointed upstairs. "He said Baxter would die of an overdose. Alprazolam and maybe vodka?"

They split up to tend to both victims.

I looked at Wolf. "What took you so long?"

He wrapped an arm around me. "You okay?"

"I'm fine."

CHAPTER THIRTY-SIX

Dear Sophie,
This will be our first Christmas without my dear father-in-law. Everyone is coming to our home for the holidays. I don't want the focus to be on him, but I don't want to forget him, either. How do I handle this?
Missing Dad in North Star, Michigan

Dear Missing Dad,
Buy a dozen or so small silver or gold picture frames. Attach a red ribbon loop to the back with a glue gun. Fill them with pictures of family members having fun times, including your father-in-law. Hang them on your tree. I guarantee it will be the hit of your celebration. But be sure you don't leave anyone out!
Sophie

Two days later, the neighborhood had

returned to normal. Natasha recovered her status as domestic diva by organizing the decorating block party.

My widowed neighbor, Francie, hadn't come home yet, but while Natasha was busy elsewhere, we replaced her purple Christmas wreath, not to mention the raccoons, with an elegant traditional wreath and lovely battery-operated lights on a timer around her front door and downstairs window so she wouldn't have to go outside to turn them on or off.

Around four o'clock in the afternoon, Claudine and I retreated to my kitchen to make vats of hot chocolate and mulled cider.

When Claudine asked for vanilla for the hot chocolate, I nearly choked. She couldn't be Brown-Eyed Girl. That was wishful thinking on my part. Plenty of people added vanilla to their hot chocolate.

Liza had contributed all her cookies from the cookie swap. Now that Luis was in jail, Pandora wouldn't be visiting. In fact, Liza planned to fly to Miami to spend the holidays with her mom and sister, and shop for her dream condo.

Chili simmered in three Crock-Pots in my kitchen. Patty and Sugar had promised to bring trays of corn bread.

Nina barged in through my kitchen door,

dragging along a reluctant Liza. "Look who I found!"

"Good timing, Liza." I smiled at her. "You're arriving for the best part. Food and lights."

"I don't think anyone will be happy to see *me.*"

"Nonsense!" Nina pinched a cookie from the tray on the table. "Okay, tell me if I have this right. Luis and Gwen had an affair."

"Apparently very short-lived. Only a couple of, um, you know" — Liza's ears turned red — "encounters."

"I thought it was a big deal, and Gwen wanted Luis to leave you." Claudine stirred the hot chocolate.

Liza sighed. "I never figured him for such a rat. He tells me that he realized she had some issues. She'd figured out that her ride on Baxter's money train was coming to a very abrupt end, and she was actively looking for someone to be her next source of the good life. She pressured Luis to leave me. When he broke everything off with her, it forced her to move to what she called Plan B. If she killed Horace and made people think Edith had lost her mind, then Baxter would be in charge at Scroggins Realty, and they would be back on top financially."

"Then why did he kill her?" asked Nina. "Sounds like she had moved on."

"He caught her coming back from Edith's house after the cookie swap. He wanted to talk with her because he interpreted her little mention in her Christmas letter about having an affair with a yummy neighbor as a direct threat to him." Liza raised her eyebrows. "And I think it was. Gwen loved to yank someone's chain like that. So at first, she was all sweet and nice and even offered him cookies, but when he resisted her advances, she became angry again and threatened to ruin him, and he hit her over the head with the stag-head candlestick."

Rapping on the door stopped our conversation. Wolf opened it. "Is this a ladies-only chat?"

We protested in a chorus.

"Come in! We were just talking about Luis," I said. "What I don't understand is why there was no blood in Gwen's living room. And no one noticed anything amiss in there. Elvin said he didn't clean it up."

"That's actually one of the reasons I'm here. As near as we can tell, the blow to the head didn't kill Gwen."

Liza screeched and jumped to her feet. "Luis didn't murder her after all?"

"Maybe, maybe not. The injury from the

candlestick definitely contributed to her death. She was on the floor in the living room when he left. Apparently, she got up, put the candlestick back on the mantel, and went to her kitchen. I guess she was dazed or confused at that point. The blow to the head caused internal bleeding. She died from a hemorrhage, what they call intracranial bleeding. Remember how the kids filled her orange box of peanut brittle with the poisoned peanut brittle? She must have eaten it from the orange box, thinking it was safe to eat. But it thinned her blood, so when she was hit by the candlestick, she bled inside her skull and died."

A squeal came out of my mouth. "She killed herself!"

They all looked at me like I'd lost my mind. "Well, in a way. The children ate the peanut brittle she made for herself and the family, so the kids replaced it with peanut brittle she made to give to Liza and Luis. It was just like the stuff she gave Horace, tainted with warfarin. So she made her own situation worse by unwittingly eating the poison she prepared" — I pointed at Liza — "for you and Luis!"

Liza collapsed into a chair and fanned herself. "Oy. I could have died, too. Gwen was far more vengeful than I ever suspected.

Luis said she wanted to poison us because she was angry with him for rejecting her. Imagine. *I* might have died from eating that peanut brittle. And I never did anything but treat her as a friend."

"Claudine, Natasha kept telling us that she saw you at the apartment when you should have been at the store. What was that about?" asked Nina.

Claudine blushed. "I've been working on a special Christmas surprise for Jonah, but that place is so small that they know everything I do. I came home during my breaks to do research, but it didn't work out."

"What kind of gift requires research?" asked Nina.

Claudine smiled sadly. "I was trying to find a family member whom Jonah has never met — but no luck."

"I hope you'll stick around for chili, Wolf." I arranged a huge tray of toppings for the chili. Salty olives, avocado slices, corn chips, chopped green onions, minced white onions, shredded cheddar cheese, oyster crackers, sour cream, diced tomatoes, spicy jalapenos, and, for the very selective, shaved chocolate. "Would you mind taking this out to the table Mars and Bernie set up this morning?"

"It's the least I can do."

"Liza, would you call Bernie and Mars? We could use some help carrying out the Crock-Pots, too."

Liza held the door for Wolf and walked out with him.

Nina leaned back in her chair dejectedly. "If only we had found Brown-Eyed Girl."

Claudine dropped a ladle on the floor.

Nina and I gasped and pointed at her. Suspicion in her tone, Nina said, "Moondoggie."

"How could you know about that?" asked Claudine.

I felt so stupid. "Of course! Horace took Edith's last name. It was her father's realty business, so Horace became a Scroggins!"

"Horace Scroggins, who is in the hospital, is my Moondoggie?" Claudine sank into a chair, her hands shaking. "I had almost given up hope of finding him."

I raced to the cookbook where I had stashed the letter and brought it to her. "Horace kept this. He asked me to retrieve it when he fell."

She clasped a hand over her heart and tears rolled down her face. "My dear Moondoggie. Oh, I can't wait to see him again. First thing tomorrow morning or maybe tonight? What a special Christmas this will be!"

"I'll drive you. I have to be there for this reunion." Nina grinned from ear to ear.

With help from Bernie and Mars, we carried out all the food.

Nina served us mulled cider. Steam rose in the air from our cups. She did a little dance. "Oh, Claudine, you can't imagine how thrilled I am!"

Kat skipped along the street with other children.

"How's Kat adjusting to two new mommies and a daddy?" I asked.

Claudine smiled. "She's doing beautifully. And it might even be easier on her when she finds out she has a new grandpa, too."

"I don't understand." I sipped my cinnamon-laden cider.

"You just solved the Christmas surprise I was working on for Jonah. Horace is Jonah's father."

"Not your husband?" asked Nina.

"Shortly after we moved, I found out I was pregnant. My husband was the only father Jonah ever knew. When he was little, I explained that he had another father somewhere, but I didn't ever think I would find Horace again."

Nina gasped. "If Horace is Jonah's father, then Horace is Kat's grandfather. What could be more perfect? Horace has a whole family he didn't know about!"

Nina and I toasted.

"Now, you girls! You have to promise to keep that tidbit under your hats. I don't want Jonah finding out from someone else."

We promised. But I worried about Edith. How would she take the news? Horace didn't want her to ever know that he had loved Claudine all these years.

A little line formed at the table as neighbors greeted us and helped themselves to food.

The town had agreed to block off the street for the day, but a golf cart appeared to be off course.

The driver wore an elf hat, and his passenger had dressed in a full Santa suit.

Neighbors and friends rushed toward them, exclaiming and hugging as they recognized elf Baxter driving Santa Horace, who handed out packages to the children.

Edith joined me. "I didn't contribute any food, so I thought the least I could do was bring the fellows home in style."

"I'm so glad you did. You made this day special."

"I want to thank you for everything you did for me."

"My pleasure. May I ask you one question?"

"Certainly."

"Why did you make such a fuss about a coupon at Rocking Horse Toys, yet you won't buy clothes if they're on sale?"

Edith blinked at me as though I had asked the most stupid question in the world. "Well, no one wants to be foolish with their money. I clip coupons like everyone else, but I've never bought last season's clothes, and I'm not about to start to now."

Everyone had their own quirks and rules to live by.

"I wanted you to know that Horace and I have agreed to divorce. Don't look shocked, dear. It's quite amicable. Poor Horace has endured more than anyone should expect of another human being. He fulfilled his promises to my father long ago. It's time Horace moved on and experienced true happiness in his life."

"But what about you?"

"I shall stay where I am, in the house I love. But I intend to move the mirror in the hallway back where it belongs. I have found a space for sale, not far from the Torpedo Factory Art Center." She smiled. "I think you'll be happy to know that it will be Baxter's first sale when he's able to work again. I may have been a bit hasty when I fired him. Little Kat brought back so many wonderful memories of the days I spent drawing and painting with my son. I am opening a children's art center staffed with art therapists who can help children through their troubles."

"Mrs. Scroggins! Mrs. Scroggins!" Kat raced toward us holding a piece of paper that flapped in the air. She held it out to Edith. "I made this for you. Merry Christmas!"

"For me?" Edith's surprise quickly turned to joy. "It's beautiful! Is this an angel?"

"That's my ma . . . Grandma Gwen singing in heaven."

She had captured Gwen's long hair perfectly.

"Is this her kitty cat?" asked Edith.

Kat became solemn. "She never ever had one, so I think she needs one in heaven."

Edith pointed to a black rectangle. "And what is this?"

"That's her earth TV. She's watching over me."

At that moment, the lights on the houses and the trees came on. All around me, my neighbors exclaimed.

While all the houses were beautiful, Mars and Bernie had outdone everyone with a snowflake machine that shone on my house, making it appear that snow flurries were dancing against it.

A cheer went up when a local man announced that Mars and Bernie had won the Clark Griswold award. Natasha would never hear the end of it.

I took a deep breath and looked up. In spite of the blazing lights on my street, in the dark sky one star twinkled even brighter, and I knew Gwen was watching TV.

RECIPES

To continue the cookie swap theme of this book, I held a contest asking readers for their favorite Christmas cookies and the stories behind them. These are the winners! I especially cherish the warm memories and love behind the cookie recipes. I hope one of these recipes will become a favorite at your house.

ELLEN-MARIE KNEHANS

I have shared this recipe at every Navy duty station we have lived. It has been a hit at several cookie exchanges and it is often asked for by colleagues. I am an elementary school teacher now, but when I taught Home Economics, at the middle school, I did have my one eighth-grade class make these. They loved the challenge of making even layers. We love these cookies so much that I make two batches right away — one stays vanilla, the other chocolate. These look fantastic on a plate and kids and adults love them. I make these so often I don't use a recipe, and I don't measure the thickness of the dough . . . I just know.

Ellen-Marie's Famous Pinwheels

1 cup butter
1/2 cup sugar
2 tablespoons cocoa powder (you can add more if you like it darker)
2 1/2 cups flour
2 teaspoons vanilla
Pearl sugar (I get mine from Rasmussen's in Solvang, California, or King Arthur Flour)

Cream butter and sugar together until fluffy. Add vanilla, blend. Add flour slowly. Blend. Divide dough into two equal portions. Add cocoa to taste to one portion, mixing until well blended.

Roll out each portion of dough between wax or parchment paper until approximately 1/8–1/6 of an inch thick. Remove one sheet of wax paper from each portion and place vanilla dough sheet on top of chocolate dough sheet. Remove remaining vanilla wax paper sheet.

Carefully roll sheets of dough lengthwise to make a cylinder (like a jelly roll). Roll the dough in pearl sugar. Wrap in wax paper and chill overnight.

Preheat oven to 350.

Slice dough roll crosswise and place slices on lightly greased cookie sheets or parchment paper. Bake at 350 degrees for 8–10 minutes, until vanilla portion starts to tinge brown. (Do save the ends of the rolls for hubby and/or kids . . . the dough is as yummy raw as it is cooked. AKA Cookie Sushi.)

MICHELLE MELVIN

I have a recipe that was handed down to me from my mother-in-law over thirty years ago. It's not cookies, but Peanut Butter Balls. These have been a staple in the Melvin household every Christmas long before I became a part of this family. My mother-in-law is now in a nursing home, but her daughters and daughter-in-law continue the tradition. My children and all of my nieces and nephews associate these with Christmas and Nanny. If you decide to use the recipe, please credit my mother-in-law, Mrs. Ann P. Melvin!

Ann's Peanut Butter Balls
1/2 cup peanut butter (I have always used crunchy peanut butter)

1/2 cup icing sugar
1/4 cup butter
1 teaspoon vanilla
1/4 cup coconut
1/4 cup finely chopped cherries
1 package chocolate chips

Combine all ingredients in a mixing bowl. Roll into balls about 1 inch in diameter.

In a double boiler, melt chocolate chips and a small piece of parawax.

Dip the peanut butter balls in the chocolate and place on wax paper. Let cool and set. Store in a covered container in the refrigerator.

KATHY KAMINSKI

Growing up, when I thought of good cooking it was my grandma Gertie that came to mind. She was my dad's mom. No surprise — before she was married she worked as a cook for the rich people in the small town of Albion, NY. However, I don't remember her as a baker. I'm sure she must have done some baking, but all the sweet recipes seem to come from my mom's mom, Lucy. Today I'll share her most famous recipe: her Pineapple Squares.

My mom, Audrey, told me her mom made these since she was a kid. She has no idea where the recipe came from; however, it was quite popular in Polonia. Who knew pineapple squares were a Polish thing? Polish ladies all made their own versions, tweaking the recipe so that each version was a little different. What made Lucy's special was the cream cheese frosting. Nana always believed in taking something when she went to visit. She'd ask, "What should I bring?" and everyone replied, "Your pineapple squares."

Lucy's Pineapple Squares

For the Crust:
3 cups sifted flour
1 teaspoon salt
1 1/4 cups butter
1/2 cup cold milk

Work dough as for pie. Use 1/2 portion for bottom of a sided cookie sheet.
　Preheat oven to 350.

For the Filling:
2 medium-sized cans crushed pineapple
7 tablespoons tapioca
1 cup sugar

Mix and spoon into piecrust. Top with remaining rolled-out dough. Bake at 350 degrees for 45 minutes.

For the Topping:
1 small package of cream cheese
2 tablespoons softened butter
1 1/2 cups confectioner's sugar
vanilla — no amount written, probably 1
  teaspoon
milk — small amount to get spreading con-
  sistency

Cool, then frost. Sprinkle the frosting with crushed walnuts if desired. Cut into squares.

NANCY FOUST
I received this from a friend and they go over very big with my family and anyone who gets a cookie tray from me at Christmastime. I have made them many, many times.

Whoopie Pies
1 cup butter, softened
1 1/2 cups sugar
2 teaspoons vanilla
2 eggs
4 cups flour
3/4 cup baking cocoa
1/2 teaspoon salt
2 teaspoons baking soda
1 cup water
1 cup buttermilk

Filling:
2 cups marshmallow creme
2 cups powdered sugar
1/2 cup butter, softened
2 teaspoons vanilla

Preheat oven to 375. Grease cookie sheet.

In a mixing bowl, beat butter, sugar, vanilla, and eggs until well mixed. Combine dry ingredients. Add to butter mixture alternately with water and buttermilk. Drop by teaspoonfuls on greased cookie sheet. Bake for 5–7 minutes. Cool completely. In a small mixing bowl, beat filling ingredients until fluffy. Spread filling on half of the cookies, then top with remaining cookies. Makes about 3 dozen.

(I make two kinds: strawberry and vanilla. The strawberry filling is made with strawberry marshmallow creme.)

JEANNE SCHUTTS

Here is my favorite Christmas cookie recipe. My grandma (Marseilla Schutts) used to make them. I know it was in a Messiah Lutheran Church cookbook from Port Byron, IL. She attended that church, so it either came from the cookbook or a church member. My grandma was a wonderful woman who never had an unkind word to say about anyone. She loved having the family get together. She passed away several years ago, and we all miss her.

These are very popular at holiday get-togethers, and we are always asked for the recipe. It is something different for people who do not like chocolate. You can take them to parties, and they travel well.

Real Good (Unbaked) Cookies
1/2 package almond bark
1/2 cup peanut butter
1 cup peanuts
1 cup miniature marshmallows
1 cup Rice Krispies

Melt the almond bark. Add peanut butter and mix well. Add other ingredients and mix well. Drop onto wax paper and refrigerate until hardened.

MARGARET F. JOHNSON
Here is my mother's cookie recipe. She was a great meat-and-potato cook, and this is the only cookie recipe I have. She wrote it in a letter to my aunt in 1942. I had just had my diphtheria shot and was cranky. She wasn't able to do much cooking after 1950, so I did most of it. Of course, I've continued

to cook ever since. *I love food!*

I think these are best with a simple chocolate frosting.

Helen Lou's Drop Chocolate Cookies

1/2 cup butter
1 cup brown sugar
2 egg yolks, beaten
1/2 cup sour milk
1/2 teaspoon baking soda
1 teaspoon baking powder
1/8 teaspoon salt
1 3/4 cups flour
2 squares melted baking chocolate
2 egg whites, beaten to soft peaks
1/2 cup walnuts

Preheat oven to 350. Grease cookie sheet.

Sift together the flour, baking soda, baking powder, and salt. Cream butter and sugar, add yolks, add milk and flour mixture. Then add melted chocolate. Next fold in beaten egg whites and walnuts. Drop cookies on buttered cookie sheet and bake for 15 minutes. Frost if desired.

JESSICA FAUST

I hope I make it into your cookie exchange with our family Scotcheroos! It's my grandmother's (Grandma Rose Carroll) recipe,

461

and it came from her mother. Generations of Christmases on this one . . . Everyone loves these. I also make them gluten free by subbing gluten free pretzel sticks for the noodles.

Scotcheroos

1 cup chocolate chips
1 cup butterscotch chips
1 cup salted peanuts
1 cup thin chow mein noodles

Melt the chips together in a double boiler, add the peanuts and noodles and stir until thoroughly covered. Drop by teaspoonfuls onto waxed paper and let set.

JAMES ASHCRAFT

The following Christmas cookie recipe was handed down from my grandmother, Myrtle Fite, to my mother, Peggy Rae Ashcraft, who passed it on to me. Myrtle Fite was given the recipe by a friend and fellow ladies' club mate, Mid Geary.

Holiday Tizzies

1/2 cup sugar
1/3 cup butter
2 eggs, well beaten
1 1/2 tablespoons of sweet milk

1 1/2 cups flour
1/2 teaspoon salt
1/2 pound candied pineapple
1 pound chopped dates
1 pound candied cherries
1 pound (4 cups) whole pecans
1 wineglass full of whiskey (1/2 cup)

Preheat oven to 300. Grease cookie sheet.

Cream butter and sugar. Add eggs and milk. Toss the fruits and nuts with half the flour. Add the rest of the flour to other dry ingredients and mix with egg mixture. Then add floured fruits and whiskey. Drop by teaspoon on greased cookie sheet. Bake in slow oven for 15 to 20 minutes.

ELAINE FABER

This is a family basic brown sugar cookie recipe from my grandmother (1920s). Because it is so versatile, it can be used all year long. Anything can be added to change the flavor: chocolate chips, raisins, dates, dried figs, persimmons, or candied fruit (for Christmas).

Holiday Nut Drops
1/2 cup shortening (butter or margarine)
1 cup packed brown sugar
1 egg

1 teaspoon vanilla
1 1/2 cups flour
1/4 teaspoon baking soda
1/2 teaspoon salt
1/2 to 1 cup of chopped nuts (or chocolate chips, raisins, dates, dry figs, persimmons, or candied fruit)

Preheat oven to 350.

Thoroughly cream shortening with brown sugar. Add egg and vanilla. Add flour, baking soda, and salt to creamed mixture.

Mix in chopped nuts (or other ingredient). Bake 10–15 minutes.

ROBERTA DANIELS

My mother received this recipe over forty years ago from a friend at Christmas. Our family loved them so much that she went out the next day to buy a pizzelle iron. My mother has passed on, but my husband and I have been making them for over twenty years as part of our cookie treats at Christmas. Family and friends love them. This year we made close to 350 pizzelles to give to family and friends. As one of our neighbors said this year, "Oh, the cookies are finally here!"

Pizzelles
Yields 70–75 pizzelles.

6 large eggs
1 3/4 cups sugar
2 sticks margarine (melted and cooled)
2 teaspoons baking powder
4 cups all-purpose flour
2 teaspoons anise or vanilla flavoring
 (Roberta uses anise)

Beat eggs, add sugar, melted margarine, and anise or vanilla flavoring. Mix well. Add flour and baking soda until well mixed. Batter will be thick. Use a teaspoon to place on pizzelle iron. Bake on pizzelle iron for 43 seconds. Time may vary from iron to iron.

HELENA GEORGETTE MANN
This is my mother's recipe, which I have altered some. Everyone liked the original. They go crazy over the altered version. It's all the teenage boy next door talks about.

Gingersnaps
1/4 cup shortening
1/2 cup white sugar
1/2 cup light brown sugar
2 teaspoons baking soda
1/2 teaspoon salt

1/3 cup molasses
1 egg
2 1/3 cups flour
1 1/4 teaspoon ginger
1 teaspoon cinnamon
1/2 teaspoon cloves
1/4 teaspoon freshly ground pepper
1/4 cup white sugar (optional)
1 teaspoon cinnamon (optional)

Preheat oven to 375. Grease cookie sheet.

Cream together shortening, sugars, baking soda, and salt. Add molasses and egg and mix well. In a separate bowl, mix flour, ginger, cinnamon, cloves, and pepper. Add to shortening mixture and mix well. Form into small balls.

If using optional 1/4 cup white sugar and extra cinnamon, mix them together and roll the balls in cinnamon-sugar mixture.

Place on greased cookie sheet. Bake for 9–11 minutes for crisp edges and a softer center, or 13 minutes for a crisp cookie.

KITTY FREE

My best friend, who passed away several years ago, gave my family these cookies with the recipe. You can make them with M&M's for holidays (red and pink for Valentine's Day, green and red for Christmas, orange and brown for Halloween). We have even added food coloring for special occasions.

Forgotten Cookies
3 egg whites
3/4 cup sugar
1/2 teaspoon cream of tartar
1 1/2 cups miniature chocolate chips
Foil

Place foil on a cookie sheet. Preheat oven to 375.

Whip egg whites until stiff. Add sugar (slowly) and cream of tartar. Beat until thick. Slowly fold in the chips. Place by large spoonful on the foiled cookie sheet. Turn off the oven and place cookie tray in the oven for 21/2 hours. Let them cool completely and peel them off the foil. Store in airtight container.

Cranberry Jingle
1 part vodka
2 parts peach schnapps
cranberry juice

Fill glass with ice, add vodka and peach schnapps, and fill with cranberry juice.

English Bishop
(modern version)

2 oranges
2 cups apple juice or apple cider
2 cups cranberry juice (if using Ocean Spray use original version)
1 cup rum
1/4 to 1/2 cup Grand Marnier
pinch of cloves (optional)

Preheat the oven to 350. Place the oranges in a pan and roast for 20–30 minutes. Combine all the other ingredients in a pot. Slice the roasted oranges and add them to the liquid. Heat but do not boil. Serve with a slice of orange in each cup or mug. (If making a larger quantity for a party, you may wish to float small clove-studded oranges in it.)